JOHN ABERDEIN

John Aberdein was born and educated in Aberdeen. After some time herring-fishing and scallop-diving on the West Coast, he taught English and outdoor education in Fife, Hampshire and Orkney.

He was the first person to kayak round mainland Scotland; a member of the Kirkland Five who campaigned for more democratic schools; and a main organiser of Labour's move to ditch nuclear power in 1985–86 – a policy since reversed by 'the divine fiat of Tony Blair'.

His first short stories, *The Can-Can, ken?*, were published by Duncan McLean (Clocktower Press, 1996), his story 'Moving' was runner-up in the inaugural *Scotsman*/Orange Short Story competition in 2004, and his novel *Amande's Bed* (Thirsty/Argyll Publishing) won the Saltire First Book of the Year Award in 2005.

John Aberdein is based in Hoy and divides his time between writing, gardening and travelling.

D1368945

'My book of the year is *Amande's Bed* by John Aberdein. It's a good blasting story, a great river-rush of language and a book made of the combination of wisdom, energy and generosity.' Ali Smith

'High-voltage . . . the language is gloriously alive.' Jackie Kay

'*Amande's Bed* is at once a *Sunset Song* for Aberdonian townies, a Doric Roddy Doyle, and a Joycean delight in wordplay and multi-consciousness. It's a memoir, a dream, a document, a quietly tragic comedy, wildly diverse yet unified – a daring and significant achievement.' Andrew Greig

'A tour de force of good writing with artful gaps in a convoluted plot, and a really sharp sense of the city of Aberdeen in the 1950s, even down to the lamented end of their tramcars. Aberdein has a really sharp ear for dialogue and a good sense of the absurd that lurks in the everyday.' Professor Ian Campbell

'Worth reading for the supple zest of the language alone.'
Jenny Renton, *Sunday Herald*

'Bold and extremely accomplished; big-hearted, clear-eyed and quick-witted . . . an elegy for what has been lost that still points to what might be.' Stuart Kelly, *Scotland on Sunday*

'A balance of humour and tragedy, tragedy ultimately traceable to social conditions, but not in any mechanical way . . . I have never seen north-east urban speech given such natural, witty and yet dignified expression.' Professor Lindsay Paterson

'The most honest, perceptive and humane description of post-war working-class life I have ever read . . . sometimes funny, sometimes surreal, often stark, but always with a luminous compassion.'
Steve Arnott, *Scottish Socialist Voice*

'Absolutely engrossing...' *Shetland Times*

'John Aberdein has perfected his art to create a modern masterpiece.'
John Ross Scott, *Orkney Today*

'To me *Amande's Bed* reads like Joyce edited by Grassic Gibbon: a humane *Ulysses*, more manageable.' Brian Smith, *New Shetlander*

'*Amande's Bed* is perhaps not the book to give to your maiden aunt. It is an excellent piece of writing. John Aberdein's dialogue is authentic and often brilliant, showing a fine ear for the nuances of north-eastern dialect.' Ron Ferguson, *Press & Journal*

'Dialogue is witty, pithy, incisive, Pinteresque ... the prose is worthy of Borges on an off day. Which is praise indeed.'
Tom Adair, *Scotsman*

'His funny, acidic, sexy stories ... are bold (and, I think, successful) experiments in pushing back the boundaries of Scots narrative.'
Duncan McLean

'Truly well-crafted work ... his narrative control in the most sensitive treatments of raw sexual behaviour is masterful.' Gerard Carruthers

'Extremely funny...' Robin Bell, *Books in Scotland*

'A book of grand dreams in little lives and of tragedy only a single breath from delight.' Katie Gould, *The List*

'A wholly authentic new voice – think lyrical Grassic Gibbon meets ludic Vonnegut.' Gavin Wallace

'A ribald, gutsy combination of smeddum and alienation ... Scottish and universal.' Professor Douglas Gifford

Strip the Willow

John Aberdein

[signature: John Aberdein]

21st August 2009

Polygon

This edition published in Great Britain in 2009 by
Polygon, an imprint of Birlinn Ltd
West Newington House
10 Newington Road
Edinburgh
EH9 1QS

www.birlinn.co.uk

ISBN 978 1 84697 119 8

British Library Cataloguing-in-Publication Data
A catalogue record for this book is available on request
from the British Library.

Typeset by Koinonia
Printed and bound by Clays Ltd, St Ives plc

For Finn and Heather

The author would like to thank the Scottish Arts Council for a bursary which enabled him to devote time to researching and writing this novel.

Warm thanks to family and friends for their unfailing support, and for their detailed and constructive criticism.

march 31

what larks

A lemon UCKU plastic bag, flat on the tar, lank in the air, hopped and gusted towards her. According to the latest story, plastic bags were the root of all badness.

Nobody will be free until the last financier is strangled with the guts of the last bureaucrat.

Get your orgasms throwing paving stones.

L'imagination c'est le pouvoir. Imagination is power. Such was the calibre of slogan she and others had printed and glued to the walls of Paris.

Mort aux sacs plastiques! It didn't quite fit, somehow.

Lucy sat on the leather seat of her Morris Traveller, on the wind-swept Prom.

She glanced at the sixty perspex pods, slow-spun on the high wheel: *UberEye.*

She gazed where concrete churned in the big orange drum, to make a matrix for the perspex surf pens: *UberSea.*

Tomorrow LeopCorp and the Council would consummate: *UberStreet.*

Tell it like it is, thought Lucy, because – and this was the crunch – she too was responsible.

It came pissing down. She drove a lap of the Prom in her Morris Traveller, for the joy of the hissing road. She skimmed past the corporate joy aids.

She parked. Guy had invited her up on UberEye for a special viewing.

– This is not really your area, he said, as they stepped into a pod, but I thought you'd like a look.

9

Guy did insufferability really well.

– It might help to straighten out some of your ideas, he continued. The hoi polloi want kicks, Lucy, individually packaged kicks, the proles are not that creative.

– Either way, she'd said, you don't give a fuck, Guy, do you?

– You do? said Guy.

– Yes, said Lucy, I give one.

– Yet you still keep your fancy job, Lucy love, said Guy.

The slur was more piercing than the far from idle threat.

As their pod rose, locked in its curve, she had to admit it was not that boring. You could see the city in relief, less as a granite warren, more as a mental map. You could see the twin rivers, Dee and Don. Between them lay the quaint hills of the hinterland, Bennachie, Scoltie, Tap o Noth – volcanic, sculpted, vitrified – that many used to tramp. Out at sea, a hazy view of the windfarms and the planet-saving kits.

– So what are you going to charge? she asked, when the pod reached its zenith.

– Twelve, said Guy, nine for concessions. Stags and hens and birthday deals. They'll flock from all over.

– No doubt, Lucy said, and paused.

And then she posed the killer question.

– But, even at that, will LeopCorp be satisfied?

If she could have turned on her heel in triumph at that point – but the pod was at two hundred feet.

– To make global impact— said Guy, and gripped the chrome rail as the wheel started downwards— we must always accelerate. Let's hit that tonight. You'll be at rehearsal?

– I won't fail the feast.

It was still barely noon. Back in the car, she paused at the bend in the Prom where the Don cut through its own sandbanks with grey and silver scissors. There used to be larks, high in the sky. She stopped, wound down the window and listened, but there were no larks, only concrete pouring and distant engines. What larks? When did you ever hear larks in the tail of winter? She looked back at her city for a good long time.

The city glinted back at its lover, was shrouded, swept with narrowing rains, then glinted again.

a violent undresser

Alison and Gwen were having a discussion, in Gwen's bedroom, about how untidy a bedroom could be and still be counted as one. Gwen wasn't much of a dresser, but she was a violent undresser. She was a great reader and writer, but not a great filer. She wasn't a compulsive showerer, but there were enough damp towels in the eclectic landslide that hid her bed to guarantee a brisk decomposition.

    – So fit's this ye've got yir heid stuck intae noo? said her mother, picking up the topmost book from the pile.

    – Fit's this? mocked Gwen. It's Rosa Luxemburg. Revolutionary and martyr.

    – We're aa martyrs in wir ain wey.

    – Are we? Even when we sell out?

    – Fa's sellin oot?

    – You for a start. You and your wonderful pal, Lucy. The Council.

    – I resent that, said Alison.

    – Resemble that, said Gwen.

    – I really div. I only dae fit I dae tae keep body an soul thegither, and keep ye, quine, in new knickers.

    – The world's not only about new knickers.

    – Ye'd be surprised.

    – The men I fuck— said Gwen.

    – Oh, aye—? said her mother.

    – Never you mind. Rosa made revolution without an ounce of make-up.

    – There's mair than ae kind o revolution.

    – Till she got shot.

    – Fa o? said Alison. Fa did she get shot o, like?

– Fa o? Fa o? jibed Gwen. You'd maybe learn, if you'd only listen.

– Bound tae get shot, of course, said her mother, if she kept her bedroom in this kind o sotter. If Bill clapped een on this, he'd dump ye quick.

– Bill will never dump me. He told me for a fact. Even if – anyway—

She always slept with Bill round his place, the staff annexe at the hotel, inhaling his post-work odours; his thyme, coriander, oxter sweat and gravies.

– Anyway, I've got an interview, said Gwen. Didn't tell you I'd applied, did I?

– Sae sudden these days, madam, said her mother. Faraboot? Fa wi?

– LeopCorp Towers, live-in assistant. I'll be out from under your feet. Bill's got one too, interview.

– LeopCorp? Rookie Marr? Ye sure?

– Yes, I'm sure. We've both got interviews and we're going for it. Get in on the inside.

– The fit? said Alison. The inside? I'm sayin nithin—

– Good, said Gwen. That's taken you long enough.

like honey under the moon

It was late afternoon. Luna came and sat near Guy on the circular couch. Rookie was close on his other side. All three sat within touching distance, without touching. They were surrounded by plasma viewing screens – three banks of twelve curved screens – on which many a trauma swam. They felt private and privileged, as they watched the world spill its entrails. They felt as sensory as sharks.

Luna she might be called, but whether she was the full Luna or not remained to be found out. And why she lent herself to a jerk like Rookie Marr impressed itself on Guy as a question.

Most dealings he had with women had their inherent pain. Lucy, for example, his Council counterpart, his sparring partner at work, was almost an opposite to Luna. Lucy refused to capitulate to the system without squawking; she was always querying Guy's actions, as though she were his freelance conscience. But then she was a child of Paris, one of those rich gamines who claimed revolution on the back of a few screenprinted posters and a fistful of cobbles.

Alison, her deputy, was another case: brittler maybe, not continually sniping, but letting her criticism boil over in fierce laughter, then buckling down again. Alison was feisty, but she knew the score. LeopCorp paid the Council, and the Council paid her bills.

He was constrained to work with Lucy for the next two nights, then he would see.

But for now it was about Luna. Luna wore a slim silver dress, doubly slit. Her legs were not in the least milky. Luna's legs, when they moved in the silver dress, were like honey under the moon.

Luna and her protector, Rookie Marr, lived in conjoined turrets. Hers was South Turret, Blissville, dedicated to joy and whatnot; his was North Turret, the Fastness, the vantage, perched at the seaward end of the city's main street.

Mile-long Union Street was a triumph of city-straightening from the nineteenth century. It was ideal for LeopCorp's needs because it was available, simple and cheap, unlike the Mall, Fifth Avenue, Sunset Strip, the Reeperbahn and the Champs-Elysées. One mile long, pretty damn broad, and with high flush walls, it was the perfect stretch colosseum, where Spectacle could cavort and be syndicated, here and beyond.

Guy had a central part to play. He had a grounding in the theory and praxis of events management. He used to write tracts about it. He used to attend clandestine conferences, where a select few plotted how the banal spectacle of life could be overturned, surrender its passivity, and come into consciousness.

Commodity slavery: *non*. Life as sharpened in situations: a very big *oui*. *Desire for consciousness, and consciousness of desire* was a phrase much bandied about.

Then, on one ill-judged foray in the *Guardian*, in a colour piece about a Situationist conclave in Islington in the early 1990s, he used that phrase without attribution, passing it off as his. He was immediately sacked from the International by its self-appointed founder, *flic, philosophe* and prat.

Henceforward, having been accused of plagiarism, he decided to inhabit his sin. He changed his name from Terry Clarkson to Guy Bord. Up North especially they grinned at the sound of that; it had an ironic slant in a Scottish accent. He offered his services wherever Spectacle concentrated its rhetoric, for example at celebrations of wishful thinking and invocations of the irrational on drained moors. Thus *Culloden 2 – The Remake*, a rejigging of historical forces, and *The Bogfire Banshee Bash*, a solstice thing, sat at the top of his CV.

But he was always on the qui vive for movers and shakers, keen to be inserted in the city scene where crowds were more readily channelled, the money was bigger and the equipment didn't blow down. And they didn't come much more moving-and-shaking than LeopCorp, the Marr outfit. Guy's presentation at interview was a neo-Situationist three-card trick. How to take a readymade city, lock it to one's purpose, and shaft it for all it was worth. That's what had got him on to the couch.

They were devouring a montage of classic hits on thirty-six DVDs. Cliff divers soloing down at blue Acapulco, multiple meerkats jabbering about a snake, a million ecstatic pilgrims up to their bits in a very brown Ganges. An attack on border police in China (studio reconstruction only), a polar bear mauling a small white whale, floods and selective searchers sweeping Louisiana. Everything was so vivid, fluid, varied, the circular couch itself seemed a coracle, spinning by Treasure Island. Guy didn't clock this at first. Was the wall spinning left, or was it the couch revolving right? But then he saw the remote in Rookie's palm. Rookie stopped whatever the spin was briefly, pointing and guffawing. Then it started again. So Guy just went with the flow, leaning, ardent for a warm shoulder. The shoulder eluded him.

In his heart of hearts, Guy knew that one day there would be no room for him on the revolving couch. It too would evolve into a cliff. He hoped he would have the timing to make his move, rather than be shoved off backwards. Or if they sought to dunk his face in rivers of shit, he would volunteer for an ankle-deep tributary. *No illusions,* he said to himself. He tried to suppress the statement that yammered behind that, *I have the illusion I have no illusions.* Because madness beckoned, the moment you let the line slacken. *I have the illusion I have the illusion I have no illusions—*

What line? The line of his hardened forty year old jaw. The taut whale-fastened line of an events manager. The line a white homes in on, when it senses injury in the water.

A bank of three plasma screens doubled as a door, though the remote had to be pressed to find out which. One of the wall-screens was rumoured to be a window but Luna had not, during her lonesome daily searches, discovered it. Torrid plasma pulsed round her all the time, except when she was in Rookie's bed or her own. Rookie Marr had informed Luna there was no need to go out. He himself made only occasional excursion. *Out* was where filming took place.

I am the Leopard, he'd said to her, on their first night. Whatever in him had wooed her earlier, this was indeed news. He was not only the son and heir to LeopCorp, he had inaugurated a bestiary. You'll want for nothing, he had continued. It was only a couple of steps from there, she estimated, to *You'll achieve nothing, You'll be nothing.* Rookie Marr. He'd made her bed, she'd chosen to lie on it.

– Well, Guy, said the Leopard. It's time to say goodbye.

– Goodbye, said Guy.

– Tonight rehearsal, tomorrow the real thing, said the Leopard, with as much grandiloquence as he could muster.

Real thing, thought Guy. He was an events man, he did *mega, way out, fantastic,* there was no need to grub around with talk like that.

– Luna, said the Leopard, with a jerk of his sub-leonine head.

– Yes, Leop? said Luna. She had once tried *Pard,* from which he recoiled like a winged gunfighter.

– See our new man out, said Rookie Marr.

– Yes, Leop, said Luna.

When Luna stood up and walked, Guy could not keep his eyes off her long skirt. Luna's skin, as revealed, was at the darker end of the honey spectrum.

– And Guy— said Rookie Marr, drawing off his gaze.

– Yes? said Guy.

– Make it good, said Rookie Marr.

– Of course, said Guy.

– Or you know what you will be?

– Toast? said Guy, in measured hope.

– Dead meat, said the Leopard.

The Leopard pressed a yellow key on the black remote.

A curved plasma screen, showing in slo-mo the trampling of a tourist in Pamplona, swung inwards, dipped hooked horn adrip with gore, and a bright stairwell beyond was revealed. Luna indicated Guy to go first. Even in the world of the shark pool, hospitality died hard. She saw him to the threshold, she saw him through the slo-mo door. She saw him down the first dozen steps. As he descended, he felt a modest number of fingers on his shoulder. He turned around.

Taking advantage of the construction of her dress, she had hoisted the lower tabard, the elongated apron. She had nothing else on, apart from silver shoes, and she said nothing.

Guy was kind of frozen. The silence, if nothing else, needed to be covered.

– Do come up and see us sometime, said Luna.

– Will. Sure. Bye.

Feet stammering on the stairs, he fled.

any wynd was of the mind

That night, rehearsal night, it was nearly twelve when Lucy, abandoning Balcony A, abandoning Guy and his remarks and the technical crew, abandoning the sea of carved polystyrene that was Union Street, blew Alison a light goodbye, and took her leave downwards by means of steep double steps. They were called the Back Wynd Steps, but were dead straight; any wynd was of the mind.

possibly losing heart

Alison looked at her departing back and shook her head. Lucy was losing stamina now, possibly losing heart. She was older, sure, but it wasn't just that. If you were someone like Lucy, there was only so long you could put your principles on the line without coming apart. From her own point of view it was different. She fought back out of reflex – *I'll aye fecht for Gwen* – but also knew when to lower her head and avoid open harm. Now, with Gwen moving beyond her, she was even more drawn to the older woman, her tough, gentle superior, who could both resist and be generous, then detach herself in a way.

Well, there was a showdown coming, they both knew that.

change would be a fine thing

There was a typical heap on the left hand side, on one of the landings, drifted about with stray white polystyrene beads. Lucy tried to pick a way down past without scrunching.

– What ye tiptoeing for? said the huddle on the Back Wynd Steps.

– Sorry, didn't want to wake you up.

– Didna want to put siller in my cup, was it? Ye must hae plenty.

– Thought it would jangle.

– Change would be a fine thing.

– Ha, she said. Hey, do I—? Do I know you from somewhere?

– From *somewhere*? he said. Ye should. I've been that place.

– I'm sure I know the voice.

– Tell me ma name, then.

– Oh, it's just the voice, said Lucy.

– The *voice*, he echoed. The *voice*. You be Julie?

– No. Been many things, but not a Julie.

– Pity.

– You cold? she said. You must be cold. What do you need for a coffee?

– Coupla quid.

– Okay.

– No coffee at this time, he said.

Not *Nae coffee,* she noted. His accent had moved towards her.

She popped a coin in his cup, but knew she should have put it in his hand.

edge of the sink

When Lucy looked in a mirror, she often did history. Comparative history: the morning and evening of a life.

'68 had been sweet and Rabelaisian, tentative, assured, a Hogmanay and a New Year's Day, a throwaway defining moment. Now here she was, in the office washroom at sixty, moisturising, dwelling on it, the city poised to tumble about her. The hard, glinting, bought and exploited city. Sixty the new forty, forty the new twenty? She peered in the mirror so hard, her moisturiser fell off the edge of the sink.

Yep, it was evening alright.

Her mobile pinged.

limping home

Up in the Fastness, the Leopard settled into his highback chair and snarled through the intercom for food. The dish was alien, Red Deer Haunch, this was not his country. Not quite, not yet.

Luna did not join him. Luna never joined him for food. His moonwoman preferred what grew in cellophane packets: rocket, pak choi, cress.

Out at sea, the *Girl Julie*, with red steel plates and brand new purse-net mounted, skipper Spermy McClung, was limping home after striking *some bloody rock no on the chart* off Boddam. A waterlogged log more like, from Sweden, Russia. It hadn't revealed on the radar's sweep and it hadn't come up on sonar. Something just below the surface, in no-man's sea, is always feared the worst.

– Fuckin pass me the blower, he said to the mate, Baxter.

He spoke on the radiophone to his new owner, and Rookie was far from chuffed.

– The investment we've put in, said Rookie, leaves me exposed. We cannot afford down-time.

– Deal wi it, said Spermy, and passed the phone back.

– Says he canna afford *down-time*, said Spermy. We've left him *exposed*.

– Cunt, said Baxter.

In on land – yes, there was plenty happening there. Eager for cash, and unabashed by work, the Poles had moved in, or been moved in. There were shops in Uberdeen now, like PriceRite and KostKutter, where half the goods were labelled in Polish.

Zupy: Barszcz, Rosol, Zurek.

Soups: Beetroot, Clear, Slightly Sour.

Maciek would have preferred to make his own barszcz, from his own beetroot. He had a plot of land now, a small allotment, overlooking the ruffled entrance to the harbour. What he wanted to plant there would take time to come to table. If salt on the wind didn't poison it first. As he made his way down to the harbour from KostKutter he dropped a coin and a word, as he often did, to the man who dwelt on the steps.

– Have faith, said Maciek, the wheel comes round.

– Wi forty broken spokes? the man replied. Doubt it.

Up in Northfield, Andy Endrie was touching the cold frame of a photo of his son, his loon, off-centre on the minimal mantelpiece. Down below, the electric fire, he could feel it beginning to scorch his breeks. He hoped Amande would come through soon and see to him, and also bring her partner, Ludwig, for a powwow about the chestnut stall. Fresh chestnuts from Spain. Old warhorses, veterans of the class-struggle, they still got out on the streets. They had to supplement their pensions somehow.

Next door – he could hear them through the paper-thin partition in the Council semi – Ludwig and Amande were having a row. They needed each other; they needed somebody to row with, to take their minds off poverty, slackening tissues, suppressed homesickness, waves of self-pity and others' disdain. One spoke in German Scots, the other in French Doric. He couldn't make out all the words. But they were good people, they had seen plenty. *Dinna tu m'accroche pas.* That was a bit cruel from Amande, she often used it. *Don't try to hook me.* And yet, when she was sitting behind Ludwig on the bike, cuddled into his back, she used to seem content. Maybe that was it. The basic huggy warmth was fine: it was face-to-face they didn't get on. He himself hadn't seen them properly for a year or two. His head was forced back irrevocably by his spondylitis, craning up at the ceiling. As he would say to you if you came by the house, *Ach, I'm a bittie mair cramped noo.*

Bing Qing was supervising in the kitchen behind Balcony A. A precise word here or there, she felt no panic, even at the thought of so many VIPs. But that was easy for her. She had fled when young from cultural revolution in Shanghai, where the greatest minds, the most skilled people, had to dig dung. Since then, for Bing Qing, everyone was a VIP.

Her kitchen staff were Chinese, her serving staff were Polish. It was a good combination: the Chinese dedicated to the chopping-knife and the hot wok, the Poles educated and polite. The Poles were starting to count hours; she was careful not to underpay.

Zander Petrakis, combative professor, was completing his monthly tour of the city boundary, as far away from the centre as possible, striding from boundary stone to boundary stone of the Freedom Lands like Nietzsche over his Alps. He was Emeritus now, and no longer taught. He would write; he would help the department win its funding with his delineations and relations of ideas, and sharp researches. Within the Department of Moral Philosophy his own chair was Philosophy pure. Although he had fought against the title *Chair of Philosophy*.

That is what is wrong with Western Philosophy, he'd said. Too much sitting. The first word of wisdom comes with breath in the lungs. He would have preferred his status to be conferred as *Great Stride in Philosophy*.

He stopped at a last stone before dusk. A grey stone, irregular, earthfast, standing at the wooded crown of the Blak Hill of Queyltis, in the picnic area at Hillview Crescent. He made out a shallow saucer mark. Its lead was melted and stolen, any useful inscription gone. The message from the past could not be read, and he moved on.

William Swink II, Uberdeen's elected Provost, was getting into a tizz in the Town House, abusing English, struggling into his *chained-off office*, as he called it. It was a thin double chain, with a monstrous bauble. Using the ermine of his robe as a polishing duster, he huffed and breathed and rubbed it.

– It's dim as ditchwater, said the Lord Provost.

– That'll mak twa o ye, said Walter Mitchell. Yir chain's fine, I Brassoed it this mornin.

He unkinked the Provost's chain, and let it enhance the absentee chest and the womanly belly-paunch. He could remember the Lord Provost when he was fitter. He rippled his hands twice down the lightly-trapped ermine, suppling it in place.

– Hey, Walty, said the Provost. Watch the material!

– Haud at peace, ye auld minker, said Walty.

Up in the Fastness, the Leopard swallowed a last dark gobbet of venison, and dismissed his Principal Taster for the night.

are you with us or against us, lucy?

Soon her mobile began a second crescendo. Guy the Accelerator. Lucy laid her brow on the chill mirror, and shut her eyes to outwait him.

She didn't reopen till the third burst of pinging stopped. Condensation had come over the mirror – so reassuring to see your own breath. Her finger made nine lines, at angles, in the fog: two rivers, a bumpy hinterland, a coast.

History grounded on its map.

Dampish settlement at first, Deen, of no account, like its close neighbour, Don. Or rather of which no account. She had searched, she had raked the record, stashed high in a tin-lined room in the Town House.

Rivermouth dwelling opportunities, Deen and Don, scrabbling about in glacial gravel. Lucy imagined calluses beaded across a young girl's palm, and a rough wooden spade gradually rounding.

Mediaeval burgh next, compact, *bijou*. Dung-strewn, wooden, a bugger to go on fire. Its leper spital a mile outside. The girl now carrying an expired hen and a cog of yesterday's milk to leave some distance away, on a cup-marked stone.

Then the seventeenth century spawned its oxymoron: *Civil War*. She imagined persecution, of the girl, and the girl's child, caused by lack of imagination of what it is to be another. The girl hiding, failing to hide, up foul alleys, from dragoons.

Lately a city, Greek, *neo*, of sparkle and severity, washed in the wind. No coal or iron ore, but plenty deep and surface stone, and grass, and near and distant fish. Hand-knitted stockings for the Crimea, mutton pies, horn combs.

Envelopes patented then manufactured athwart the river, from fresh pulp, for bills and billets-doux. She imagined the lass's tongue, licking a gummed triangle. It was the same girl, harried through history, strolling free a single moment.

Then the whining bombs tumbling home, on Urquhart Road, Cattofield; the stanched mutuality of stretchers.

After that particular war, called *the last war* for unclear reasons, it was rationing, typhoid, mild depression, oil.

Old shops swingballed, to maximise malls. On the day she learned of her mother's death, Lucy saw, from the top of a dizzy bus, a lurching iron ball, splattering through the lath and plaster of an outdated draper.

The new glassy halls were christened, and post-christened, with propitious names: *St Nicholas, Bon Accord, Sonsy Quines.*

Santa Claus, Happy to Meet, Big-Breasted Women.

To attract big cargo. And lo, big cargo came. Tall kirks got converted, into pubs and clubs. Once the folk were Picts and Celts, wild, blue, artistic. Then they fled hell as Papists, Episcopapes, Seceders, Receders, and phlegmatic Protestants. Finally they were

Long Throats, happy in their cups.

Now Spectacle—

The last of the mirror fog had gone. Her phone began that rising ping again. She plucked the mobile from her bag, flipped the lid and took the call. It was Guy, of course, wondering *where the ten bells of fuck* she was.

– Keep your hair on, Guy, she said. I wasn't aware there were that many.

She and Guy, never notably adhesive, were coming unstuck.

– Are you with us or against us, Lucy?

She pulled on her coat and tied the belt in a flamboyant knot; the kind favoured by younger women.

the 37 million quid thing

Union Street, specced up specially for Spectacle, had long been closed to normal traffic. Instead, a slow-revving rotating belt had been installed, as may be stood on, or stridden on, in the newer terminals of bigger airports. A mile of belting above the rollers, a mile of belting below, made of high-tensile, non-slip pavementette.

Pavementette: a marvel first fabricated to make the pocked skin of the moon amenable. Due to New Formula Fluon nothing could mark pavementette, whether gum, gunge or rocket peroxide. Woven into the fabric, every fifty metres or so, was a local brand name.

Mountain Heart

Mountain Heart

Mountain Heart

What do you think? Guy Bord had asked, that day when the members of the Joint Working Group were on their tour. The revolving belt was remarkably smooth.

Moved, I am, said Lucy.

Good, he said. Oh, I see, ha, *moved along*—

No, it's philosophy, Guy.

Which one are you on these days? said Guy.

Cogito, sed non ergo sum. I think, but do not therefore, necessarily, exist. Moved, I am.

Give me a break, said Guy. That's 17 million quid you're standing on. Correction, 37 million. It overran.

Thanks, Lucy had said, I'm moved.

It lay stopped now, or stoppedish, the 37 million quid thing, softly vibrating. Not a soul was being carried to a horizon against that soul's particular wishes.

Lucy aimed a path across the vibrating band and jiggled into the boozy crowd.

– Fuckface, fa dae ye think ye're pushin, eh? Hey, I'm spikkin tae ye—! a woman said.

Fa meant *who. Ye* meant *you. Fuckface* meant a variety of things, principally *Fuckface.*

– Sorry, she said, and coughed. Could I just squeeze—?

– Dinna ye fuckin sorry me! said the woman. Loser!

Lucy shut up, as was implicit in the last instruction. *Loser*, as a catch-all term of scorn and abuse, seemed to have scourged the language recently. Financial misfortune, negative equity? *Loser.* Sacked due to global downturn? *Loser.* Down because of romantic fracture? *Loser.* And if, despite your own travails, you showed sympathy for others, other *losers,* you were a *double-loser* yourself.

It was not the law of the jungle, which was probably quite humane, and based on good housekeeping.

It was the law of the shallow pool, where a lame creature attempting to ford is reduced to a skeleton in no time flat. By the hidden piranha. The new lingo told Lucy all she needed to know about the legacy of the Sixties. There was none.

All you need is love? *Loser!*

Yanking her coat-knot tighter, she took fresh aim towards two huge bergs of jagged polystyrene, lodged on the far edge of the pavementette. The bergs were bright, basically white, but aquamarine back-lit for truth to nature.

The first had a ledge chipped out, for green bottles of Stella to sit. It had a legend chiselled above. *Chill!*

Smart. Cool. Self-centred. And the greatest of these is cool, she thought. Cool had been cool for fifty years, possibly longer. You are a long time dead, she thought. And before that, you must seek to be a long time cool.

There were three green bottles left.

The second iceberg had a double set of stencils forking up, the left hand-prints small and red, diverging, the right footprints vertical, big and black. Some leftie perhaps, in mourning for socialism, or love poet who had kicked ass with Death.

She wished there were more. There were plenty more bergs and Lucy wished the other blanks had been chiselled or inscribed or daubed; customised with people's meanings. But meaning was something you bought into now, not something you did.

Squeezing between abusive boozers was bad enough. She sidled now between squeaky, clean, artificial bergs. They *scraiched*, when you frotted them, like electrocuted winter hares.

Lucy entered the granite building behind, went up the carpeted stair, and through the ante-room declining canapés – *Dzienkuje bardzo, Thanks very much.* She came out on the hospitality balcony behind where Ten Bells of Fuck stood with his arms folded, and where a couple of acolytes, with cream gloves on the parapet, fawned over the scene. There were more than a hundred poly-styrene bergs in all, a hundred and eleven, the whole length of the pavementette on their side of the street, their faintly-greenish sheen melding to barely-tinted white, like the mint spectrum of a fold-out Dulux paint catalogue. The bergscape creaked in the south-easterly that slid in off the North Sea, and sought to draft a haar into proceedings.

Guy must have heard her arriving, but Guy was too stiff, with pride probably, to swivel. His bold maleness, male baldness, glistened under the lights.

– *Sea of green, sea of green,* chanted Lucy, just above her breath, *in a ye-ellow submarine.*

– *As we live a life of ease,* said Guy, still not swivelling, *every one of us has all we need.*

Did he believe that? He wasn't daft, Ten Bells of Fuck. Just that the times made him shrink, accept the envelope; that was common enough. Guy was an events manager, who accepted events.

She wondered about the seat of honour.

servicing leopcorp

She wondered aloud.

– Why is the Leopard not with us? Lucy said. If I may be so bold?

Perched in the centre of the balcony was a gold throne, gifted to the Leopard formally by the city.

The throne, it's no real, it's just a replicant, William Swink II had whispered to Lucy moments before the presentation, skirting her radical views.

Replicant? Much like its recipient for all we know, she had replied, spurning his clumsy sop.

This gilded throne was raised on a dais so that the occupant might see the bulk of Spectacle pass, and so that, from down below, any slack or weakened participant might see the Leopard's dismissive thumb move, should verdict be required. Guy laid a hand on its arm, as though, in his master's absence, he were more than mere retainer.

– We are under his auspices, said Guy. He thought of temptation on the revolving couch, then Luna's tangled offer on the stairs. Guy had been in the business long enough to know there was no such thing as a free offer. Or was it instead, from Luna, a wild cry for help?

– Under? said Lucy. You may be.

A smirr of rain was pimping across his dome.

– Mr Marr, said Guy. Mr Marr is no doubt observing it all from North Turret.

Lucy glanced to the east end of the street where LeopCorp Towers, the former Salvation Army Citadel, reared, like a poor man's Balmoral. The Salvation Army, in a variation on tradition, had been forcefed brass the previous year, by LeopCorp's moneymen, in order to scram. When they had thrashed out a new mission and business plan, the Army might devote themselves to a less baronial central soup kitchen. A revamped Army HQ might send Band Aid and a feeding programme out in turn to the city's provinces: Mastrick, Northfield, Middlefield, Summerfield, Heatheryfold, Garthdee, Kaimhill and Kincorth. And, though they were wall-to-wall Catholics, to the new Polish quarter in Torry. Lucy agreed with the core Salvationers that there was nothing more fundamentally Christian than a square plate of broth.

As part of her own outreach work with ReCSoc, the Council's ReCreation and Social Engineering Department, she had worked briefly alongside the Salvation Army, in a scheme to incentivise the unemployed to keep goats on unshorn grass. This plan, essentially a milking scheme, was still being evaluated, although the large number of al fresco roasting pits, and a new fashion for drilling the bricks above a front door to take a set of horns, were not seen as overly healthy signs.

Lucy was caught between dovetailing with the Salvationers and landing up, wittingly or unwittingly, servicing LeopCorp.

Getting the Sally Army out of the centre, according to Rookie Marr, was *win-win*. Outdated competitors in the street spectacle market they needed *like a hole in the head*, he'd said graciously, in his civic throne acceptance speech.

– Observing? said Lucy.

– Like I said, said Guy.

– Or taking it in on screen, said Lucy. He'll never catch his death.

An acolyte pointed to an umbrella in the corner. She patted her hair; it was fine and damp. She shook her head.

– No thanks. I was only remarking.

– What do you ever do else? said Guy.

– LeopCorp, said Lucy. Every time I hear the word, I chill inside.

Guy said nothing.

When you read it on a page, it put you in mind of a big fat spotty cat. *LeopCorp*. When you heard it, though—

Rookie Marr. To be fair, Lucy had only ever met him once, at the phoney throne presentation. Immaculate in black. Except for the tie.

Pleased to meet you, Lucy had said. I like your tie.

The tie was orange.

Rookie thought it was a come-on. Vast wealth – though well within the dreams of avarice – had sheltered him from the rough and tumble of the street.

Thank you, Ms—

Legge, repeated Guy, who was responsible for the intros.

Thank you, Ms Legge. I understand our paths may cross soon. What is your role in the current set-up?

Outreach Officer, she said. Chief.

He smiled at the compliment and passed down the line.

That which is uttered, and that which is heard, do not always inhabit the same planet.

Afterwards, Guy had told her that the colour scheme was a kind of livery. Rookie Marr liked to be known as, but not addressed as, *Leopard*.

He could get help for that, she'd said.

She learned he wanted the town's name altered too, as though he were Lenin or somebody. *Marrdom* he was keen on, *Rookton* wasn't ruled out.

Why be shy? Lucy said. Call it *Leopardeen* and be done with it.

Hmm, Guy had said. Just occasionally it's good to know why we keep you on.

So, Leopard. In the scheme of things, he was a cloud that blotched the moon. He was a juggler with borrowed balls. But what could a city do, thought Lucy, waiting, attending, for cloud to pass or balls to drop? It took the whole of the Spanish people thirty-odd years to get rid of Franco. Franco had to die peacefully first – they didn't even get round to helping him do it.

– Where's Alison for any's sake? said Guy, jumpy now, peering down over the balcony. You Council people, really—
 – Alison's been spending time with her daughter, said Lucy.
 – Quality time no doubt, said Guy.
 – Helping her prepare. Gwen's got an interview on Monday in LeopCorp Towers.
 – Really? said Guy.
 – But you knew that, Guy, said Lucy. Don't come the innocent with me. You're probably on the panel.
 – It would help if Alison was here, said Guy. We need someone we can rely on, to monitor.
 – You lot have CCTV coming out your eyeballs, said Lucy.
 – No, but to evaluate, from your side, the Council side.
 – The Council can look after its side, said Lucy.
 She knew that wasn't true. The Provost and his cash-strapped Council were desperate for LeopCorp, and would do anything.

The City Council's Chief Executive, for example, was chairing the City Bypass Group, and had done so for the past dozen years. The Bypass was *his baby* and, because the baby had not emerged yet, from any of its many tubes of planning paper, it needed so much of his pre-natal attention that he chose not to be locked up in nitty-gritty committees with LeopCorp, or indeed its offshoot, UbSpec Total. He could thus avoid dirt, and abstain from controversy.

Instead Lucy and her deputy, Alison, were landed with the representative Council role, as *front officers.*
 What kind of *front* shall we put on today? she'd said to Alison before one meeting. Foo aboot *black-affrontit*? Alison had replied; she was seldom short of a breezy answer.

Lucy had been instrumental in fighting a LeopCorp plan for a citywide spaghetti of flumes. Swink had suddenly broadcast his enthusiasm for *The Flummery Option,* as he called it, on Echo TV, before it was even heard of by committee. The plan seemed as follows.

Item: Long bendy translucent flumes, to carry Spectators steeply from Cairncry and the like, more sedately from the likes of Cults, in a rush and whoosh of coloured water *to fairly get them into a mood,* according to the Lord Provost.

Item: Spectators unable to access flumes with a favourable slope to be pumped up in capsules from nearby suburbs, *to arrive gushing.*

Item: Those dwelling in distant Torry, principally Polish workers, however, *would not be pondered* to, he said, *and would have to arrive under their own steam.*

It would be a merde and an abandonment to allow this rubbish, Lucy decided. At the next meeting, she had confronted Guy.

What are these flumes supposed to be for, when we get down to it? she'd asked him.

Simple, said Guy. Firstly, to stimulate the customer base.

Yes, they should stimulate a few bases, she said.

Secondly, to integrate the surface transportion and entertainment agendas.

There was no answer to that. Guy didn't get where he was by an inability to jam abstract nouns together.

But, centrally, Guy said, to multiply value for all Spectacle, and, crucially, the inaugural Spectacle we're sponsoring, *Calving Glaciers.*

Thanks, she'd answered.

Apparently the water in the flumes was to be quite warm, a little below elbow. And, of course, similar warm water in the globe's plumbing was deemed to have precipitated the current rash of glaciorum praecox and glacier-wilt, the rather damp results of which threatened to overwhelm the dunes at Balmedie and drive to their few hills the folk of Bangladesh.

The proposed flumes, therefore, Guy had proclaimed, will maximise Spectacle through heightened client awareness—

Yes, Cairncry is a bit above sea level, said Lucy.

In supersomatic modes of virtual realism— said Guy.

Yeah, she'd said. Wet T-shirts: empathy for a drowning planet.

Guy had put on a show of fuming. Then he'd let her deploy her small moral thunders and, on this occasion, win.

She spoke against *throttling the whole city for the sake of Spectacle.* It would be *like a Salvationer strangled in his own euphonium.* Some councillors' eyes lit up at this. She moved smartly on. The flumes would *grip and drape the city,* she said, *like garish octopi, long after the glaciers are gone.*

Ye played a stormer, Alison said afterwards.

Yes, I was afraid I'd come out with *drip and grape the city,* said Lucy. Like Swinky might have.

Or *trip an rape,* said Alison.

Indeed, said Lucy.

Lucy had known that, by a quirk of rhetoric, it is always tough for your opponents to put the case *for garish octopi.*

But she suspected none of the LeopCorp UbSpec Total people were serious anyway. On grounds of expense alone. They had just lashed out on pavementette. Most of them abstained. They had probably just been playing a dummy, flushing out oppositionists to lull them with a meaningless victory.

What was the pavementette really for, though? When pressed, all Guy said was that it was the coming thing. It had a thrilling top speed, apparently, still awaiting trial.

it's aabody's show

Alison arrived on the balcony briskly, shaking her hair like a retriever fresh from a bog, and knocking moisture off her sweater.

– Hi, aa. Hi, Luce, she said, nae coat me, wish that rain wid pack it in. I micht as weel hae come by flume.

– Right, said Guy, I'm messaging the Fastness now. And, by the way, ladies, inaugural Spectacle or not, this had better be good.

– Weel, laddie, said Alison. It's nae jist us, it's ye as weel. It's aabody's show.

– Canton, can do, said Lucy, deliberately glib, to Guy's face. But can they? she thought. Can the cantons do?

lightly pregnant

In fact there was quite a history to them, as Lucy was in prime position to know. The city's natives, in so far as *natives* still had meaning, she had divided, from the electoral roll, into a dozen cantons. A bright informative card to that effect was sent to every door. She should have known her people. Most seemed built for durance, being on the stocky side of slender, the dark side of light, and the hornyhanded side of delicate and effete. The natives were not to be confused with Athenians, Venetians, or Ancient Egyptians, and seldom were. Only precocious recent arrivals fell for the canton trick.

In the main thoroughfare, what had been once been the odd Victory Parade or Going Away to Iraq, what had once linked hearts and minds in a May Day march for the working class, or had wiggled a fishnet thigh in the annual Charities Procession for the relief of conscience, was now maturing, *morphing* was probably the word, towards a series of regular Spectacles.

The plan was this. Each of the dozen cantons was allocated a month. Some apparently random word or phrase, as though arriving by junk mail or fortune cookie, would set the canton fretting. If there must be Spectacle, thought Lucy, they should be good ones. Lightly pregnant with art, politics, science and history, they should embody a call to action. For example, the first one: *Calving Glaciers.*

A large sheet of paper was procured, for the sake of argument white, and laid along the length of the Prep Hangar, which had been plonked in the vacant quad of Marischal College.

Tables with substances, tea, coffee, vodka, cocoa, were ranged along one long wall. Under the table, coke was available. For human consciousness, unjolted by chemicals, was deemed to be a waste of time, and on the boring side of banal.

Along the other long wall was a series of perspex cages, deliberately kept dark, then suddenly and singly illuminated by strobe lighting for about fifteen seconds, to reveal some icy phantasmagoria. Many and zany might be the notions hooked from the unconscious, frantic and furious the dreamings.

Music was thrust from speakers at the far end, just enough bars to infect the spirit, never enough to soothe. Alternate bursts from the pair of scherzos in Maxwell Davies's *Antarctic Symphony* were favourite.

Scents, naturally, were not neglected, and were hurled into the hangar space by blower. They had consulted their Attenborough. Essence of emperor penguin sweat, extract of polar bear cub poo.

The temperature was the one thing that never, or very seldom and by very little, varied. The best temperature for creativity being 33° Fahrenheit below blood-heat, so that brain may cool but bits don't freeze, every effort was made to maintain this. They used heat-pumps in dialogue with the tawdry, shifting residues of the outside world.

Notwithstanding such huge provision, the meticulous consideration of creative needs, and the astonishing range of boost, only a small proportion of incomers, and thus only a tiny proportion of eligible cantonians, took active part.

Ideas got smudged on the white paper with a brittle stick of charcoal. Polystyrene bergs, moulded by hot knives and heat guns, were the result. If such a tedious outcome occurred again, Lucy knew, LeopCorp would thrust the last vestige of community aside, and fill the gap with their own agenda.

Canton, can do! was her underdespairing slogan.

Lucy, on the hospitality balcony, shuffled from foot to foot. Alison was beside her.

Guy Bord spoke into his lapel. She heard the words, Mr Marr, I believe we're ready—

– I'm so glad you believe, Lucy whispered in his left ear.

– Shh, said Guy, for once, would you—

There was a pause.

It was the early days of Spectacle, thought Lucy. There would no doubt be better days, more vivid, more involving, days to come.

An early draft, thought Guy. When the technical side was up to speed, and all the contracts were in place, what he and Rookie would produce would be far fiercer.

A voice came over the loudspeaker system.

– In the name of LeopCorp, and of the City Council, I name this street *UberStreet*.

White blossom in a colosseum, bubbles eddied in the air.

Bubbles alighted, the affected roared. Rice-cakes fell, as if, and frangible meringues. Then the strung charges of Semtex broke out bigger suggestive lumps to skirl at. Airy fridge-doors, bantam anvils, a slow white van. Tumbling like a car boot blessing, a street baptismal.

As pluffs and whuffs continued above, folk whacked each other with joky clubs, till they were in white bubbles, into white bubbles, really high.

– Ooh, said Alison. I fair fancy that.

– What? said Lucy.

– Bein in ower the thighs, said Alison. Floatin voters hae aa the fun.

A green bottle flew through the air, and there was blood. Other bottles flew, and there was quite a flow. People started swimming across the top of the bubbles to get to each other.

– Hmm, said Guy.

– Hmm? queried Alison.

– There go your floating voters. Thrashing around in the bloody nursery, trying to bump each other off.

– Guy— said Alison.

– Yes, Alison—?

– Get a life.

Lucy had had enough. She turned her back on proceedings, and left soon after. She thanked the staff in the ante-room and bid them *Dobranoc, Goodnight*. She didn't see Bing Qing, who was in charge, and was in too much of a hurry to seek her out.

After an hour or two, the last of the bergs was clawed to atoms.

The Leopard, on behalf of LeopCorp, from his high perch, having first pressed the orange button to detonate concatenated Semtex, now pressed the black, and the invisible drifted belt that was UberStreet began to vibe eastward, down, then faintly uphill, towards his vantage.

Just below in the Castlegate was a carved, blackened, hollow sandstone crown, where former traitors were beheaded. Now it was topped by a white marble unicorn on a tall pedestal. You could have gone a long way round the city, no doubt, asking what a white unicorn on a tall pedestal actually stood for, or rather pranced for, horny beast. The whole kit and caboodle was called the Mercat Cross, namely, in modern abstract, *Intersection of the Market*. Rookie Marr had not yet intimated any need to rename that.

At the moment the rotating pavementette began its progress, the Mercat Cross, mounted on hidden hydraulic jacks, began to move upwards, mm by mm, so that a useful crevasse began to yawn.

This facility was titled, plain as you like, the Hole.

A million million bubbles came dancing along, to be siphoned off. Gradually the woven legend was revealed: *Mountain Heart, Mountain Heart, Mountain Heart*. But the solider débris of pleasure still had to be sorted. Not just the empty Stella bottles. Most citizens who weren't rat-arsed, paralytic, smashed, totalled or out of it had the sense to attempt to flee down side streets. Others, prone or supine, vibrated along.

Down the Hole, masked Nigerian doctors and Malaysian nurses and Polish scene-shifters began to choose from the two issues of glove, red rubber and white latex.

half-zipped

Lucy got down to the Station taxi rank cursing Spectacle, cursing the damp, cursing herself mostly, then cursed again; there were no trains at this time of night, not even the Virgin Bullet. So no taxis. She turned back and there was one coming out of Carmelite, with its light on. She hailed it. She had beaten the crowd.

– Rubislaw Den, she said. South. What's that smell?

– Need ye ask, said the driver.

She skrunshled tight to the door in her smart coat. There were white beads stuck by static to her ankles. She thought of the bloke on the Back Wynd steps, Mr I-Guess-Your-Name, Mr Disturbing. He hadn't been there tonight. Just a thin brown nylon sleeping-bag, half-zipped, and a rumpled blanket. Perhaps he was caught up in Spectacle; perhaps he had sought a deeper darkness.

She left them to it, the lot of them. She switched off her phone.

april 2

Most of the injured from *Calving Glaciers* were quite unhappy. There were three broken arms, two collarbones, assorted broken toes, an out of kilter hip and suspected pelvis. Aggravated alcoholic concussion aplenty. There was an initial exchange of numbers in A&E at Foresterhill, between the compos mentis. If they hadn't gone off the boil when they got home in the early hours, they would have rung round, formed a support group, and a concern group, set up a boycott of UberStreet and sued for compensation, depending on who was up for taking a lead.

They were still waiting.

these are not our times

Lucy chaired the debrief in the Council Chamber, surrounded by portraits of mainly men, sitting on gilt identical chairs. There was a Motion of No Confidence pending on the décor, from the genderistas.

Guy was doodling on a piece of paper, then scoring it out.

– Welcome, said Lucy. I'm glad we could all make it. What's the initial reaction?

– Hmm, said Guy. As I think I said, far too womby, extremely samey. The thick end of not a lot.

Lucy gave him a look. *The thick end of not a lot.* A comment like that about summed LeopCorp up. If you could ever sum them.

Guy Bord was now Acting Director of UbSpec Total, the public-private partner of the City's ReCreation and Social Engineering Department, whereas she, Lucy Legge, ReCSoc's Chief Outreach Officer, was Chair of the Joint Working Group. UbSpec Total was a jaw of the Leisure Division of LeopCorp and was trying to swallow without trace a dodgy firm of longish standing, Swink Stillwater, which had its sticky fingers in Mountain Heart and many local pies, when LeopCorp as a whole moved in.

If it wasn't possible to follow all this, that was what was intended. What *public-private* meant, what *partner* meant, when the chips were down, was anybody's guess.

At this stage, at all stages, LeopCorp's wider plans were unknown.

– Samey? said Lucy.

– Samey, said Guy. Canton One didn't really run with the idea. Polystyrene, polystyrene—

– The hose of polystrene balls was not so good, said Otto, tracking his boss's lead.

– I didn't see that, said Lucy.

– Leaving early doesn't help, said Guy.

– There wis a burst hose suddenly sprayin, said Alison. A lassie breathed some in and it cloggit her lungs. I went doon til her, she wis gaggin. I tried tae phone ye. She gey near croakit.

– Guy? said Lucy.

– No, that was within parameters, said Guy. That's why you do risk assessment. Without risk, Spectacle is dead. Correct, Otto?

– I had tae dae mooth-tae-mooth, said Alison, and I dinna even like women. Had tae turn masel intil a human hoover.

Guy gave her a hard look. The more she spoke in the Doric, the spikier she got.

– She okay? said Lucy.

– Otto got her to sign a disclaimer, said Guy. He chequed her out, two thousand.

– I wasn't referring to money, said Lucy.

– She wis fine, said Alison. But I'm still spittin.

Guy was thinking of Luna, naturally.

– I must say I didn't like any of the ending, said Lucy.

– You didn't see it, said Guy.

After the spontaneity on Blissville's stair he was still wondering.

– Because I didn't like it, said Lucy. I knew about it. It was grim, degrading.

– Leave the endings to me, Lucy, said Guy.

He wondered if his mad fleeing had caused her pain. How could he get in touch, apologise?

– Have ye got ither endins? said Alison. I dinna want tae land up every full moon wi a moothfu o baas.

– Similar ending, better effects, said Guy. I think we can really feature the ending, bump up the balcony tickets at the LeopCorp end.

He could ask for a summit with the Leopard, have a fresh chance with Luna.

– This is a community Spectacle, said Lucy. I'm not buying into dearer tickets.

– We've had all these arguments, said Guy. Your Council won't wear deficit. Nor will the muppets further south. UbSpec has to stand on its own two feet.

– And knock folk off theirs? said Lucy.

– Off what? said Guy. He must be off his head. Luna was only setting him up.

– Their feet, said Lucy. Tumbling them into a pit—

– In mediaeval times this was understood, said Guy. You Sixties people still cling to your lovey-dovey vision. It doesn't put bums on seats.

– I don't want to put bums anywhere, said Lucy.

– So what are you really saying? said Guy. You want cuddly spectacle but not Spectacle? You want a menagerie, but not real circus?

– It's not a circus, it's a long straight street, said Lucy.

– True, Alison said. And it's nae aboot cuddlin a menagerie, we leave that tae ye, Guy. Ye havena a clue far we're comin fae, in ReCSoc. We've aye been mair ootreach, the educational side o things.

Alison could be pretty staunch.

– *Outreach*, said Guy. What can I say? *The educational side of things*—

– Let's take a break, said Lucy.

During the break Auto Otto, as he was known, Guy's chief assistant, spent some time plying Alison with bourbon biscuits. Though an airburst of wet brown crumb from him weakened his case. Alison retired to the Ladies and was late when they reconvened. Lucy waited for her, while Guy rolled and unrolled his set of minutes.

– Let's move on, said Lucy.

– Indeed, said Guy.

– Canton Two is waiting for the word.

– Or phrase, said Guy.

– We've done contemporary for starters, said Lucy. I wonder if we shouldn't delve into history now.

– The Civil War, said Alison, wis gey bad roond here. Nae mony folk ken that.

She and Lucy had researched it together.

– Perhaps because nobody gives a monkey's, said Guy.

– Well they damn well should, said Lucy.

– Believe me, said Guy. Nobody gives a stuff for the Covenanters.

– Thae Royalists did— said Alison.

– Maybe this is old helmet now? wheedled Otto.

– The Battle of the Bridge of Dee, said Lucy, meant a lot, we know—

– To nobody, said Guy. Small battle, not many dead.

Otto opened his palms towards Alison, to console her. And to signal their probable defeat.

Few councillors were contributing, but that was standard; at least they were awake. You could pick up your allowance without being caught in awkward crossfire.

– During the Civil War there was raping in the streets for three days, said Lucy coolly. Unchecked rape. Thought that might appeal, Mr Bord?

– Raping is heavy, said Guy. The genderistas nodded. There are better ways, more consensual. He sensed them turn to look at him.

– Here's the title for next month, said Guy, it just came to me. *Underwater Sex.*

– Jesus— said Lucy.

– Beyond him, even, said Alison. In aa probability.

– If we must blow bubbles in the street, said Guy, let's blow them to better purpose. Just you watch, *Underwater Sex*, it will pull them in.

– Consumed by Spectacle, said Lucy.

– Way to go, said Guy.

– Unconscious with lust, said Lucy, lust for unconsciousness.

– Steady, said Guy.

It was becoming a ping-pong match, between the Situationist with '68 stripes and Debord's much later reject.

– Any other ideas? said Lucy. But after Guy's last contribution, only a single species of imagery was surfable in the Chamber.

Silence.

– La lutte continue, said Lucy.

– Give it a rest, said Guy.

The meeting adjourned.

The genderistas rushed to an ante-room to take a line.

Lucy left the Town House, using the old plush lift with the hand-operated mesh doors. She offered to take Alison to the Art Gallery for coffee.

– *Underwater Sex*, said Lucy. I'm on the way out, it's obvious. These are not our times.

– Na, said Alison. I'm there ahind ye. But I've got a date.

– Who with?

– Nae sayin.

– Fair enough. Tell me tomorrow.

– Aye, right, said Alison.

freedom for dissenters

Alison headed off to see Gwen first, give her some last-minute coaching for the interview. Gwen was reluctant to emerge from her bedroom, while her mother was trying hard not to revisit it. With a bit of resolve they could get closer.

She spoke from the hall.

– Gwen, luve, I've an appointment for yir hair. Come ben an I'll tell ye.

– Tell me through the door, said Gwen, it's not important.

– Hey, said Alison. Ye canna go oot for interview like that. Nae bloody wey.

– Rosa says freedom means nothing unless it's freedom for dissenters.

– It's nae freedom we're bletherin aboot, it's a job.

– Rosa says—

– Rosa says sweet Fittie Airms about interviews. Wise up, quinikie, I've got tae ging oot in a minute. Yir appointment's three-forty. Here's fifty quid sae ye can get some decent claes.

– Fifty, said Gwen.

– I can mak it eichty, Gwen, but that's ma limit.

– Eighty, said Gwen.

– I'll leave it on the table. A hunner, that's yir lot. I'm oot the nicht, mind?

No reply.

– That's me, then, said Alison. See ye. An tidy that room o yirs, please, or the landlord'll rip oor lease in flitters. Okay?

– I'm outta this dump anyway, said Gwen.

– Yeah, said her mother. Very Rosa. Bye.

The more effort she made, the further they seemed to grow apart.

Like the time they took off together, camping and walking, when Gwen was sixteen. And Gwen just sat at the top of Devil's Point for hours, glowering up and down the Lairig Ghru, as the clouds swept lower. Come on, she'd said, time tae ging doon. Time for you to go down? Gwen had replied. Look, Gwen, she'd said, if there's somethin— There's nothing, that's the whole point, isn't it? Gwen had replied. There's either something or nothing, you either go for it flat out or stay up here for ever. I dinna get ye, said her mother. I wish you hadn't, said Gwen. Who's my father anyway, is he dead or just fucked off? Alison turned away from her. Did you bore him to death? said Gwen. When she was able to turn back, Gwen was little more than an outline, in the grey heart of the cloud, three feet away.

On the way down, Gwen had sent chunks of scree skittering into the abyss with her boots.

Lucy walked slowly alongside the stilled pavementette. The odd polystyrene bubble was still flirting in and out of shop doorways, in the eddies and gusts. For the next two weeks the street would be open again, a pedestrian precinct. Then it would be closed off and kitted out with all the aqueous scaffolding of idle gratification.

She quickened her pace. Between O2 and Orange she started down the Back Wynd Steps.

She could see immediately it was him there, a way he had of hunching his blanket, like a chief-in-exile rather than the manky bauchle he seemed to be. Though when he spoke, he did seem more alert, attuned somehow.

– Hello again, he said. I recognise these lovely feet.
– But I was in heels last time.
– Can't have everything. What's my name, then?
– Don't know, she said. Still can't think. Possibly never knew it.
– But you know me?
– Seems that way. How do you exist like that?

She did keep one pace back from him.

– You exist. Your day's been hard, he said. Fact?
– How do you know? said Lucy.
– Tell by the way you scuttle. Pressured, emptied, unbalanced.
– I try not to show it, Lucy said.
– Did you scuttle along with me ever?
– Wasn't much of a one for scuttling.

Pause.

– What do you need for a meal tonight? she said.
– Company would be good.
– Here's a five – a ten.
– Places that cost a ten wouldn't let me in.
– In case I don't see you again, here's twenty.
– Is that the plan?

– No, it's not the plan. I've got plans up to here, other people's plans, sick of them.

– What do you do? he said.

– I'd rather not say.

– Are you fulfilling a life's ambition?

– Somebody's maybe, not particularly mine.

– Does it matter?

– I think I used to know the answer to that. Look, have to go.

– One of us always has to.

– What do you mean by that?

– One of us always has to go, it's what I believe.

– Does that count as belief? said Lucy.

– Sit down.

– Can't.

– Sit down, he said. It's a city, isn't it?

– That's not the meaning, said Lucy.

– That's what's wrong, people don't know the meaning. People don't sit down together.

– I was at a meeting all morning, she said.

– Call that sitting? Sit down.

– On these filthy steps?

– You're talking about my home.

She took a small step back, the better to survey him.

– You do this deliberately, don't you? said Lucy.

– What?

– Useless beggar. It's an act, it's a got-up act that absolves you.

– What from? he said. Absolves me from what exactly?

– From making the shitty decisions the rest of us have to.

– If only you knew.

There was a sort of hovering in the debate, if it was debate.

So, wait, he said. Wait, who you really angry with—?

– It's— No—

– I know, you need to go. See you next time. Mebbe I'll have moved.

– You won't, she said. You won't have.

– Might have changed landings—

– What for?

– Gone up or down in the world.

– Ha.

– Your name's Iris, isn't it? he said. I knew an Iris.

– Must confess, said Lucy. Not cut out to be an Iris.

– Oh, sad, he said.

– So then—

– Have to go? he said.

– Need to— yeah, said Lucy. See ya.

as they hit bottom

Guy had dumped *Underwater Sex* by next meeting, for a mercy. Couldn't get swift enough delivery of plexi of the right flex and strength to take the weight of water.

He flung his interim defeat aside. He saw the genderistas grinning at each other and their male sidekicks, and counting victory. Hoping to see Luna again, if *see* her was the term, Guy had texted the Leopard for an extra meeting, but had got, well, nil in return. He hadn't dare to phone.

– Let's offer Canton Two a Mel Gibson sequel, Guy said. *Faintheart.*

– No, let's get back on track, said Lucy. She had decided to tough it out. Let's open it all back up.

– Ooh, the Covenanters are coming, said Guy. Please, Mama, no Covenanters—

Guy fixed Otto across the table with mock-wide eyes, and wobbled his shiny dome like a novelty toy on a parcel shelf.

– Before Guy has a fit, said Lucy, here's an idea. Let's have a Spectacle about the Harbour. There's plenty to celebrate there. Aberdeen Harbour Board is the oldest company in Britain. Uberdeen now, of course. Oldest limited company.

– Whoopee-woopsie! said Guy. If it's not *educate*, it's *celebrate*—

– Get ower it, Guy, said Alison.

She really could be remarkably staunch.

Guy glanced at Otto. Otto shrugged.

Lucy cleared her throat. Davie Dae-Aathing, she said, rid the Harbour of a huge blocking rock by lashing to it, at low tide, hundreds of barrels. Early sixteen hundreds.

– Holding my breath here, said Guy.

– The ropes came under terrific strain, continued Lucy, but when the tide rose to maximum, the rock lifted too.

– Relieved to hear that, said Guy.

– And when the tide turned to go back out to the North Sea, so did Davie's rock. Craig Metallan they called it. We could have Craig Metallan ebbing and bumping the length of UberStreet, then all the new boats coming in, trade opening up.

– What a spectacle, said Guy, for those days. Rubbish now. Papier-mâché lumpy thing bopping along UberStreet, under some helium—

– Sponsors, said Alison, we could easy get, surely? For aa the balloons—?

– All the balloons? said Guy. If it's anything like last time, they'll be burst inside five minutes.

He could imagine bursting inside Luna, in far fewer than that.

– Try to imagine various vessels, Guy, gliding along on your pavementette, said Lucy. Coals from Newcastle, lace from Brussels, esparto—

– Guano— said Guy.

Lucy inwardly gave him that. She had that sinking feeling. She knew she was on rightish lines, but without the heart or thrust somehow. She lived in a sea city, sure, but wasn't really up to speed, if that was the phrase, as a sea person.

They attacked, from opposite directions, ten more ideas, without truceing once in the middle.

– Running into a big shortage of days now, said Guy. Decide.

The minute a decision was made, he could text Rookie again for a meeting.

– Let's sleep on it, said Lucy.

– Lucy, eh, a bittie better? said Alison, once they had clashed shut the black forfex of the ancient lift.

– Maybe, said Lucy, as they were on their way down. Guy's only biding his time. Soon he'll really provoke us. No way he wants us

50

stymieing UbSpec that much longer. It's UbSpec Total, after all. Ultimately, it's not the Council's show, far less the people's.

– Yeah, said Alison. Suppose.

– Remember, said Lucy, as they hit bottom. If I'm forced out, you've got to find a way to stay. Alison—?

Alison was distant, slightly smiling, like she was looking forward to a somebody else who would make up for everything.

– Who is he? I recognise that look.

– Who's who? said Alison, adopting her boss's accents for once.

– Come on, lass, said Lucy, responding, I'll buy ye a drink.

animal recognition

The leopardskin chair swivelled round to the tall slit window. The Leopard had just had that window reconfigured to give a perfect sightline down UberStreet.

Above him on the battlement roof was a replica working cannon and a tall flag, snapping in the wind. Although there was still indecision over renaming the city so soon a second time, there had been no tussle over the flag. By happy historical chance the flag came crested with two rippling leopards already.

Rookie Marr opened the slit window and trained his SAD rifle, the Swiss Army Digigun. It was a SAD 3, the one with the rifle, telescope, camera and mugshot database combined. SAD 1 had earphones and music-player bundled with the rifle, but music did little for him. SAD 2 had animal recognition and laser lock-on, but he knew his animals anyway, having eaten most. SAD 4 had the whole damn shoot, but it put the overall weight up, and brought on wobble.

By looking down through SAD 3's scope, Rookie could see whoever came in or out of the Town House, the City's formal HQ. The lift itself was fully bugged. He'd heard the chat, but the picture scan was set too fast, reducing the evidence to fuzzy glimpses.

He'd come across this Lucy once at a reception. He needed to suss the Alison out. After all, he had just employed her daughter.

a female polar bear

They went in the pub with the longest bar in Scotland, The Prince, rechristened by Alison *The Price of Mince*. There was about twenty years between them, nothing really. Alison found a gap at the bar to get the drinks in. Lucy sank into the snug cushion of an open cubicle. Alison came back, set down the glasses, fluttered four fingers towards somebody bar side, then wriggled in.

– Cheers, said Lucy. Well—?

  – Very well, said Alison.

  – Does he want your hand in marriage?

  – At the very least. Hey you, behave!

  – Hey me nothing, said Lucy. It's time you had a bit of stability.

  – Thanks a heap. Hey, that reminds me. There wis this polar bear, see, said Alison.

  – Polar bear, said Lucy. Really?

  – It wis in the White Star offices in New York.

  – Oh yeah? When would this be?

  – Lang ago. Afore my time. 1912.

  – Before mine too, madam, said Lucy, I'll have you know.

  – Sae it was the White Star offices in New York, see, 1912. And there's this great lang queue shufflin alang the lobby, an shufflin up the stairs. An they're weepin and wailin.

  – Weeping and wailing?

  – Weepin and wailin. An this woman in black at the front of the queue gaes up tae the mannie at the desk on the third storey an she says, *D'ye have word at all*, she says, *d'ye have word at all*, she had a mant—

  – Mant?

  – Stammer. *D'ye have word at all*, she says, *on Patrick McGonagall? No, missus, very sorry*, says the White Star man. *No word.*

  Then a guy in a top hat steps forrard an he says, *I say, my man*, he says, *do you have any word of the Countess Cosmo?*

An the mannie at the White Star desk says, *No, I'm terribly sorry, sir. No word.*

An aince again the queue starts shufflin.

Just then there's an affa kerfuffle fae the bottom of the stairs, followit by a heavy *clump-clump*, up through the first storey, up through the second, an finally, clumpin on tae the third storey landin, in flies a female polar bear, and elbows her wey tae the desk.

An the polar bear taks a fair grip o the desk, an leans richt ower. An, as the White Star mannie shrinks awa tae nithin in his seat, the polar bear says—

– What you stopping for? said Lucy.
  – Big paws—
  – Get on, you!
  – The polar bear says, *Ony word aboot ma hoose?*

– That'll go twice round the world by Christmas, said Lucy. We could do a Spectacle on it. With a cardboard *Titanic* like Fellini's *Rex*.
  – Foo many wrecks did he hae like, Fellini?
  – Not *wrecks: Rex. Rex Rex.*
  – Ye soond like a corncrake on heat.
  – Alison, please, I'm a bit past being on heat— said Lucy.
  – Dinna kid yirsel, said Alison. Humans are aye on heat.
  Lucy looked into her own distance.

– It's funny, said Alison. We've just deen Calving Glaciers. But if we doved straight intae Polar Bears—
  – *Doved*? said Lucy.
  – They'd accuse us o being frigid or somethin. Ken fit they're like, the Gender Beasties—
  – Never mind the genderistas, said Lucy. They do their best. How's Gwen? Did she get the job?
  – Workin in North Turret, start straight aff. Under Information Officer. *Publicity and other duties*, the descrip says, live-in compulsory, free accom. LeopCorp provides the uniform. Black slacks, orange blouse. Her partner Bill's gotten a start as well. Assistant Principal Tasting Officer, he doesna even hae tae cook nithin.

– She pleased? said Lucy.

– Think so. I am an I'm nae. She's nae as tough as she thinks, wioot her mither.

– G & T, love? To toast Gwen.

– Sure, said Alison. As it comes.

random attempts

In South Turret, in Blissville, Luna made a set of random attempts at finding a key sequence. She punched the remote, but it didn't reveal a window. She thought of, what was his name? Then she plumped down on the circular couch and resigned herself to the plasma. She did this three times a day, sometimes thirty.

In the adjoining turret, Rookie Marr was on the phone to TV interests. Global interests, there was no other kind. The extreme brilliance of the UberStreet package seemed to have got their juices working. All he had to do was bring them to auction.

There had been a few calls back and fore, but the *Calving Glaciers* support, concern, boycott and sueing group still hadn't met. *Spectacle Concern* was mooted as a name. Somebody thought somebody else was going to write to the paper.

Spermy went champing down to the shipyard and through security to check how they were faring with the *Girl Julie*. She was deserted. A dark and light grey minesweeper had come into drydock. All the wrights were gathered round her.

– It's the Gulf, said the manager.

– The Gulf is it? said Spermy. The Gulf will aye be there next year, maist o ma fish winna.

– Possibly true, said the manager, but we have to take our orders where we can get them.

– Foo can a man like me compete wi a navy?

– Well, defence contracts are special, said the manager.

– Aye, said Spermy. At cost-plus, they fuckin wid be.

Maciek had arranged to meet Pawel for a walk, beyond the allotments and out to the Battery and the South Breakwater.

– This reminds me of Gdansk, said Pawel. Westerplatte. My grandfather was killed there. Cavalry.

– I've been there, said Maciek, it is important.

– So why are Poles still running round? said Pawel. Now we got our country back?

– We got our choices, said Maciek.

– But not our houses, said Pawel. I'm a skilled builder. There are fourteen people in my flat. Am I black or something? Am I some sort of Jew?

– Pawel, said Maciek, if that's how you feel, I don't think you and me can work good together.

– We're Poles, said Pawel.

– Being a Pole is not enough, said Maciek.

– Not enough? said Pawel. You some kind of traitor?

– No, said Maciek, I'm not a traitor.

– Well fuck you, man, said Pawel, you're wasting my time.

The chestnut stall was back in good nick. Andy couldn't attend to it any more; he couldn't look down at all, with his disease, could only touch things. But Ludwig was a good hand with the WD-40 and a set of spanners. He cleaned and tightened the whole shebang.

– Coals are through the roof, Andy, you know this? said Ludwig.

– Fit I aye said, Ludwig, man, said Andy. Closin the pits wis a real brainwave.

Amande had gone down the town on her bus pass to try to buy conical bags. In conical bags, it looked like you were getting a bargain, and the chestnuts were nice to hold, like a treat. The cost of imported food was going up fast, with fuel and all, chestnuts were no exception. She and Ludwig had bought thirty kilo from a stall in the Green, but she wasn't sure about shelf-life, so she'd exited everything from Andy's fridge. Poor Andy was well beyond fridges anyhow, he was a menace to life and limb just spreading a piece.

Bing Qing was having trouble with her Poles. She paid them the minimum wage, and made sure a clear system was there for sharing out tips. But they claimed they could get more in their own country. Lech was the spokesman.

– Sometimes you have to think about that, Bing Qing said. You have to feel for yourself what is best.

– Six pounds fifty, said Lech, we think would be best.

– Six pound fifty, very nice money, said Bing Qing. Six pound fifty I cannot do.

Zander Petrakis had a meeting with Lord Provost Swink. He wanted the city's support for something. Well, Town and Gown have always gone hand in glove, Swink had remarked to his dresser, Walty.

– Come in, Mister Protrakis, he said.

– Petrakis, said Zander.

– What can I do you for?

It was a ludicrous expression for the occasion.

– You can do for me a great thing, said Zander. My Crete is facing the ruin of Knossos. You know Knossos?

– But it's a ruin already, is that no so? said Swink.

– A film company, said Zander, want to trick it out with knock-down walls and three-sided chambers. For their filming, the old labyrinth is too tough.

– But your Crete will fight that? said the Provost.

– No, said Zander, that is sadly the point. That is why I seek, and others seek too, international support for heritage values.

– Oh, said the Provost. We're hardly international, we're only Uberdeen.

– Nobody is international, said Zander sharply, unless in the mind.

– And except the big boys, surely? said the Provost.

– That is the point, you have hit the point, said Zander. We can only resist international with international.

– Well, I've just called through for tea, said the Provost, tea and a scone, if you'd care to join me.

– That may not solve it, said Zander.

Zander had had forty years of couthiness and its claustrophobic by-lanes. He took his leave.

– Well, cheerio, Mister Protaxis, if that's how ye feel. I'm sorry we're no up to mythical standard, like you lads in Crete.

mister kitoff

This time Lucy didn't hesitate.

A quick goodbye to Alison in the pub, Alison wanting another, then she crossed UberStreet at Market Street, and inclined up, till she got to the heart of mobile phone land, where Orange, O2, Lug, Link and Vodaphone all had premises.

She could remember past shops, declined emporia: Lipton's, Woolies, British Home Stores. But now, apart from mobile phones, there were only four other species of shops left on the street. Fast food, walk-in insurance, charity and cheapo.

There were two branches of Cod Zone Fritter, three of I Do It Fried Way and four of British Heart Trust. At British Heart Trust you could pick up a willed sofa for sixty quid or a reconditioned telly for fifty, and feel good, boosting research funds for such a worthwhile cause. Close by were a few insurance firms you'd never heard of, some back-of-a-lorry quantity discounters like 99 and Twist, and several board-ups. All the prestigious branded shops, like UCKU, Plus, Next Butt One, were tucked in malls.

She went down the steps. At first she didn't see him.

Because he was down a landing.

– What you doing down here?
   – Got moved on, didn't I? They tried to take my particulars.
   – Your particulars?
   – Except I don't have any. *Name?* No chance. *Address?* Here. *Next of kin?* You tell me.
   – Did that satisfy them?
   – No. There was only one. Promised he'd be back, before *the close of play* he called it. With what he called a *colleague*.
   – What then?
   – Night in the jail if I'm lucky, Lucy.

Pause.

– It is, isn't it? *Lucy*?
– No, said Lucy.

Pause.

– Yes.
– *No, yes*? he said. I thought it probably was.
– Think you should come with me this time, she said.
– Musta been a real bad day. It's okay, money's fine.
– I insist.

The taxi driver wouldn't countenance it. Nor would the driver of
OediBus, which was now truly global, having gobbled Greyhound
and other majors. OediBus was the Halliburton of wheels. They
carried millions now, civil and military, but not palpable lice.
– Hey, min, you're jumpin, said the driver-conductor.
– So? he said.
– So, jump.
He dragged along in her wake. She walked a fraction ahead
anyway.

It was difficult for Lucy not to say *Let's get you into the bath*, as soon
as they got through the door.
– Let's get you into the bath, she said.
– Who's we? he replied.
– Don't be difficult, she said.
– I don't know what I'm like underneath. It may be difficult. You
may need scissors.
– I'm sure I've got an electric saw. If that's what turns you on,
Mister Kitoff.

Getting the boxers off alone would have required a charge of black
blasting powder, or else some plastique pressed in the fly. Under the
sink she found a pair of wooden tongs.
– If your name was ever inside your underpants, if you ever
went to that kind of school, it is now officially obliterated, she said.
– The school or the name? he said. Jolly D.

– It'll take a Dee to wash this off. I should have marched you up to the Linn and chucked you in.

– Did we ever go there? he said.

– Go and just stand in the shower, she said, while I set fire to these.

Any bath would clog with that amount of tar.

She was able to flush muck away as it delaminated off him in dauds. Off his torso and buttocks and legs.

– You seem to have preserved quite well, she said. Bog person.

– Thanks, he said.

– Now the head, said Lucy.

He flinched and drew away.

– We might as well go the whole hog, she said.

The head was mankiest of the lot.

– Must we?

– We must.

She made sure it was only warm. He flinched again. She reduced the flow. But again he drew back.

Only after slow advance and quick retreats did Lucy divine what was up with him. Most skulls are eggs basically, but his was nothing like. It was jaggy with dykes and dents. Crenellated, like a ridge deformed on the ocean floor; oozed, congealed with lava. In its heyday, possibly, sulphurous bubbles danced.

– What the—? breathed Lucy.

– Is there a problem? he said.

It went way beyond amateur forensics. Lodged between her hands was a jigsaw. A fragile 3-D jigsaw, all the colours facing in.

– So did I ever sleep with you? he said brightly. Now that you see me in the altogether.

Altogether, she thought. There's an *altogether* here?

– Did you? he said. Did I?

– Come on you, get dried.

– How much is missing? she asked, as she tucked him up in the spare bedroom.

– A few decades, he said. That's nothing on big ships.

– Decades— said Lucy.

– Perfect name for them, he said.

– What happened?

– The memory function got squeezed the most. I don't know what happened. Very little of what's happened since connects. I can't hack into it.

– Don't say that, said Lucy. *Hack*. It sounds horrible. But you remembered me. Three days in a row.

– I remembered your feet. I thought I remembered your name. It's orientation that escapes me. And how my story hangs together.

– What hope is there? she said, sitting on the far end of the bed. She nearly said, *So is there no hope?*

– When the NHS was flush I was down for a series of three ops. Neuro-surgery on the hippocampus. The first one worked, the second was aborted due to side-effects. The third one never came to the top of their list.

– What do you mean *worked*?

– I got a lucid spell, hyper-lucid. The hippocampus, the short-term store, suddenly started flashing buried stuff over to the neo-cortex. Boy was it flashing. It was like I was in my own film. Lots of supporting characters dancing in and out, with plenty to say for themselves. But the flashing was all concentred on one day.

– What day was that?

– January 1st, '68.

– What a year—

– Was it?

– They say if you remember it, you weren't there, said Lucy.

– That's not much help, he said. Anyway, in the recovery room they took tape after tape of me, warbling happily and unhappily on. The technician made a sort of story from them.

– The technician? Was that part of his job description?

– No, but he moved around doing lots of jobs, moved all over.

Always poking his mike up people's noses. Any good stuff he got, he tried to weld that into stories. And into the *front ends* of novels he used to call them.

– Is that ethical?

– What, only writing the front end of a novel? I shouldn't think so. People want to know how it all works out.

– No, I didn't mean that. I mean turning people's lives into fiction?

– I wouldn't know if it was my life or not. It was certainly very vivid. But he had a way with words, did Tam. The surgeon reconstructed my brain, and Tam reconstructed my story.

– Very neat.

– Think so? he said, pointing to his skull. As he took his hand away from the crash-scene, she noticed something she hadn't seen during the mucky episode in the bathroom. His palms were kind of gnarled, sort of corrugated, criss-crossed.

– Horny-handed, eh? he said. What do you think? I must have put some work in, in my day.

– Hold on, she said. I thought of something a minute ago. Never mind Tam's version, did you never listen to the tapes yourself?

– Patients hadn't accrued those kinds of rights. It was their tape, the NHS.

– It was your memories!

– They were reserving them for use in psychotherapy, but when the second op blew up, they put me out in the long grass. A home overlooking a soothing landscape and a bendy river. I escaped of course. Holed up on an island, other places. And the rest, with my memory, is not history.

– Tam— said Lucy.

– I don't think I'm *Tam*—

– No, but where's he now?

– Oh, he tried to make a go of writering but nobody could make money from him. He's down at Left Luggage. He keeps the drafts in a spare locker. They all have a locker or two they work themselves for bonus. It's understood.

– Will he still have your *front end*?

61

– Lurking, I daresay. He took care of it. I spoke to him only last week, when I drifted back. He did offer me the draft. But doubt very much that I could face it.

Lucy stood up.
    – Hey, been a real big day.
    – Like *Need to go*, over again?
    – No, like *Goodnight, buster.* Sleep tight.
    – Night, he said. Thanks for the douche.
    – Forget it— said Lucy, and bit her tongue.
    – Already have, he said.
    – Okay, you, she said. I'm off early, Edinburgh tomorrow, so I'll leave a breakfast out. Oh, and a shirt and pants from the chest. Of my late father.
    – Breeks too would be good, he said. Some sort of trousers.

the inner or the outer man

He spent part of next morning baggily wandering the house. There was a lot of sculpture, some busts, some abstracts. He got lost several times, and kept seeing the same photograph or painting where he didn't expect. Kept dunting his shin on some kist or chest in a darker hallway.

He got frightened of the house and came back to his room with a tray of stuff from the larder and fridge.

He wasn't happy in his room either, so he went through to Lucy's. He looked for matches on her bedside table. He found them on the black marble mantel and lit the old gas fire.

He put his hands on top of the marble and toasted his chest and points south. His right finger traced and retraced the pale veins on the mantel, the twigs and branchings.

It almost reminded him, but of what?

From downstairs a grandfather kept dinging.

He wanted to go down, arrest the pendulum.

But wasn't sure about finding his way back up.

The gas fire was still giving out its low blue roar when she came in from the evening train.

– What you doing on my bed?

– Sorry, I was away there. My room was cold.

– It's centrally heated.

– I couldn't see that.

– I've brought us tea. I got Marks and Sparks kippers at Waverley. Build you back up.

– Couldn't look at a kipper, sorry. Smell.

– Do you want to go down to the station now? See Tam? Tam must know your name, surely?

– I was *A13* to him, he said. Before they picked me up for the first op I had been wandering. Nobody had an earthly where I'd been. No papers or nothing. *A13*.

– He calls you *A13*? Hardly.

– No. *Jim*. As in *pal*. Tam's originally from Glasgow.

They went down in her Morris Traveller, going round by St Machar Drive and the Prom to avoid the centre.

– This car's a throwback, he said. It's not like the other cars I see.

It was a modest, pleasant estate, with curved ash external framing.

– It's an honest trundler, she said. I don't take it to work. I keep it in the garage against rust, away from the haar and the salt air.

– What crap is that? he said. Down there. *UberSea*?

– A set of surf-viewing chambers, said Lucy. Not everybody can enjoy surf on their own. It evens up the opportunity. The Uberdeen Buddhists have endorsed it. The season ticket works out quite cheap. You can reserve a pen.

– To watch surf? he said

– From the inside, said Lucy.

– To watch surf?

She hadn't a clue why she'd given the spiel, she'd no wish to defend it.

Half an hour later they were back with three manilla folders, tashed and faded, in a red UCKU bag. UCKU did a range of colours, Cool Lemon, Passion Red, and so on. He'd given Tam the last of his change. Tam didn't want it. He gave it to him anyway.

– What would you rather? said Lucy. Read or eat? The inner or the outer man?

– Eat, he said, cheese. Cheese is fine, I know you've got cheese. Cheese and ham. A sandwich.

– You're easy put by.

– Then, I think, an early bed.

– Really? said Lucy. I'd hoped—

– Tomorrow's the 1st of January.

– No, it's— Oh, yeah, '68. Absolutely.

– Let's see what the day brings.

– But I'm off first light to Glasgow till late tomorrow. UbSpec Total voted me to go.

– It might be ramblings, he said. By the time you come back, I might just burn them. What point is there trawling amongst the past, at this stage?

Lucy didn't reply. She fussed at the window and busied herself. She seemed to take an awful long time to shut a pair of curtains.

that sweet ignorance, forgetting

Next morning his face was chilly. He snuggled under till he heard the front door click and then got up.

He moved down to the kitchen and poked around. From time to time, the grandfather dinged.

He made a pint of coffee. She had white pint mugs.

He unfolded a slatted blond chair and set it down at the side of the Raeburn. He took the top manilla folder from the plastic bag on the worktop and laid it broadways across the slats. He fetched the coffee and put it on the stove, on the asbestos mat.

He laid his bum to the stove's heat, as close as he could, and then swayed away. She must have banked it up specially.

He clasped his biceps in opposite palms, and kneaded them with his thumbs.

He repeated the previous bum manoeuvre.

Running out of things to do, he made an excursion to the loo.

Out in the hall, the grandfather dinged.

He lifted the folder, to balance on his lap, so's he could sit. He reached for a swig of warm coffee. Last moment of freedom; freedom of that sweet ignorance, forgetting. He twisted to check the door was closed. He thought of a different Tam, well-mounted on his night mare Meg – mired to the stirrups indeed – jolting her rider into storm.

There was such a thing as dread of the almost known.

He flopped the first folder open. Withdrew one sheet.

Which was blank, possibly a cover.

It gave him pause for all that.

A second sheet, he drew out. Blank.

A third. Ditto.

A fourth, a fifth—
All the snows of amnesia come again.

of human nature

Alison knew the relationship with Finlay wouldn't work. What she didn't know was why she was drawn always to repeat such doomed experiments. It taxed her optimistic view of human nature, to find her own so prone to stupidity. Younger men, why was she drawn to younger men? Sure, they had their famous vigours. But what could you talk about when you took a break from fucking? It was wrong to generalise but, by and large—

They had arranged their second meeting in Ma's, Ma Cameron's, and there he was. Sitting in the alcove on the left, in a rugby jersey and red long hair like a Celtic bard.

– Hi, Finlay, luve, she said.

– Hi, hun, he said. Usual?

don't try to control me

Lucy got back from Edinburgh in mid-evening and found him sprawled on the kitchen floor. He was in a slack form of the recovery position. She could have taken a felt pen and traced his proneness, with the volume of white paper splayed beneath his body.

– This is terrible, she said. You need to build yourself back up. Or you'll be no use to man or beast.

No comeback. No gay repartee.

– So were they ramblings? she said. Shall we just burn them?

– Very funny.

– Oh, she said, picking one up. They're not upside down, then.

– Do you think – Tam? she said.

– Leave Tam out of it, Lucy. It's hardly going to be Tam.

It was not a discussion. It was a very short circuit.

He woke in the middle of the night and went through to her room. It was locked.

– Lucy, he said. Speak to me. Tell me what you've done with them.

No reply.

– Lucy, he said. You're perfectly safe, I don't have a hard-on.

No answer.

– Lucy, he said. Whatever you do, don't try to control me.

He went back to his room and lay with the light on, looking at the ceiling.

april 9

my space

She was surprised next morning to find him down at breakfast. He had made eight pieces of toast and propped them in the stand.

– Sorry about last night, he said.

– What?

– Sorry that you felt you had to lock your door.

– I think you should get out of the house today, said Lucy.

– Get out—?

– Of the house.

– You don't want me snooping, is it?

– I think we need to give each other space.

– That's another of my beliefs, he said. People always give me space. People give each other space. But what are you meant to do with it? Had my space, more than enough, thank you.

– Don't take offence, it isn't meant that way. I have things I need to adjust to, come to terms with. Some are at work.

After tightening his belt and asking for additional braces and the address written down and a map and a little money, he set off. He went the easiest way, downhill. Crossed the road. He saw a bus coming and took it. Hazlehead. There were huge trees and massive banks of rhododendron. He found a maze.

– It's the only municipal maze in Scotland, the attendant said.

– What's *municipal* got to do with it?

– What the brochure says, *The only municipal maze in Scotland.*

– New on the job?

– Student.

After an hour and a half the student attendant mounted the wooden safety tower. He shouted down to the figure grazing and pausing amongst the privet.

– You lost, mister?

– I think I know where I am. Still in the maze, amn't I?

– Aye. Get your money's worth, I would.

nae problem

Lucy got into the department with her briefcase tucked under her arm, and was a bit short with Alison.

– I've really got piles, said Lucy.

– Funny place tae hae them.

– So can we leave that meeting till after break?

– New problem wi Guy we've got— said Alison. Okay, okay, nae problem.

Lucy got into her office, opened a spreadsheet on-screen, reconfigured some calculations, dealt with seventeen emails, signed three letters, and made out her expenses for the week before.

She unlocked a bundle of papers from her briefcase.

is that where we're going

She had glanced through odd pages in bed, two nights ago, and had glimpsed some stuff. Unsettling, very. She hadn't risked Tam's text at all night two. Now she took the first sheaf and shuffled the pages, then banged the whole wad tight. It was all shouty and bold, the Sixties for you. Here goes, she thought. It was straight in, there wasn't a title page.

Icarus '68

He was a strange character, the man I met, the man whose life I tried to record, if *character* is the word. But what else can you say? He was a strange *lack of character*? He was a strange *useless character*? That's hardly fair. Even useless characters have their uses. He was a *windy character*, that's for sure, that's what I feel most. A strange *windy character*, in at least two senses.

He blew with the wind at times, with as much control as a piece of paper. He was bold at others, but easily frightened off, so windy in that sense too. But then you can never sum somebody up, you never quite get them. Because, listening to him, listening to A13, which is how I first knew him, listening to Jim as he became, I knew there was more. For a wind blew through him too, as though he was a harp strung from a tree, an Aeolian harp that a gust might snatch a chord from.

Yet the various gusts that blew, after his accident, for I only met him afterwards, sometimes made him seem not so much a harp as an empty hall, with hollow echoes of glory and servitude. No, let me get that figure closer. There were portraits on his wall, and French windows flung open, at both ends. Wind made the portraits rock where they hung, to gouge thin grooves in ancient plaster.

The first portrait that sprang from his throat threw me. Not that I was supposed to be thrown, my job was just to keep the tape-machine running, put in new spools, thread them through the recording head, and start again. Sometimes I missed some of the stuff that came from him, because he wouldn't stop. He was in a trance after the operation, and he wouldn't stop, nor could he be shaken from it. Lady Macbeth, sleep-talking. So I tried to remember that stuff, some of it no doubt lost for ever. You have a life, maybe momentous, maybe not. Yet if the moments go, you might as well not have gone to the trouble of living them. Without a proper connected story you start to decline to a kind of newspaper, each day new, that never gets a second reading. The ecstasy of your soul and all its troubles start to fade, like so much drawer-liner or scrunched absorbent for wet shoes. I exaggerate, but you get my drift.

Well, the first portrait threw me, because it wasn't his father. No doubt his father made a huge impression on him, a huge depression too, but it was of his father's friend Ludwig that he spoke most at first. Ludwig had lost a hand, that was probably what made his portrait stick, Ludwig had lost a hand in an industrial accident. He nearly bled to death, after his wrist was shorn by the whirling blades at the top of a fertiliser hopper. The bleeding stump they stuck in superphosphate. His ex-hand they plonked in a Time-and-Motion inspector's briefcase, before they rushed both to Casualty. It was easy to see how this would stick in a young Jim's mind. Not that he was a witness, but he heard about it at table, after meat, and he marvelled at Ludwig's hook.

The next portrait threw me too, because it wasn't his mother. His mother was dead. Jim's mother died when he was not much more than a lad. He remembered releasing her ashes out of a glider window, as they overflew a mountain. Was that a flight of fancy, as some might say? I don't think so. It seemed, as I taped it, remarkably real. But it wasn't his mother he spoke about at first, but of two other women, Amande and Lucy. Amande could be fairly intense, which seemed to embarrass Jim. She was an older woman who had come across from Brittany in the war, married a whitefish skipper, then been bereaved, a shocker of an accident at the mouth of Aberdeen harbour. For which she was not consoled. Yet isolation and consolation became her themes, and it emerged she and Jim had been mighty close, mighty close in some lifesaving sense.

Then there was Lucy, the portrait of Lucy. To say she was the love of his life is to understate. But love is the home of all extremes, I think, and this love was so full of truth, for so short a time, so full of imposture and needless harming, that even extremes became beggared.

Jesus, thought Lucy. Is that where we're going.

With Lucy he seemed to want her so much, he was able to imagine her inner life, though how accurately we can never know. He would be running along with his own story, and then there would be something like *At her window, gazing* or *Meanwhile, in bed* and it would be about Lucy. But then men are notorious projectors, as my wife Iris is never slow to point out. (Whereas she is so rooted in circumstance, locality and practicality, it makes your eyes water at times. And a complete anarchist.)

Then again, with his long-time nemesis, Spermy McClung, a similar thing applied. Not that there was *inner life* to imagine where Spermy was concerned, Jim didn't spend a whole barrel of time looking for that. But *where* Spermy was, what he was *doing*, who he was *bawling out*, how many million of which marine species he was currently *murdering*, that he did have a knack for. Envy of man-of-action by full-time wimp, I suppose, simple as that. Spermy had pained him before, and would be instrumental in savaging him again. No doubt you do well to develop a sixth sense for the swerves and shifts of a man like that. (Did it verge on hero-worship? Because that's dangerous ground, as the moth finds out every time it shuns moon and worships incandescence. Though *are* moths drawn by moonlight? I have to admit I'm guessing here.)

The third of those to get seriously under Jim's skin, so to speak, was Julie. Julie Swink. Only the Lord Provost's daughter, so help me. Scientist, toughhead. About as sentimental as a barnacle. (Mind you, apparently Charles Darwin, I nearly said *Dickens*, Charles Darwin spent about eight years studying them. *Nora Barnacle*, who was that again? Sometimes I wish I had more time for research, instead of wandering around sticking microphones under chins. Transcribing? It takes so *long*! No way you can skate it: it's all in real time.) As I say, Julie got under Jim's skin. But whether it was empathy or something less exotic, it sure turned out a stormy time. Hang on to your hats, gentle readers. Julie Swink was either a scientist fallen amongst rogues, or she was a diver and she took him down. For the moment let us leave it at that.

Marilyn knocked and came straight up to her desk.

– Bundle of stuff for signing-off. UbSpec want a meeting tomorrow, they're open as regards time. Are you okay?

– Oh, fine, she said. I think so, yes fine. She had been careful not to bundle up the papers guiltily when the Admin Sec came in. When did you say?

– The time's not decided yet. Marilyn looked over the typescript briskly and back at Lucy.

– Research, said Lucy. The Civil War. I understand we might do it after all.

– Never heard that, said Marilyn. I think they want something far, far bigger. Do you want coffee bringing? You've been in here a while.

– No, no, I'm awake. It's fine.

– Suit yourself. We can check timetables for tomorrow later. Come past my desk.

Well it was a draughty hall the wind blew through, rocking the portraits. Ludwig, Amande, Lucy, Spermy, Julie. The way I've set it out in the final text, they're hung in that order. There were, of course, quite a few more.

His father, Andy. Andy was upstanding, integrity carried to an annoying degree, that nobody (not Jim for sure) could hope to live up to. Sober, practical, pretty selfless (not that Jim thought so), Andy was one of those Communists who resigned on principle after the Russians invaded Hungary. Jim's sister Annie, a bright spark, was briefly present, but if there were other siblings, brothers perhaps, they didn't appear in the audio record. (Mind you, it was Hogmanay, they might just have been out, carousing the night away, in other houses.) Then a professor from Crete, Zander Petrakis, and a caterer from Shanghai, Bing Qing, that he bumped into. Though the longer I go in this game, the less I believe in random coincidence. Then Iris, I've mentioned already, my second wife Iris. Jim and her went back a long way, in the school chum sense. Iris knew Jim's real name, of course, though by the time I met her, I'd just about finished typing this. Thanks, Iris, I said. It was just after she came out of prison, I wanted to do an audio-feature on her, but she refused. Then, in the course of our increasingly warm discussions, *Jim* came up in some context or other. They both wrote plays at school. Such a detail by this stage was not even ironic.

Anyway, let's gather this. All the time, as Jim spewed out his trance on tape, and as I transcribed it, then shaped it up in the way you'll soon read, I had been trying to piece together who this piece of wind, this part-time harp, this draughty portrait hall could be. By *could be* I didn't mean just his name. Names are a bagatelle: *Jim, Shem, Hamish, Hamlet*, what can it possibly matter? No, it wasn't his *name* but *who he really was* that I was after. That was the core of my project, long after the cheques from the NHS were gone. There was even that other quest he'd fondly flirt with: *Who he could have been, given luck and a fair wind.* We can all indulge ourselves in that sort of thing. But it can also throw some interesting beams. Well, I had to be frank with Iris. My typescript was as good as finished. No, I said, your information has come too late, get your tank off my lawn. *Not* the way you want to speak to a recently-freed anarchist, let me tell you. I said to her, I've done the best I can, it would weary me past conscience to reorder all my stuff.

You might ask what it is, this *best* that I've done. Well, I've done the basics. I've turned all first person into third, in order to turn Jim into someone more distanced. No-one wants to hear *I, I, I,* hammering on. I've moved some recordings around to where I think they belong in the original chronological sequence. Nobody's that keen on reading jumble. And I've edited out most of the repetition, I hope. Because sometimes Jim moved via trance to a strange kind of incantation. A dream to listen to, but if you ever try setting incantation down, a thorough bore to read.

That's about it really. I've added interior decoration, a few descriptions of the city from my own knowledge, and some sketchy topography so you can keep a hold of the journeys. But it's the *feeling* that's most important, and that's what was there on the tape. What it *felt* like to be this man. If you don't sense that, then it is my fault: he blew me plenty, I shaped too much. Does it in any way *touch* on the novel? Perhaps all biography must. This I attest above all: I fleshed out scenes only where that seemed vital, and in ways I thought consistent and reasonable.

Icarus '68 opens at the outset of a year. That may seem daunting. Courage, reader: it is over by the end of the first day. This is one of the swiftest accounts of a fall you will ever meet.

Let me begin.

In the moment the year started, Jim slipped through the warped door and started

Icarus, thought Lucy. Always keen to get out of the old house.

In the moment the year started, Jim slipped through the warped door and started running through fresh, powdery snow, unfree, yet with the momentum of freedom. He wore a zipped top, blue cotton shorts, and lightweight Japanese road shoes, Tiger Cubs. They made a *shima-shima* noise through snow as he drew to his pace. A voice sounded at his back, for indeed the warped door still stood open. A voice came. Back and nae be sae damned selfish! But Jim kept running. *Shima-shima,* his shoes repeated. Then that voice again. Back and tak in the New Year properly!

77

Properly? thought Lucy. A while since she'd heard that one. Why they had to have the Sixties. *Properly* indeed!

Jim turned around. There stood his councillor father, framed in the brick council house with the cold iron windows. He did look trapped, he looked tired and, though Jim didn't like to acknowledge this, there were elements of despairing. There was something between them that was invisible. Slanting between them lay the ghost of snow, his mother's ash, falling on the mountain top, released from the glider window. It was time to get away from all that.

Time indeed, thought Lucy. The world is full of dead mothers.

But something in him made him go back. Something in him made him go back and try to contend with the whole procession. He was no sooner back in the hall, getting a row for melting, than the bell went and it was Ludwig. Come in, come in, said his father. Ye're ma first foot, Ludwig man, Happy New Year! Happy New Year, Andy, said Ludwig, who was attempting to stamp crimps of hardpacked snow out of his black oxhide motorbike boots. But these prints also, said Ludwig, pointing down with his hook, there is someone before me? Oh, just the loon, said Andy. He was awa oot runnin but I grabbed him back. Eh, loon? Shak hauns wi Ludwig.

Jim seethed. He wished the earth would open and swallow his father up. Common feelings in a lost young man. He shook left hands with Ludwig, awkwardly, and watched him struggle out of his leathers. Good tae see ye, Ludwig, said Andy. How've ye been? Still doon at the bloomin Fertile? Yes, big promotion now, said Ludwig. I clean out the boss's office, not just the canteen. I am suitable for paper clips, look. His father inspected Ludwig's hook. That's a fair fancy rig ye've gotten, said Andy. Battery magnetic, switch on, switch off, replied Ludwig. They want me soon for the Scottish play. Fit, *Macbeth*? said Andy. No, *Peter Pan*, said Ludwig. *Doon the Pan*, mairlike, said Andy. That Royston and his bloody stopwatch. Yes, said Ludwig. I never forget the Time-and-Motion men, Andy, you know that. But I try to, even the War, forgive. The importance is to analyse, prevent recurring. So, still in the CP?

said Andy, as he ushered Ludwig through. He motioned Ludwig over to the cut moquette Cintique armchair, with the Dunlopillo cushions and light teak arms.

Fuck me, moquette! The real moquette. Now it was all coming back.

Yes, still in the Communist Party, twelve years, said Ludwig. The Cintique had the best view of the TV, which had its volume turned down and exhibited the formal bows and silent leaps of the White Heather Dancers. There was a pause in the conversation while the room's occupants caught up with this. And how is being a councillor? said Ludwig eventually. Just trying tae warsle awa, dae what I can, that's aa a Labour councillor can dae, said Andy. You always do your best, Andy, said Ludwig. That is the metal they make you from. But being Labour is always struggling through heavy sludge, no? Aye, weel, said Andy.

The doorbell went again, this time a double tinkle. Jim was on hand to open the door. It was Amande. She moved forward to give him a hug, but again he felt awkward. She had once rescued him from being trapped in a butcher's freezer, and she had used her body chastely to warm him up. Now she managed no more than to press cold cheeks together. He lifted the camel coat from her shoulders, and then, as she turned around, hoping to look in his eyes no doubt, he nodded towards the living-room.

Come awa, come ben, Amande, said his father. He was always a bit too ready with the joyous welcomes, thought Jim. For those *outside* the family. A Good New Year, ma dear, said Andy. Happy New Year, Amande, said Ludwig. Happy New Year, said Amande. Sae, what's it to be, aabody? said Andy. Ye'll tak a snifter? I have my bike also, said Ludwig. A bike is not ideal for schniftering. Just the one, said Andy, a wee one surely? Ach, only if others, said Ludwig. Amande doesna drink these days, said Andy, and I'm nae bothered. I am very good, said Amande, these days. Three lemonades it is, then, said Andy, that's easily poured. Loon? he said to his son. Nothing, said Jim, I'm out again in five minutes. Four lemonades, said Andy. I'll give Annie a

79

shout. Annie! She'll probably handle a small sherry. Annie! Jim felt the pressure begin to build.

Andy poured a very small sherry into the bottom of a conical glass, and four lemonades into engraved tumblers. The lemonades fizzed over the top. Fit's a few draps? said Andy. Here's a toast, fit'll be, qu'est-ce que c'est, Amande? Nouvelle année! said the unremarried widow from Britanny. A very frohliche '68! said the bereaved ex-prisoner-of-war. Come on in, Annie, ye're just in time, Andy said to his arriving daughter. Aabody got their glass? Here's tae it, then. Here's tae these days. Here's tae absent friens. Spermy, far's Spermy? At his fish, said Amande. Here's til that loon o yirs, then, said Andy. They tried to sip the fizz as it pringled their nostrils. It would be bad luck not to. Jim didn't touch it.

These days, thought Lucy, *these days*. Social history, yes, she was into that, but not family blethers. Eager for larger patterns, she preferred to skim-read.

Oh, my sainted Jesus! She had just glanced ahead.

Lucy stood at the mirror of night's window,

She slammed the paper face-down on the desk, waited ten seconds, and then flipped it back.

brushing up and combing through the gold in her hair. She contrived a hollow hive, live and crackling. But where was the *buzz*?

Her guts. They were going tight, turning to water. She gripped the desk and tried to stand up.

She should be in Prague, where it was happening. Like magma, the Plastic People of the Universe, their music, molten, desirous, bursting free.

Scared to hell of the truth to the point of sickness, she gripped the desk harder. Fuck, fuck, fuck, fuck, fuck! The door opened.

Alison stood there. All Lucy saw was her mouth moving. Alison was giving her hell for something. *Otto. Lack o support. Bust-up.* Say something—

– Sorry, love, said Lucy.

– *Sorry, love*! said Alison. *Sorry, love* doesna come near. Come on, fit are ye at?

– Sorry, said Lucy, thought I'd just, you know, work on through. You don't know how bad things are.

– They're shite, said Alison.

– Being away. Stuff, you know. Need to catch up, make it noon?

– Mak it midnicht if ye like, said Alison. I've just stuck the heid on Otto. What a sickener that bloke is. He's like that daftie pup on His Maister's Voice.

– Noon, then? said Lucy. Can it wait till noon? Then we can concentrate—

Alison looked at her, saw weakness for the very first time, said nothing, and went out.

my life life

Coiffure piled, Lucy pressed on the window-sill. Below in the blanched garden, that humpy sculpture of his. Theo, her widower dad.

Pressed on the windowsill—! No, no, Tam, too near the bone, too near entirely! She needed to fly to the station, interrogate Tam. She read on, flushed, riveted.

Lucy couldn't abide Theo's sculpture. Theo didn't officially belong, yet he belonged, as Stalinists always did in this society. He was Head of Sculpture at the College, well-named Gray's. She spun and flung the brush on the bed. It bounced to crack the fluted lamp. One shard rocked on the polished table like a psychotic scallop. One moment everybody else seemed mad, the next, you were. A bare bulb glowed on.

She scribbled a yellow Post-it for her screen, flew down the stairs past a startled Marilyn, grabbed a taxi outside ReCSoc, and hit the station concourse at a rare old speed. She slewed to the left, past the soft porn and choc shop, the turnstile toilets, and brought to a halt at Left Luggage.

– Where's Tam? she said to the man.

– Off the day, missus.

– When's he on?

– Believe he's on holiday.

– When's he back? When?

The guy had whiskers coming out his ears.

– He's gettin his leave in, he's due to retire. Cleared his lockers. He's off the rota.

– Where can I get hold of him?

– I'm sorry, missus, that's no for me to say. That's private.

– Private! The bastard's pinched the story of my life! Not just my life, my life life—

– That's between you and Tam, missus, nothin to do with ScotRail.

– Come on, it's not about Tam, it's somebody else—

– I telled him, said the man. I telled Tam plenty times, It's only left luggage, it's no worth cuttin your throat for, don't get involved.

She took a taxi back up. It was 12.13.

– Where's Alison? she said to the Admin Secretary.

– Gone for an early lunch.

– Did she say where, Marilyn?

– No. She said you were due to meet up with her at noon.

– Blast, was I? Thanks.

could you fling me

He was still in the maze. The student shouted again, after climbing the tower.

– I'm away to get a sandwich from the café. Do you want me to get you something? I could fire it over?

– That's good of you, he said. Could you fling me a cheese-and-pickle?

Alison sat in a snug in The Prince. No sign of Lucy. Pain, ignore. She phoned Gwen. Off, busy. She texted her. She was waiting for Finlay to heat up her bacon, brie and cranberry ciabatta and bring it through.

Maciek came out of KostKutter and walked along UberStreet towards the top of Market Street. He had just come out of the manager's office. He had arranged a bulk discount, big bulk, big discount, with the stuff delivered free to the communal flat in Torry. Being a catering squad foreman himself had helped. Now he would spread the word, picking his people. He had to counter Pawel and Lech. Pawel in particular was always pushing for action. Housing, transport, underpayment, illegal hours. Pawel was right. But there would be bad reaction against Poles if things went wrong.

Guy Bord had a date with Lord Provost William Swink, director of Swink Stillwater, owner of Mountain Heart. There were still aspects of the deal to tie up. It was probably best defined as *private-public-private-private,* the stage it had got to. They dined at the Elms, at a discreet table near the window. Guy had booked a posse of five tables in a semi-circle, like empty wagons, just to be sure no-one would overhear. He had paid the manager off.

William Swink preferred to be known as William Swink II, Yankee style. But even after forty years of black gold flowing, lots of the locals were still stuck in their ways.

– Guy, he said. Want a wet? I'll get it.

– Table water, said Guy. I have to keep one eye on UbSpec's partners, you know, when I get back. Lucy for one, he thought. Alison to an extent. Luna? Both eyes on her.

– On the rocks? said Swink.

– Absolutely.

– Two Mountain Hearts, dear, please, plenty ice, said William Swink. What specials do we have today?

Mountain Heart was the brand name many now used for the thing itself, for bottled water, like saying Coke for cola. It denoted pure spring water from the Cairngorm plateau, rushed cold and full of natural minerals to your table. It was pretty forward-looking when his father, a previous Lord Provost, had set it up in the late Sixties. Apart from Vichy, and that had unfortunate connotations, there hadn't been that much of a market for – well, water.

– All the best, said William Swink II. This is the dog's bollocks, eh, no healthy adjectives or chemical shite.

– Adjectives? said Guy.

– Cheers, said the Lord Provost.

– Oh, said Guy, right. Cheers.

The Leopard cursed the pair of them. Their specially planted button-hole cameras kept swinging round, Bord and Swink. He couldn't check their body language.

But the sound worked, the sound usually did. And at least the waitress in the Elms was tasty.

fuckin loonies

Guy was summonsed immediately, the minute he had paid the bill and said farewell to Swink. He flagged a taxi and promised the driver a fiver if he hit the gas. The driver was cursing UberStreet's new pavementette, which would keep him off his favoured route permanently.

– Yes, terrible, said Guy.

– Fuckin loonies, said the taxi man.

– No way round? said Guy.

– Jist narra wee roads, Waverley, Thistle Street. The fuckin lights at the Library, they're aye against you.

– I know what you mean, said Guy. Step on it, please, I'm tight for time.

He flipped the man a fiver, even though he was late, got through security by peering into a box in the wall, and sprinted up the North Turret stairs. The cylindrical stainless lift was reserved for, but seldom used by, the Leopard.

– Luna? said the Leopard, when Guy arrived in the Fastness, panting.

– No, said Guy. Just got here.

– Will I call her through, I mean? said the Leopard. Look, there she is.

Guy could see Luna, repeated ninefold on the console off to the side of the Leopard's desk. She was curled up on the couch in a gown, with a good book or something. It must be a real tear-jerker, her shoulders were heaving.

– No, it's okay, said Guy. Wouldn't want to intrude.

– I think she likes you, said the Leopard. I thought there was evidence of that.

– You're very lucky, said Guy. Then, with quick amendment, You deserve her.

– Not your sort, said the Leopard. Plenty between the legs, nothing between the ears. Now listen.

accident waiting

Lucy got back in her office, opened her top drawer, and detached a couple of hankies. She was lashing with sweat from the dash downtown.

Julie went to bed after midnight,

– Who the fuck's Julie? Oh, her—

Julie went to bed after midnight, after filling her twin 70 cu ft alloy bottles out in the shed by the tennis court, and after saying goodnight to her father's select Hogmanay party. She intended to sleep through that party and be up early for her New Year dive. Her scientist partners had flunked out, particularly Jamie. A real *keep-your-powder-dry* one, Jamie. She would dive alone. In her bedroom she ensured that the O-rings of her Calypso underwater camera were greased. Then she checked her wetsuit zip was free and working.

Julie a diver? thought Lucy. With that zip so free, Julie sounded more like an accident waiting to happen.

She might dream of strange fish. She might dream she was up close to

a filling bottle, one hand on the handle of the portable compressor, watching the needle judder to the red. Knowing she could be blown apart, kneeling to observe. Well, a girl could dream.

Lucy found herself stiffening.

They had no sooner demolished their lemonades and, in Annie's case, her small sherry (Jim, of course, drank nothing), when the bell ping-ponged for the third time. I'll get it, said Annie, who had left her Forestry revision upstairs and was now really perky. Andy went with her to the door anyway, in case. They opened the door to his brother-in-law. There was a new woman standing beside him. Come awa, come awa, Hughie, said Andy, I see ye've got your squeeze-box? I beg your pardon? said the new woman.

Good for her, thought Lucy.

His accordion, said Andy. Your accordion, Hughie. They laughed. Jim grimaced at the level of humour. Georgina this is Annie, and this is Andy, Madge's man, said Uncle Hugh. Hi Annie, hello, Andy, said Georgina, I never met your Madge, but I heard a lot about her. I heard she was a lovely woman.

Lucy paused, why and for how long she didn't know. Then she went through and got a latte from the machine. And a diet bar.

Aye, weel, come in, the pair o ye said Andy. Dinna wear oot the step, eternally standin. They went through. Ludwig, Amande, this is Georgina. Happy New Year, Georgina, said Ludwig. What do you work at? Not a big lot really, said Georgina. I clean kirks and control taxis. There were a few exchanges, then Annie said, Hey we've got seven now and an accordion. If one more comes, we'll have enough for Strip the Willow. Daft, said Jim. The accordionist has to play. He can hardly dance at the same time, stupid. Watch it, said his father, apologise to your sister. Well, she deserves it, said Jim.

Lucy dropped her sweaty tissues in the bin.

Strip the Willow. The ultimate social dance. Line of women, multiples of four, equal line of men. Travelling steps to get you up and down the lines, plus pivoting steps, whirling your own and every other woman's partner round, weaving with crooked, uncrooking arms. You could hardly go wrong but, if you did, it just redoubled all the laughter.

She danced it first at those Communist socials, the socials her mother Marcie took her to till she was nine or so, and then, when disillusion, drink and death kicked in, never again.

Andy, said Ludwig, sorry I have not seen you this long time. Aye, we've missed ye, said Andy. Each arm of Ludwig's Cintique chair was angled modishly, like a nursery ski-slope, so Ludwig had to coddle his lemonade single-handed. You know I never go back to Hamburg yet? I ken, I ken, said Andy. Sonia, Wilhelm, Eva, I always hope they die quickly. Nae use tormentin yersel, Ludwig man. But I know there are those who fire not yet touches, said Ludwig. They scream for air, suck draughts, they press low to the floor. Horrible, said Andy, horrible. They drown dry in their own house, said Ludwig. Terrible, terrible thing, war, them that have kent it, said Andy. Tough tae thole, tough tae endure, tougher tae leave ahind, said Andy. Dae we ever, man? Sometimes I think we jist repeat, repeat.

Then on top, last January, said Ludwig, I get a letter from a woman I never hear of, in Germany. She has been going through her husband's papers, and finds my name, some family cuttings. She finds something else too. This is the worst. This woman's husband has been in the camps in Poland. I don't wish to listen, said Amande. Come, Georgina. They went through to the kitchen. The others stayed as Ludwig continued.

The very bad camps. And he is there in uniform. Birkenau, the Birch Wood, the big camp of Auschwitz. And did this woman's husband hae a brither, said Andy, is that it? My brother Kepler, I always had fear and doubt, said Ludwig. My own brother, to do such stuff. Aye, if only they'd kept Birkenau as a birch wood, Andy said. There's certain folk should be kept stuck on the flat o their erse, till they learn tae leave things be. Good idea, Andy, said Ludwig. To make fascists stay in the house, wear always carpet slippers. Absolutely force them tae wear them, said Andy. Eh, Ludwig?

Jim had always admired Ludwig, the way he had recovered from his accident with the hopper and rotating knives, but now he felt distaste rising, focussed on that hook. The hook seemed to attract tragedy and to signal too much defeat. He felt guilty about deserting Ludwig, so he went through to the kitchen.

Alison poked her head round the door.
    – Sorry, sorry, sorry, said Lucy. I know we said noon.
    – It's okay, said Alison, I ken ye're – preoccupied.
    It sounded as though a person had been taken over.
    – I am, I am. Three, then?
    – Like I said, said Alison, there's been this bust-up. Otto's trailin new stuff for Guy. I dinna ken fit's behind it.
    – Not *Underwater Sex* again!
    – No. Funny thing is, I think they're aa set tae concede on the Civil War.
    – Marilyn doesn't think so.
    – Pity, because we've deen that muckle research. Specially trackin that early Lucy—
    – Ur-Lucy, said Lucy. She'd be three hundred and eighty, I think, this year. If she'd lived, poor lass.
    – Aye, said Alison, I mind ye were fine pleased. Findin anither Lucy fae days lang syne, anither Cooncil worker—
    – Right. But what exactly is UbSpec after?
    – Otto's sayin they want a freer hand.
    – *A freer hand*. Well, we knew that was coming.
    – And they want the Joint Working Group to be jist an annual review body. *Annual* review! I tellt Otto tae ging an fuck himsel.
    – Did he?
    – He cam back an said, *Quarterly?*
    – Okay, but what are we saying?
    – I've aaready gone an said it.
    – Yes, but that's just another of their dummies. What have you said to the free hand nonsense? We need to play this. You and me.

There's no point calling in the Chief Exec. He won't come. Three o'clock? Four?

– Let's leave it, said Alison, till the morn. I've a special date wi Finlay the nicht, an I want tae nip aff sharp an get a fresh blouse an things.

– Congratulations, dear. How old is he?

– Auld enough tae be oot on his ain.

– Tomorrow then, first thing. Enjoy the boy.

i'll hoover beneath you

Jim entered the kitchen. There was a loaf out on the table. Amande was slicing it. The year could not be expected to proceed much further without sandwiches. What kind of sandwiches are you proposing? said Georgina. I don't know, said Amande. Andy wasn't expecting people. You're never sure, are you? said Georgina. He is equipped with eggs and bacon, but has no ready pastry for the quiche, said Amande. Could you let me through to the sink, please, said Jim. Mais oui, said Amande. Yes, a quiche is nice sometimes, said Georgina. Why don't you make boiled egg sandwiches? An endless hollow crystal drummed on the metal sink. The people will let fall petty morsels on his carpet, said Amande. Oh well, that's out then, said Georgina. What else has he got? said Georgina. Some cheese, Brussels sprout. Jim made the water drum louder. Brussels sprouts? Oui. Probably just the cheese then, said Georgina. You could grate it so it sits fluffier and goes further. On his carpet? said Amande. The water was on full blast. What? said Georgina. On his carpet? said Amande. Yes, grated cheese is bad to get out, said Georgina. I remember an occasion when. Would you shut up! said Jim. Would you shut up about cheese and carpets, and speak about something serious for a change? Hélas, hélas, attention, said Amande, you are not so kind. As my father? said Jim. Not so soft, I think you mean. Not so kind as you used to be, said Amande. Well things change, don't they, he said. Do they? said Amande. Why is this? Dunno, he said. Parce que, Amande. I'm Jim, that's all I know.

– Are you fuck, said Lucy. Aloud. She surprised herself.

The door opened. A cleaner said, Oh, I thought there was no-one here. Then I heard voices.

– Do you need in? said Lucy. What time is it?

– Three o'clock, said the cleaner. I'll just be five minutes. You're not usually messy. I'm cleaning early today, I've got special leave for my sister's henny.

– I'll go and sit in reception, said Lucy.

– No need. When I come back, just lift up your feet and I'll hoover beneath you.

– Thanks, said Lucy. That's a big help.

Jim poured himself a glass of water, now that the tap had run clear. When he turned with his brimming glass, Amande was pulling at her ringless finger and Georgina had put her head in the larder. That's me, he said, plinking the glass down. Bye, ladies. He was just pulling the back door closed behind him, when his father came through. Fit's aa this nonsense, his father said. It wasn't a question. Come in back in this very minute. It wasn't even a coherent command. Fit on earth's the point o goin oot an gettin frozen? said his father. It's totally brass, ye must be aff yir chump. Ye're nae Admiral Byrd. I never said I was Admiral Byrd, did I? said Jim. I'm only out for a flamin *run*. Dinna start bawlin at me! said his father. Well, that's what I need, *a flamin run!* Jim shouted. Selfish brat, ye're aye oot on some ploy, said his father. What's the point o the Council buildin this hoose for ye, an ye winna even bide in it? Some of us are not the Council's puppet, said Jim.

Get you, thought Lucy.

– D'ye mind? said the cleaner, who had trundled back in.

– No, said Lucy, and lifted her feet.

Vera smart, said his father. The Council is welcome to my share of the house, said Jim, if that's what bothers it. Bothers it! said his father. I dinna ken why we bothered tae win the War, said his father. Eh, Ludwig, fit's this, ye aff already? said Andy, seeing who was through in the hall, climbing into his leathers. Bye, said Ludwig. It is a big pity, all this shouting. Bide, bide, Ludwig man, said Andy Endrie. The quines are just makkin the sandwiches, look. Bide. I think I go before it over freezes, said Ludwig. Annie's eyes glistened, standing beside Ludwig. She was helping him with his difficult fastenings. Now we'll never get that dance, she said. We'll never get enough folk to be in the house at the one time.

Ye see that, said his father, when Ludwig had gone, ye spile aathing. I think you'll find there's somebody better at that than me, said Jim. I'm sick to the teeth of the way you treat me, he said to his father. His father swung the flat of his hand at his son's impudent face. He telegraphed it, so that it missed. Get oot, he said, and never darken this door again. Until ye're prepared tae say a sorry. You'll be the one that says a sorry, said his son, and made good his slam.

The snow had crisped, like Ludwig feared.

– Bye, said the cleaner.
    – Bye, she said to the cleaner. I didn't catch your name, you're new aren't you?
    The cleaner thrust the *Margaret* security tag on the breast of her tunic towards Lucy, at the same time saying, *Maggie.*
    – Bye, Maggie.

That was the end of the sheets in the first folder. She reread the last sentence again.

The snow had crisped, like Ludwig feared.

She liked that somehow. She liked Tam's straight hard style. They were getting somewhere. She opened the flap of the second folder. A knock on the door. Marilyn popped her head in.
    – I won't poke in, she said. That's me away. The meeting with UbSpec's at nine sharp tomorrow, confirmed.
    – Thanks, said Lucy. Thanks for everything. I'll let myself out.
    – The janitor's here till seven. Goodnight.
    – Night.

She was suddenly tired. She couldn't take any more anyway. The family stuff seemed about over, and the good stuff couldn't be far. Time to go.

She stuffed the three folders in her case and set off home.

a fast chrysalis

That night Guy was called to another meeting, a briefing. It was important stuff, about how they were going to structure the real Spectacle, now that the dummy runs were over. The big boys were due to show up soon. The pavementette had been properly tensioned and was capable now of working at full throttle. Guy put his tuppenceworth in early, so that he could detach himself from the meeting and pop next door to Blissville.

– Hello again, Luna, he said, when she had managed to find the key sequence for the door to let him in. Hello, it's really good to see you.

– Hi, said Luna. You ran away from me last time.

– I had to, said Guy.

– It was rude, she said. You ran away when I was offering you something I knew you wanted.

– Luna, said Guy, Luna, there were absolutely bound to be cameras.

– Yes, she said. In the old days there was God's eye staring down, now there are a few cameras. You men. Which are you most afraid of?

– Luna, said Guy, there must be somewhere better for us.

– There isn't, she said. There isn't anywhere. If you want to swim with me, you have to swim here. Leop is busy just now. Just here in the doorway, look, under the arch. There won't be a camera in the actual arch. Come on, come on, I can see you want to—

– Luna, said Guy, as she let her silk gown drop, like a fast chrysalis, you brighten my sky.

– How was your day? she said, when she got back in.

– Which one? he said.

Typical answer.

She didn't dignify it with immediate response.

– I only ever had one proper day, he said. Feels that way.

– Did you get fresh air?

– It seemed quite fresh, he said. I was in a maze.

– A maze—

– I would have got the tea, but I'd no change, I gave it to Tam for looking after my stuff.

– I could have given you more, if you'd said.

– I don't like to beg, he said. I wasn't on those stairs all that long. I lived on an island. There's always something to live off, on a decent island.

– I daresay, said Lucy.

– But no island is an island, entire of itself.

Right, she thought.

– I owe the mazeman £1.80 for my cheese-and-pickle, he said. He's just a student. Would you remember that, in case I forget?

– I thought a lightish tea, said Lucy. I'm sorry I'm late.

– Are you late?

– There's a ready Caesar and a quiche in the freezer. Do you want wine?

– I don't risk booze.

– By the way, she said, did you ever run?

– Run? Just run? Yes, that was quite popular. Running along. Yes, I did the odd bit, I'm pretty sure. On the island the heather was thick and the bog got in the road. I mostly would have walked, I think. Except when chasing sheep, with my knife. My running must have stood me in good stead, but I never caught any. One I drove over a cliff. Salt-caked sheepskin, sogged guts.

This must have been what it was like, the hyper-vivid too-much-information stuff that Tam taped way back, Lucy thought. He seemed to have flashes still.

– Happy to walk now, till I get lost. Then I stop. You walk, I've seen you. Did you ever run?

– Run, no, said Lucy. There are other things I want to ask, but later.

– The famous later, he said. I found four sorts of berries, cowberries, crowberries, blaeberries. Rose hips. Are they a berry? Or halfway to a fruit? Hips.

– Uh-huh, she said. Will you be happy watching TV?

– Is anybody? he said.

– Good point, she said. Soon they'll all be watching Spectacle.

– Do you have to watch it, or can you take part?

– Both, said Lucy. There's your plate, your knife and fork. There's an extra sachet of Caesar if you need it. Now, I have to go up to my room. I'm not hungry.

– How do you get into the sachet?

– Work at it.

– But don't overwork, he said. I think that's always been my secret.

– Those horny hands?

– Ah, there you've got me.

The state of mind he seemed to be in, she was reluctant to leave out scissors.

a bag of bones

She put on the gas fire low; it was a bit sharp in the bedroom, she'd left the window open wider than she meant. She took the second bunch of papers out of her briefcase.

Shima-shima-shima-shima. He was on the road again. He'd had enough of New Year. He left them to munch their fat sandwiches and sip bland chemicals.

Lucy smiled. She remembered some of the more advanced chemicals, particularly in Paris. Before she had to hurry home. Paris was over by then, anyway. *Sois jeune et tais toi. Be young and shut up.* It was partly De Gaulle saying that, partly the Stalinists. But without the young, without the hard line of the Situationists, *rien*, fuck-all.

But then she had to come back. Her own situation just sort of closed in. Theo had been surprisingly good, over the whole affair. Why did Marcie die, she'd asked, the day she came back from Paris. At this stage in my life I need to know. She lost her belief, said Theo.

Don't marry anyone else, said Lucy. That would be my decision, said Theo. I don't care who you sleep with, said Lucy, as long as you don't do it in this house. Again that would be up to me, don't you think? said her father. Don't anyway, Lucy had said. There are too many memories. And he didn't, old Theo, he was careful to be careful with her. Or if he did it was silent, or she was out at the time and didn't know.

Jim sped through the white and arid Byron Square, with its grocers and cop sub-station, its community centre and betting shop. There was a break in the sky, a starry gap, a silver jet-trail arrowing over. Probably angled for San Francisco, where the good stuff was. The sky arrow grew fat, then bendy.

She almost paused to comment, but then passed on. *Good stuff* was what she noted.

Far e fuck's e fire? rapped a local drunk, as he ran past. Remains to be seen, comrade, he replied. Fruit! shot the drunk, as he receded. 1968 was an hour old, yet already horns were locked. *Selfish! Come back! Fruit!* et cetera. Jim tried to let that language slide but it took him over. The Interim Committee On Solving Lovelessness was due to meet that evening, at the Monkey House. INCOSOLOV.

Two-three idealists stamping about, waiting for followers, getting chilly. Been there, thought Lucy.

Jim kept running. He curved up a white hill. He ran along the top road, striped by recent buses, Provost Fraser Drive. He possibly wouldn't speak at the Monkey House. Not that he couldn't speak. Just that he often didn't. Because on the building site the topics were boring.

Tits, beer, bonuses, and the uselessness of bosses. The uselessness of students who didn't finish their degrees was also high on the list.

Yesterday, when they'd caught him scrawling a poem on a pie-bag, while he was supposed to be making the tea for break, they went about spare. It wasn't even a pie-bag, it was a bradie bag, all oily with fatty flakes and difficult to write on. Difficult to make an impression. Because of the oiliness. You'd have thought plumbers and sparkies and chippies and brickies would understand these technical points. A poem in honour of his native city. It even rhymed, mostly.

There was a taste of blood in his throat from the frost, but he was moving smoothly now, he was getting grooved. Jim switched from the long dismal drive onto the Ring Road. It half-ringed the city. The sea did the rest. After the tea-break yesterday, when the Ready-Mix arrived, the drum on the back of the lorry had sounded like short harsh waves endlessly churning. Then the drum tilted and spun, spewing concrete over the rods for the warehouse floor. They had to shovel it level.

Speeden up, ye scrawny bastard, the foreman had shouted at him, or the cunt'll ging aff. Nice. *The cunt'll ging aff.* Just when he was composing. Why don't they mix it on site by hand? he'd said. Cut down on all the panic? Oh, aye in a panic, that's them, said the geezer next to him. It's a real killer. Come on, ye prick! bellowed the foreman. Cuntin poets. Eh boys, fit hiv we ivver deen tae deserve a cuntin poet! Even the grumpy old labourer, Killer they called him, grunted at that. The foreman threatened to get him shifted, out to the new incinerator site at Tullos. Fuckin dae less harm oot there, said the foreman. Poems burnt pronto, part o the service.

Beauty, when it does not hold the promise of happiness, must be destroyed. Who said that? Debord or Raoul, somebody in Paris, Debord she thought. She repeated it to herself. *Beauty, when it does not hold the promise of happiness, must be destroyed.*

On Jim ran. *Shima-shima-shima-shima-shima-shima.* There was a ring of hard-pruned roses there on a roundabout. Downhill now, easy and smooth he ran, mind slidingly idle. Hunters, proper hunters, had been running long before folk ever squatted down to pullulate in cities. Hunters of spirit would still be running when Paris, London, Rome, Berlin had been abandoned as scribbled drafts of a bad idea, on a greasy bag. He passed the Grammar rugger pitches, where the moon slanted *H* after *H* after *H* after *H* on the snow. Binding in scrums and raking in rucks, in the game of high advancement. He was in a freer line of evolution, running.

Christ, thought Lucy. If I want doughball philosophy, I can buy it on Amazon.

Down Jim swung through Rubislaw Den. The snow came on again. The sweat of tea and rubber coolies had been exchanged for well set back, proportionate mansions. The snow drove harder. On an instinct he ran up one short drive and sheltered at the side of a big bay window. The tall curtains were drawn, except for a crack of light. The window was open at the bottom, as though to allow a cat freedom. There was a wooden bowl of apples sitting on the inside ledge.

One squint through the crack showed him Lord Provost William Swink, he was forever in the local papers, plus a few stuffed shirts of a certain age, probably councillors. Nobody knew what Swink's politics really were, was he Social Progressive or Progressive Social? He was a pie-man. Coming back to the town from his time in England, he had bought about twenty bread shops and turned them into pie outlets. He had taken shares in other food concerns, fishing-boats and abat-toirs, cold stores and sausage houses. He wanted to break into drink too, that was the word. That was the handle most folk had on their current Provost. Jim got his ear as close as he could to the bottom of the window to try and fill in the gaps.

Now image. It's high time we attacked image harder, the Provost was saying. Typhoid hurt us more than we knew at the time. Five hundred in hospital, and then the deaths, well trade took a dip, you'd expect that. Granite, fish, paper and comb were already in decline, we know that too. Tourism dropped like a tradesman's plummet, as we ken fine, eh lads? Jim wondered if any of the councillors were really tradesmen, or whether they owned tourist-related businesses. But before I go further, said Swink, will you try a dram? Senator, a whisky? said the Lord Provost. I'm a bourbon man, but when in Rome, said the Senator. It's Fiddich, said Swink. I'm sure it'll hit the spot, said the Senator. Men? Aye, aye, Bill. Just a suspicion. Nae too much noo, William. Heave awa wi't. The councillors, if that's what they were, had spoken.

Lord Provost Swink went the rounds with a tray of drams swilling golden in their cut crystal. He went round a second time with a silver platter of shortbread fingers. Then he announced himself ready to spill a few beans. I think it's time we rid the city of its identity with alienated beef, he said. Alien beef? said the Senator. Exactly, said Lord Provost Swink, because that's what did for us, with the typhoid. We need to give ourselves a good sluice, and for that there's nothing better than water. A good sloosh, said a councillor. Cheers. Cheers, said Swink. Now, pure water, where do we get it? Nae oot o a tap, said a second councillor, there's nithin in that tap nooadays but chlorine. From springs isn't it, said Swink. Best of the lot, a spring on a mountain-top. That's an affa lang wey tae ging for a suppie water, said the second councillor. Granted, said Swink. So that's where the Senator comes in. We would need one Chinook per week on manoeuvres from Edzell, that would cover it for a start. We've spoken on this. Aberdeen Pure. Sorry, I dinna get ye, said the first councillor. The name of the water, said Swink. We build a bottling-plant at 4,000 feet on Braeriach, and fetch it down in the Senator's chopper. Three thousand bottles a week for starters. Wells of Dee equals Aberdeen Pure.

Soonds aaricht, I suppose, said the second. Rescue wir reputation an ye ken fit ye'll be minded as? Lord Aberdeen? said Swink. Na, said the second. Clean Bill o Health. Ha-ha-ha, said Swink. Help yourselves to cheese and a perforated water biscuit. It's a cracking new line we've just brought out.

Plot aplenty, sure, but where was *Lucy*? Terrible when you were well through life and all you wanted was the chance to re-read your youth.

So to cap the whole thing, said Swink, there's three parts to this. Investment, transport, marketing. If the council will join me on the investment side, if the Senator can smooth the way to accessing airborne help with the transport, and if we get into the marketplace first with a bright new product, I think we're made. Hear, hear, said a third councillor. We'll all be made, I'll make sure of that, said the Lord Provost. There's only expensive bottles on the market now. Their pitch is wrong. What we're after is a popular water, to refresh the swine and lift the buggers up. So that's the slogan: *A People's Water: Aberdeen Pure.* Here's to it!

Jim had heard enough, more than enough. But it was still snowing. When the toast and the briefing stopped, the councillors started leaving and drifting out. Jim kept tight behind the bay window. His knees were seized, and his calves felt stiff. Only the Lord Provost and Senator were left in the room. The Provost was pouring two really big whiskies. Then it came out. It wasn't just mountain spring water they were plotting to snaffle. It was North Sea oil.

Just as the Wells of Dee at the top of Braeriach would *earn their keep*, so also the black reserves under the ocean crust, as yet not huge in proof, might *transform certain finances*, so long as certain finances were *in pole position* long before the off. Publicly-owned real estate does need to be managed creatively in the new situation, said the Senator. Planning controls will need to be more imaginative, agreed Swink.

As long as we keep the long nose of the press out, said the Lord Provost. That *Echo* drives me up the wall at times, with all their probing. *Tarves Man Finds Rat in Flour, Buckie Wife Breaks Tooth on Biscuit.* A free press is a luxury when business needs to expand. Buy in then, said the Senator. Do your own press thing, your own title. Time for you to diversify from bread and water. Let them eat news, eh? said Lord Provost Swink. Or something, said the Senator.

Then they huddled by the fire like a pair of Ebeneezers, and Jim could hear no more. He soft-shoed down the drive again.

Thank flaming fuck, thought Lucy.

Lucy pressed against the windowsill and looked down from her bedroom window. Two linked couples, lax, laughing, not letting go, came skittering down the near side of the road, and passed safely on. Up from the lounge came a clink as Theo entertained some first-footing guest, someone from Gray's School of Art or, more likely, the continuing rump of the Communist Party.

Then, on the opposite side, she spied some slender creature in shorts. She watched him loping along behind the mature trees, hidden then reappearing, with puffs of breath going up and scuffs of white afly at each ankle. Glancing at her, the youth tripped, and spilled quick in the snow. She went and drew him, supporting him, shooshing him up the stairs. Nah, he lolloped on past. God!

Cheek! To suggest she fantasised about some half-clad guy passing by. An unknown guy. A bag of bones, if truth be told.

Jim reached the Brig of Dee. There were little embrasures where you could stand safe from traffic. East was the glimmering harbour. West were the louring hills. He remembered the time with Spermy, the time the Dee was frozen, nudging along in huge plates, on which his wild pal skated. Spermy was the type could sort Swink out. Because West, on the Cairngorm plateau, was where the Dee welled up and where Swink planned to plonk that bottling-plant to make his pile. Some breezeblock bottling-plant: just where his mother's ashes lay? Grotesque. Aberdeen Pure? No chance.

Aberdeen Pure, yes, for a while, thought Lucy. Slow to catch on. Till rebranded as Mountain Heart. But all water holy. If sealed in a nippled bottle with a use-by date.

Jim stood on the Brig, over the upswirl and swallow of dark waters. He thought of Nan Shepherd's book *The Living Mountain*. Flakes of white came swivelling down, blanking his thinking.

She seemed to have been reading all day. What time was it? Nine. She had.

He was bound to come back, her runner. She let the needle hover above *All Along the Watchtower,* from the brand-new Dylan. After his electric sell-out and bike smash-up, back to the true acoustic. She lowered the needle and went back to the window. She imagined bunching up her ribbed polo like a coiled python *None of them along the line / Know what any of it is worth.* She would crab backwards at her bra *No reason to get excited / The thief he kindly spoke* and he would clock her full-on *But you and I we've bin through that /And this is not our fate / our fate / our fate* shit, the needle. The door had clashed downstairs, and a heavy suck went through the house.

A horrible dented Brezhnev hat and pilled black coat, real dead lamb or nylon, was on the path below. Theo was going too, buttoning himself. Well they could go, well rid. All she wanted was for her runner to come back, silent, genuine, urgent.

She left the bedroom, at that point, she remembered, and went downstairs, kind of determined.

Jim would soon be level with the Swink place again. Hell, his foot-prints under the window.

There came the sound of a light knocking.

He was the only runner out tonight, they would be lying in wait and catch him easy. Their plot would be safe then.

A second knock.

He remembered Admiral Byrd at Advance Station, his father's book. He had a lot of feeling for Byrd suddenly, for all the self-isolated; desperate to act, to save the world, traversing white wastes, gassing themselves sick in huts and rooms.

There was a third knock at her door.

He could do with somebody to discuss this with.

She went and unlocked it.
— Can I come in a minute? he said.

read on, don't stop now

— You've got it here, haven't you?
She compressed the corner of her lip under a canine.
— Let's read it together. I'll take a chance.
— Don't know if I could face that, she said.
— I've read very little of it for ages. Mankind cannot stand too much reality. That's why I always left it with Tam.
— Well, she said.
— Well?
— Well, said Lucy. Come and sit down. Watch, the chair's a bit squeaky. You sit there, I'll sit over here.

— I would read it to you, he said, but my glasses must have got smashed.
— I'll read. But I have to say this. Whoever told Tam about me, and made stuff up, it's pretty outrageous. Was it you? I may have to stop from time to time, and ponder. That's what I find.
— It's not a page-turner then, from old Tam?
— Oh, it's a page-turner. But I still have to stop. Privacy is a major casualty. Are you sitting comfortably?
— No. Bloody wicker. The bones of my arse are nipping.
— Well I am, said Lucy. So I'll begin.

Someone appeared the other way. They were both on the lightly-beaten track, on the Ring Road pavement.

— Who's that? he said.
— Guess, said Lucy.

At the very last both dodged, but in the same direction. Oomph! His pace brought them both down in a slither, till her iced shoulder veered and rapped a tree.

– That I do remember, he said.
  – Oh good, said Lucy.

Oh, thorry, he went, muffly. What the! Faith full of hair. Yeuf! she went. Totally obliv. You certainly were, she said. Sorry! he said.

He rolled off and by dint of a knee here, a hand there, they fetched to their feet. He looked back up the road. He'd been really zooming, convinced the Provost and Senator had found his prints and would be out tracking him. A car came over the hump slowly. She tugged him round and laughed in his face. Hey, you! she said. Pay attention!

She began to give him a brushing-down. All he really saw was the hair he'd had threaded in his teeth. Red-blonde under the sodium lamp. Are you running from something? she said. I thought you were Mercury there on a mission. He turned again. The car had stopped, and switched its lights to sides. I am, he said. Or just no home to go to? Not one you'd be in a rush to call home, he said. Come in for a cuppa, I'm just across the road. It wasn't the sort of word he expected. He had expectations already. *Cuppa.* Where, that huge house? Yes, the light upstairs, that's me.

– That's you, he said. That's you speaking.
  – You got it, said Lucy.

You sure? he said. Whether it's me or not? Whether it's okay? he said. Best be quiet when we get to the stairs, she said. Okay, he said. In case my father is back. She pushed the black wrought gate. Which creaked. I hope the bed doesn't do that, she said. Don't you know your own bed? he said. Never had sex in it before, she said. She levered the front door handle, mock-quietly. We've hardly been introduced, he said. Soon change that, whispered Lucy. What's that big lump in the garden? he said, stalling. *Sisyphus*, said Lucy, my father's sculpture. Come on.

Been watching you this year, she said, when they were safely in the bedroom. Sit. Not on the chair, it's squeaky wicker. Over here, where it's comfy. Do you like my hair? Me at the window all night combing it, you running past. I won't sit on the bed, he said. Too sweaty. Do you? she repeated, do you like it? Must tell you what I've just heard, he said, it's scary. He sidled up to the tall window and checked down at the Ring Road. It's drastic, he said, really drastic. The angle was restricted by the trees. Hey, never mind that, Jumpy, look. What? Do you like it or not? Uh-huh. *Uh-huh* is not an answer, it's my hair we're talking about. I do, I do. I haven't asked you to marry me yet. What do you like about it? Don't usually go for beehives, he said. Get you! What do you go for about it? There's red, a sort of reddy, through the gold. Better. And? It's brilliant. Shiny anyway, she said. Well, now the intros are done, are you going to get your gear off, or am I? I'll do it, he said, my kit's siping. His father's word, meaning *wet through*. Me too, said Lucy. Look the fire's on. You can toast them over a chair. It's very good of you. Good's not what I had in mind, she said. Ooh, I thought you'd have a few more muscles. I'm a distance guy, not a fish humper. A what? Distance runner, he said. Hey, steady! Don't you want me to? she said.

– I should not be reading this, said Lucy.
   – My glasses are smashed, remember.

Yes, what about you though? I feel naked.

– Who says that again? he said.
   – Not me, she said.

You nearly are, said Lucy.

– Lucy says that? he said.
   – Yes, Lucy in the story.

Chest for a chest?

– Does he say that?
   – Listen for Chrissake!

Good idea, she said. She hoicked her ribbed top up in a coil and dipped her head out, disturbing her hair. Wow! She patted her hair in place, unzipped a boot or two and a skirt, and stepped out. Together, she said. Now.

– I cannot read this, said Lucy.

She slipped off a last wisp, as he flipped out of his Ys.

– Come over here. I feel utterly daft broadcasting this.

At last, she said. *At last*? he thought. They were going at the speed of light. Where was the average first-night fumble on a draughty porch? Ooh, you're icy, said Lucy, don't touch me. That was more the style. She pulled him by his bemused firm-on towards the burping fire.

– I got the burp sorted, said Lucy.
    – I'm glad.
    – A fitter came. After Theo died.
    – Can I hold your hand?
    – No, I need both hands to be able to flip the pages. Arm round my waist, best. Not like that, duh. Like so.

Wait, need to get a.

– Is that you started again?
    – Fuck's sake. Yes! said Lucy.

Wait, need to get a. What? she said. Hold it! he said. Johnny-come-lately thingy. I hate that latex smell, said Lucy. I'm starting the Pill. Never in the hottest of dreams was it this simple. They just about made it back to the bed. She pulled him down.

– Very romantic, and I don't say, said Lucy.
    – Blame Tam, not me.
    – I will if I can get hold of him.
    – Read on, don't stop now.

He propped briefly, on his bony bits, over her bonny bits. It had been a short engagement. Lucy, who raved for poets, hunks, philosophers and rockers, closed her eyes against the skimpinesss of her conscripted lover. Fuck, fuck, o fuck, Jesus! he panted, three at best minutes later. Thaaank you!

– Conscripted, eh? he said. He squeezed her middle. Hey, there's more to you than I recall. Lucy rocked against him for luck.

Don't thank, it's rude, said Lucy. Save your breath to get your strength up. Strength? he said. Seconds. You're amazing, he said. Might need thirds. I was away, sorry, did the bed creak? he said. Not for me, said Lucy. Anyway who gives? If Theo comes back, he'll have to handle it. Theo? My father, we live here together, I don't think he's back yet. And before you start, she said, I don't do jealous. Wee silence. Am I your first? she said, seems a bit that way. I was in bed with two when I was eleven, he said, well, eleven plus. Don't boast, said Lucy, I don't dig it. And I don't do troilism. You don't even look like a troil, he said. But I'll eat you for my supper, she said. You up for it yet? Nymph or summat? he replied. No, just that you seem like a shiftworker. One minute on, ten minutes off, or something. Do you you like my back? It's warm, he said, it's lithe, it's. Smoothtalker, stroke!

He stroked, and as he stroked, she talked about herself, her life, the tough bits, tastes, desires. Starting, stopping; asserting, agreeing; dreaming, this and that.

– A shiftworker, he said. Cheek.
    – Let me see that paw a second, she said. This lump of roughcast never stroked my fair flesh, not ever, look at it—
    – Expelled from the Garden of Eden wasn't I. Son of toil.

They were going too fast.
    – I'm putting *Icarus* down a moment, she said. Okay, I don't want you to do anything. Just kind of hold me.
    – Do anything? Moi?
    – Sssh, for goodness sake, said Lucy.

– Are we having a textual relationship or not? he said.
  – Don't interrupt, said Lucy. Or we'll lose the place.

Jim did as he was told for a while. He stroked. Jesus said leave your
father and mother. But just so's someone else can give you orders.
In the fullness of time she turned back, revolving. Help yourself, she
said, v-ing her thighs. He wasn't sure if it was personal or impersonal,
whether he was cast as lover or bit-part player, and he didn't care. Too
much, he said, as he sank in. He thought of saying, *Remind me to get in
a good union.* But let the verbals go. They both did.

Fuck – she said quietly. Fuck, fuck, fuck. Commentary and command
commingled. Come – he said. You absolute fuck – come!

Feel like a human now, she said. I'll get you one. Don't, said Lucy. You
started it, he said. And aren't *you* glad, she said. Glad or gone, I haven't
checked, he said. Hope it's the second, she said. Why? Because you *do*
need to go. Already? Thought you'd picked me out? Yeah, picked you
out from all the loners running about in shorts in the snow on the first
of January. You were the one. Pity I didn't get the same chance, he said.
You're just somebody I bumped into. Just think, said Lucy. Choosy
as that, you could have landed up with somebody's auntie. Already
landed up with my pal's mother, he said. I hope I didn't hear that, she
said. I slept with my pal's mother when I was eleven plus, I told you.
You what? she said. Ye gods, that's disgusting! Slept with her. Well I
was more unconscious. That's no excuse in a court of law. She took me
into her bed. Yup, she said, might be a theme here? She fetched me
out of an ice-box. Now I do feel dirty, she said. It wasn't the ice-box at
home. So that's okay, she said. We couldn't afford one, a fridge I mean.
It was the deep chill down at the butcher's. Now she's come to live next
door. Kept a torch for you, did she? she said. You really put it around.
Come on, your stuff must be hot and damp now, the way you like it.
Time to go, she said. Really? Really.

Can I see you again, explain all this? There was a nurse involved too,
Dinah. Not if I see you first, she said. I'm going to an important meeting

tonight, he said. Counselling? It's the inaugural meeting of the Interim Committee to Solve Lovelesssness. You want an acronym with that? she said. INCOSOLOV, he said, at the Monkey House. Natch, she said. Want to come? You always say that, said Lucy.

He got up and crossed to the window. Again no sign. No lights, no purring. Not that that guaranteed anything. What time? she said. Eight. Unlikely. The Monkey House is just a rendezvous, he said. Then they'll decide where to move on to. Depending on numbers or if anyone has a flat. Sounds organised, she said. Actually they've mended the name. Before they've met? I think they're going for GUST, Group to Unstick Stuckness. Still don't know yours though. On a first date? she said. Have some respect.

They looked and laughed, a bit more with than at each other. She thought, *Sweet naif.* He thought, *No way can we ever untangle.* This pal's mother thing's not what you think, he said. What is? she said. I'll get some stuff of Theo's from the airing cupboard on the landing. Thanks. He lay back, knacked, and lapsed into a doze while she went about her researches.

Try these? What? Try these old clothes. You've been out of it the past hour. Zonked, I just zonked. You've taken it out of me. They're a mile big. There's a belt, said Lucy. Can't I stay till my own stuff's dry? Stay where? Under your bed even. I've got the real guys there, she said. They've kept quiet. They don't usually. Albert, Simone, Jean-Paul, and their clever wee pal, Colin. What about Friedrich in that case? he said. Friedrich is off up an Alp just now. Friedrich believes it is impossible to develop an exalted philosophy wedged under a young woman's bed. I'm more than willing to prove him wrong, he replied. You'd have to pass the audition, said Lucy. As an outsider? he said. I'd manage that. Outsider is only part of it, she said. Granted I fetched you in from the outside. But the school I hold to. You hold to a school? he said. But the school I hold to, despite Colin Wilson, is not Outsiderism, it is Existentialism. Like, you know, in this empty vale, it's down to you to prove you exist. Prove, and keep on proving. Sez who? he said. Sez my '68 resolution. Roll on soixante-neuf, he said. Can we discuss this,

Madame la Philosophe? Nope. Can I lie and listen to you till my gear's dry? Nope. Harping on. Nope. Thought you seemed more Molly Bloom. Yes-I-said-yes-I-will Yes? she said. Uh-huh, he said. Nah, said Lucy. So, who broke your lamp? he said. No, I meant to ask, was there a fight in here?

She swept pearly shards of light shade with the heel of her hand onto a sheet of paper. She clattered the fluted scallops into a bin. Sad, he said. That's Venus fucked, then. She bent across and gave him one. A kiss. On the cheek. You get a poem for that, he said, if you'll pass me that sheet. And a pen? Let's see, said Lucy.

Aberdeen
In Aberdeen the granite is no façade,
I feel ghostly,
I leave my flesh when I walk abroad,
Or mostly.

But you don't *walk*, Lucy said, reading over his writing arm, you run, *mostly*? It's a form of expression, he said. A form of fibbing? said Lucy. Ghosts don't run, he said. Merde alors, nor does your poem, said Lucy, leave it. Time to go, things to do. Us? he said. Maybe us, mais à ce moment mainly just me. Vamoose, Twig.

I feel I exist through you, he said. Maybe we only exist through each other? Go, Twiglet. Can we talk about this? he said. We'll see. I want us to ride together, he said. Beat it! I already probably love you, he said, I'll write better poems. On yo hoss, cowboy. Ride you into the sunset, if that's what you want. It's the middle of the night, she said, I'm not some pitiful sex-maniac. Pity, he said. I tried to dry your shoes, she said. On the canvassy, plasticy side aren't they? Tigers, he said. Lightweight. Tiger Cubs. Right, said Lucy.

The first breath he took, as he walked past the round *Sisyphus* sculpture, crystallised in his lungs. Then his first exhalation rose like a speech-bubble, empty as happiness. He thought of a name for her: *X-maniac*.

He was barely three steps further, when he remembered he'd forgotten to even mention Swink. Forgotten to seek her advice, enlist her aid. Those powerful bastards across the road, about to con the water and oil from everybody, and thieve half the planet. He swung round. He spun in the snow. But spun again. Leave it. Nothing. What could you do? They'd gone through each other pretty damn quick, and come out on the other side. Or at least she had. The cold hit him.

She stopped and looked into his eyes.

– Wild, he said.

– So why the *Nothing* at the end? Did you tell it that way to Tam? It wasn't *nothing*, it was a lot more than *nothing*—

– You say that now, he said.

– It was, I assure you. A lot more—

– Good, he said. I'm going to sleep in your bed tonight. Don't worry, on top of the covers. We needn't open any more pages.

– I feel you should come in, said Lucy.

– Only one thing, he said. I can't promise anything.

– What's new? she said. Between me and you.

april 10

pretending the world exists

– I'm not going in today, she said.

   – Really? I'm glad.

   – I should.

   – We should do lots of things.

   – I should be angry with you but I'm not.

   – Oh ditto, he said. Absolutely totally ditto.

He kissed her forehead.

   – Sorry I pressed on your skull, your head, a couple of times.

   – The excitement. Everything's understandable when you're excited.

   – Was it good for you?

   – When?

   – Whenever. Now, then—

   – Lucy—

– Why did you tell Tam everything about us?

   – I didn't tell Tam, as such. I was in intensive care.

   – Sounded more like intensive grilling.

   – No. The surgeon managed to hook up some of my broken wires and a lot of stuff went across real fast, apparently. A wonder Tam was able to change reels quick enough, you'd think he'd have lost some.

   – Why did it stop? You must have been like Homer on speed.

   – Told you. Mankind cannot stand too much reality.

   – Did Tam say that?

   – One of the Tams. TS Eliot.

   – I'm glad in a way, but I think he's a user. Your Tam.

   – You tell him.

   – He's already gone, I checked. Tam's fled the coop.

   – Oh.

– Or at least he's left Left Luggage.

– You going to phone your work?
   – Don't start talking about work, said Lucy.
   – The world exists, I am reliably informed.
   – Don't, she said.
   – I won't. It's just a defence. Talking big, pretending the world exists. When we know it's only us creates it.
   – I'm going to forget Guy and make breakfast, said Lucy. And turn up the fire. And the stove. And we're going to feast today, as though it's the last day on earth.
   – Jings.
   – You so deserve it. Total crumb—

– Now read on, he said. With any luck we'll find out the hero's name. Probably not Jumpy or Crumb. Or Twiglet, I shouldn't think.
   – Will we? said Lucy.
   – Did Tam and you ever meet?
   – Tam? said Lucy. Don't be ridiculous. Never. Two days ago was the only time.
   – You'll maybe meet him some time.
   – Yes, she said. I'd like to ask him one or two things.
   – Likes of what? he said.
   – How much was tape and how much inspiration.
   – Perspiration too. He was never shy of that, you could smell it off him.

– I find it incredible, your family, they've not kept in touch? said Lucy.
   – Maybe they did try, initially. But I'm such a loser. A loser of the place, of tracks and names. I can't remember going to my island. I can remember being there. I can't remember coming away.
   – Do you want to try tracking them tomorrow? *Andy, Annie, Amande, Northfield.* The clues are there.
   – They might be dead. They might be hoping I am. I like the way you do the voices.
   – Do you think Tam meant to write a play? said Lucy.

– Who knows.
– One folder to go; I'll read straight on.
– Be my host, he said.

what do we know about memory anyway?

Jim was suddenly happy again, plain leapingly happy. He existed at last. He could change his mind and the whole direction of his life. He could turn round, go straight back, snow flying from his heels, and tell her. Without knocking. Straight in and tell her about Swink, his fatal plan to rob the city blind. Together they would fight him and his kind to the death. Their love, invincible together. And no more nonsense about running. The Runner was okay as an identity for the first three-four hours of the New Year, but now he could put that behind him as adolescent. Horizons were moving faster than that. But would she have him? What did she accept of him, apart from sex?

– Ouch, said Lucy.

For her he didn't exist, not fully. They didn't know each other's names. She'd hinted *thin*. It was a hint, maybe more than a hint. So he couldn't go back to X-maniac, not with any sureness, and, tail between legs, could hardly go home. He was all over the place. His feet were free to levitate, or gravitate, in successive instants. They would be out looking for him, once they discovered his snowy footsteps. They would lie in wait, overpower him easily, and thrust him into a whorl in the river. The Dee was a lovely river, but he had no desire to explore its depths.

– I haven't even checked the weather yet, said Lucy.
   – Keep the curtains closed, he said. In case it's sunny. *Busie old fool.*
      – Marvell?
      – Donne, I think.
      – *Donne, I think.* You know perfectly well.
      – With my memory?
      – What do we know about memory anyway? said Lucy.

– That we haven't mostly forgotten. Mother of the Muses, one hundred and ten per cent. Total Mother.

don't you ever listen?
He could have done with the snow starting again, but it didn't. A car's lights swished past. He felt himself in very plain view. New tracks in the middle of the night would be pretty few. He got *concrete overcoat* into his head. It was the kind of thought you couldn't really get rid of. Did they fit you for one, a concrete overcoat, while you were still alive? Did you have to watch, while they mixed it by hand?

– So is that it? Is that what happened to your skull? Did they beat you up?
    – I don't know what happened to me. Don't you ever listen?

He started through the mesh of streets, Morningfield, Forest Road. He heard a figure catching him up. He started zig-zagging. Hamilton Place, Fountainhall. He didn't run, his knees were stiff again. The figure was catching him up determinedly. Hello, said the man. I'm Zander Petrakis. I wish you a Good New Year. Oh, said Jim, Happy New Year. You sound more sober than the people from whom I have recently departed, said Zander Petrakis. I am more sobered by some I've recently left, said Jim. Your university lecturers and their husbands and wives, said Zander. Not my university, said Jim, not any more. I tried to talk to them of philosophy, they talked to me of bun, said Zander. What kind of bun? said Jim. Black, said Zander. I talked to them of my native Crete, about Icarus, they talked to me of *fleein*. Fleeing? said Jim. They were good enough to spell it for me, said Zander. *Fleein*. It is a New Year custom, *to get fleein*. I talked to them of the Minotaur. One claimed they have a Maze in Aberdeen but the climate militates against Minotaurs, he said. They asked if I was *settling in*. I said the duty of an intellectual is not to *settle in*, but to oppose. Oh, said Jim. Perhaps you will come along to tonight's meeting, continued Jim. INCOSOLOV. What is INCO-SOLOV? said Zander. The Interim Committee to Solve Lovelesssness, said Jim. I will go along to oppose it, said Zander. First we must extend and endure lovelessness. Oh, said Jim, I don't fancy that.

I am more on the side of the beetles, said Zander. Only creatures with hard shells that can live under stone can survive nuclear war, that is well-known. And survive the other war too, he added. Vietnam? said Jim. No, the unclear war on which the young are embarked, the war of sentiment against sense, fashion against discipline, mumbo-jumbo against the material facts. I was, said Jim, going to ask your help. What for? said Zander. They're going to sell off the water and sell out the city, said Jim. They should get a few drachmas, said Zander. It seems quite solid. Not sell it, sell it out. I am aware of the distinction, said Zander. To the Yanks, said Jim. This is what happens in war, said Zander. But we're not at war, said Jim. The Americans are, said Zander. Even when they are isolationist and full of Mr Monroe's doctrine, they still attack. Only it's more insidious. Not that the Vietnamese are complaining of insidiousness.

Jim filled the stranger in with what he knew, but realised there were still big gaps. And so what do you do now? said Zander. Go to the police? The newspapers? My father's a councillor, said Jim. Perhaps he is part of the conspiracy? said Zander. You've obviously never met him, said Jim. In Crete sometimes these things resolve themselves, said Zander, sometimes never. Most people now are not so vigilant. The more democracy spreads, the more they expect solutions to be a kind of guaranteed magic. To be truthful, even in the old days, venturing into a labyrinth to kill a minotaur was not that popular. The trade between social good and personal extinction is easier to make in hot blood than in cold. Well mine's cold, said Jim. I need to find a caff or something. It sounds as though these people think they have found the golden one, said Zander.

However, I must continue my walk. I will think about your problem. It is easier to think walking. You can find me at the old University, where they specialise in bun and wine and sitting down mulling. Ask for Zander. Are you the only one? said Jim. The only. A few subsidiary Sandys. Ask for Zander Petrakis, Assistant Lecturer in European Philosophy. Thanks, said Jim. They had zigzagged further into the town. Thomson Street, Watson Street, Short Loanings, Leadside Road.

As soon as Zander left his side, the night seemed bristling. Richmond Street. He could even smell it. Hutcheon Street. There was something in the air that shouldn't be. Sharp and pungent. He came to a halt under a high brick building. There was orange in the top left window. Orange danced in the adjacent window. Painted white, high along the full length of the building he could make out COMBWORKS. Uncle Hugh worked here. He used to deliver fags in a van, till his eyes let him down. Uncle Hugh had taken him round. Orange flame was in four windows when the first window broke.

Fire curled out a fierce tongue that licked off part of the C. Almost you could read it as TOMBWORKS. But the next two windows broke and OMBWORKS it had to be.

Ivory combs didn't burn, but they didn't make combs of ivory now; elephants fell for different reasons. Combs of tortoiseshell didn't catch fire, nothing about a tortoise ever did. Even the modern keronyx, and nuroid and aberoid, that Uncle Hugh praised, were non-inflammable. Not like packing straw, oily machine rags, and pitch-pine stairs and floors.

Flames surged down, flames shot up.

ORKS the legend read now, as the flames raced along. He bet from which window the fire would burst forth next. Second floor, sixth along. Wrong, seventh. Bottom floor, sixth along. Wrong, fifth. Top floor, twelfth along. Correct. More and more glazing melted or gave a shocking crack in the dance of heat, flame, smell, smoke and destruction.

Three fire engines arrived from King Street and blocked part of his view. He moved to the side. But there wasn't much shouting. The crowd as it gathered was awed. It wasn't really a people fire. There was no-one working. Oh, but where was the watchman! They perched a man and a limp canvas hose on a turntable ladder, which spun and shot him skywards to pish like a boy on a bonfire. He thought of Ludwig again. He guessed a canvas hose wouldn't have worked too well in the firestorm at Hamburg.

He smelt it coming before he saw it. Really acrid. He put a flap of his floppy coat to his face as a filter. His Tigers got warm, hot, instantly hotter. He looked down. Rivers of plastic – black, pink, lime, scarlet, jade, azure and indigo in streaky, garish whirls, treacling and twining over each other like garter snakes in the mating season – were flowing from the fire.

His shoes would be moulded, then they'd be melted. He'd fall and be psychedelic in fifteen seconds. That wasn't his scene. He hopped it.

writing to your family

When he arrived at the beach, there was a solitary figure down on her haunches. Lucky there was a decent moon. She seemed to be drawing in the sand, her back to the land. He went down, to try and scour the tackiness off his shoes. Aberdeen Beach was not a beach that held much driftwood, so she was using her finger. She looked round as she heard him approach. Happy New Year, he said to her. Thank you, sir, she said, New Year later. Ah, he said, so you're not out celebrating? Celebrate each day, said the Chinese woman. Go to beach, face East, do Tai Chi. Great, he said, my name's Jim.

Lucy paused, then let it go.

My name Bing Qing, she replied. Brilliant, that's a lovely name, he said. Thank you, Jim. What are you writing? said Jim. She made two bent strokes intersecting, then a straight line across. Crab? said Jim. Zhei shi *nu*. Jesh shi, excuse me? Zhei shi *nu*. And she pointed to herself. Oh, writer, artist? She drew it once more. Woman, see? Woman on knee. Alongside *nu* she drew a swaddled form. And this? said Jim. *Zi, child*, answered Bing Qing. *Woman* and *child*. Together mean *good, excellent*. I think the tide is coming in, he said. Always somewhere tide come in, always somewhere tide leaving, said Bing Qing. So why did you leave? said Jim. In China many instruction, not many wisdom. You wonder why I write on sand? In my country, sand permanent as bone. Red Guard hate me, hate family. My father is high civil servant, put dung on field. How can China become great if it does not value intelligence?

117

said Jim. Mao say, said Bing Qing, only if wrong idea destroyed in intelligent person can China become great. Do you agree? said Jim. No. Wrong idea. Wrong idea in all must be avoided. Lao Tze teach this.

Do you work here? said Jim. Work Yangtse River on Bridge Street. Is it hard work? Six year since uncle set up in city. Accept now, many patron. A hundred last night good tipping. One party loud, make big joke. About *Chow Mao*, so funny for us, and sexual about duck. These people weak, my staff unhappy. Do you send your family money? said Jim. Money not reach. I send poem from sand. When we share beauty, world has justice. Simple as that? said Jim. More simple than god in heaven. I call my poem *Somehow Somewhere*. I don't know how to approach that, said Jim. Will know later. Goodbye, Jim, I must write to family now.

He walked up the bleak Boulevard without looking back, looking at the hard immediate city skyline of turrets, towers, Town House spire and university. As he walked towards the town, he noted how the skyline shot up quick to mask the hills.

– Go on, he said. I like Bing Qing. When I need peace, I try to imagine her. Yet I only came across her once.
   – Perhaps that distinguishes her, said Lucy. But that's it. That's the second folder.
   – Fancy writing to your family like that. On sand.
   – Straight on?
   – Yes, we seem to be coping.

nice man

Spermy McClung couldn't wait to be away. The *Spare Me* had been slipped for the last four weeks of the herring season, after a fouled prop burst the gland, buggered the gear box and left her trailing across a skerry. Now she rocked at Pocra Quay, while he was wending his way north to Fraserburgh on crunch-white roads in a blue Bedford van to pick up the dregs of his laid-off crew. If he couldn't find his regular crew, he might have to take on pierhead jumps.

– Excuse me, said Lucy. I'm tempted to say, *Who is this spunky fella*?

– Didn't Tam mention him in an earlier folder? Spermy McClung?

– Oh yeah, got him. Jim's special something or other.

A problem like that was nothing to him. As he said himself, they didn't call him Spermy Jed McClung for nothing. He paid them. I dinna care what state ye're in, get in the fuckin van.

– Nice man, Mr Spermacetti, said Lucy.

Jesus, Jed, said Alec. I ken, I walk on water, said Spermy. All I'm askin is, get in the fuckin van. Tak a dram, Jed, it's the New Year. Ye ken I never touch poison. C'mon. Whit's the panic? said Alec. The panic is, said Spermy, we've been lyin on the slip the last month. I got Hall's tae launch her special yesterday. The rivets are still glowin in her keel and belly. Ye widna sit here rottin your liver, when ye could be oot makkin a pay? One day, Jed, one day in the year. Collect your gear next time ye're doon, I'll get somebody else. Okay, okay, said Alec. Smart then, said Spermy. I'll be back at five when I've picked up young Gibby and them.

Young Gibby wasn't in. The house was dark. He found him round at Jock's. Come in, come in, said Jock, a good New Year. Here's Spermy, boys, here's Jed. I'll wait on the step, said Spermy. Wait on the step? Ye canna dae that, said Jock. That's bad luck. Weel that's jist ma bad luck, isn't it, said Spermy. Ye mak your ain luck at this game, Jock. Fa else is in there wi you? Gib, that's young Gibby like, Nat, an a hale lot mair. I mean men, said Spermy. Just young Gibby, me an Nat, said Jock. Fishermen, said Spermy. Me, Nat, an young Gibby, I tellt ye, said Jock. Five minutes, said Spermy. Stuff yir bags an let's get mobile. I want to be through in the Minch the nicht afore the turn o the tide. Whit, said Jock, nae the Pentland Firth? It's only wattir, said Spermy. I'm aff tae rouse Baxter. Be ready for me, right?

Baxter was the mate. He lived further out. Out amongst the fenceposts of wind-swept Buchan. I was knocking on your door three times there, said Spermy. Oh, hi, Jed. We had the radio up full blast. I heard,

I knocked three times. Whit's up like? said Baxter. We're for oot, said Spermy. For oot? said Baxter. When ye phoned last, ye said we wouldna be oot till the 2nd or 3rd. Dinna believe aathing ye hear on the phone, said Spermy, have ye seen the forecast? It's northerly 8-9 imminent, nor-west 10, storm 11, possibly later. Better leave it then, is that what ye're sayin? said Baxter, should fair up later in the week? Weel, in ye come. There's a sprawl o folk, but maist o them's decent. Spermy took one step inside the outer hall, as a concession, to drive his point home. Baxter, I dinna think ye're gettin ma point, I dinna think ye're really listenin. I am sut, said Baxter. Ye are not, said Spermy. Look, Baxter. I've only had the boat six weeks, an she's been on the slip for ower muckle o that. There's herrin oot there wi *Spare Me*'s name written aa ower them, but they're fed up waitin. I dinna blame them, I'm fed up waitin masel. We've a chance tae get through the Firth afore the warst o't. Once we're oot Wast, in some o thae Gaelic holes, it'll be like a mill dam. Ye're the boss, ye ken best, I'm nae arguin wi ye. I'll wait in the van, said Spermy. Come in, said Baxter. At least say *hello*. *Hello cheerio?* Fit's the point? Na, I'll come intae yir hoose an gladly, Baxter, when baith o us hae a few bricht scales aboot us, a few scales. Please yersel, said the mate. I'll get ma thingies.

Half an hour later, a bunch of guys, sheer dregs, the best available, were trying to prop up on or spew beneath the bare benches that lined the back of the van. Slow doon, Jed, I'm pukin ower somebody sleepin I think, I canna see in the dark. Eat mair carrots then, Gib. Cunt.

– Cutting edge, said Lucy.

Never say *can't* tae me, Gibby ma loon, nae even in a whisper. The word *can't* is nae in my vocabulary. Pull in for us, Jed, said Alec. I'm desperate for a pish. Ye'd be a target on the open road, said Spermy. Ye micht get run ower, an me already twa men short. Wait till I hash on tae Ellon. Canna wait till nae Ellon, said Alec.

By the time he came into Aberdeen, still two hours before sun-up, and across the Bridge of Don, most of the human stuff in the back had, in its own sharp stinks, subsided. Is that you still drivin? said the mate, blearing an eye against the sodium lights of King Street. Na, this is me eatin candy floss, said Spermy McClung.

a red bandana

When Jim got down the harbour to the red-roofed Shack Café, it was probably nigh-on six. He was still feeling light in the head from his adventures and encounters, and tingled by her challenge.

– Still? said Lucy.
    He nodded.

He'd tried sex, air, ice, fire, Cretan philosophy and Chinese poetry. But fear of the powers-that-be closed his horizon in. With a last check round for Provost or Senator, and a hoist of his baggy breeks, he made to open the black door.

– Are those the same clothes you gave me this time?
    – Don't be a twit, said Lucy. You took them away. I never saw them again. The things that people will do for a free set of clothes.
    – No doubt, he said.

The door tinged as he went in. He made his way to the counter. There was nobody attending. Fat hanging in the air betrayed the menu. A woman with iron-grey curls detached herself from a seated customer. Hi, he said, morning. Could I get. Hailstones bulleted across the corrugated tin of the roof. Sorry, dear, speak up. He mimed lifting a mug of tea in one fist. Mimed clawing a bacon roll to his face in the other. She turned away to attend to his whims.

– *Whims*, said Lucy.
    – Yes, thanks, Tam, he said. *Whims*, I'm famous for them. Terrible man.

There were three frying pans, plus a deep pot, on four gas rings. Pan one had its bacon, sausage, wheels of black pudding. Pan two displayed sunny-side up egg, and clouded egg. Pan three boasted half-toms, collapsed, red, seedy, watery. Deep pot for beans.

He turned to look at the other occupants. Three old farts, nodding and smoking, inclined to each other, without speaking, over a chipped, formica table. For all he knew, not speaking because of the hail, the bullets. Not speaking because they were fatigued beyond tiredness, with faces like scorched ravines. He wasn't that tired himself. Not speaking because they were all out of yarns, stories, whys, becauses.

Young woman in a red bandana, fawn duffle coat, green woven midi, and black knee-boots at another table. She was sideways on to him. He knew her, couldn't place her. That happened all the time in the city. She stirred round. He made his mouth open cautiously towards her, half-a-hello without commitment, then turned to see how breakfast was getting on.

– Who's this then? said Lucy. Another conquest? Wait, I know, there's one missing. This'll be Iris.
   – You'll be peeping at the ending next.

Iron Curls was using a fish-slice in pan one to deal with hopeless casualties, and drag them across to one side out of triage. Burst sausage, scab of bacon, cauterized blood pudding. In a clearing she carefully laid a fatty rasher, as though stretching out a pale victim after an air-raid. She turned her surgical attentions to a white softie, a species of bap. She half-slit it and tore its pith. She spread it with a fluted metal-handled knife from a half-pound block of Stork, with its wrapper open like a greasy nappy. She wiped her fingers on each other, the better to mingle the dust of raw flour from the top of the softie with the oleo of pig, ox, possibly whale, and vegetable fats.

– I'm not sure I like the tone here, she said. Lord Snooty springs to mind.

At last the hail stopped drumming. Was it a bacon roll? It was. Was it a cup of tea? It also. A mug, if you've got one. We only do mugs. That seemed to him sufficient philosophy.

– Or very early Beckett, that bit, he said. We all have our influences. Surf 'n' Turf, Tam 'n' Sam.

– Do you still read?

– I did in exile, if that's what it was. Only two problems. Couldn't remember characters' names from one page to the next, couldn't follow plots.

– What else is there?

– Style, sudden incident. Lucy, you know that.

– Ye gods, she said. Here he goes again.

The bacon, searing away like Joan of Arc, was denied a moment's peace. It sizzled, arched, frazzled, on both sides and along edges. That's fine, he said. Just say, she said. Spot on, he said. I can't stand cinders, replied the woman. Murder, he said. Fit? she said. They're murder, cinders, he retorted. Charcoal's supposed to be good for you, she said. I'm bothered wi ma stomach. Your stomach? Aye, it's no right. My auntie's the same, he said. She posed the frizzle on the spread softie, and shut the pliant lid, pressing it down with the flat of her fingers. A docked tail stuck out one side. Did you want ketchup? No, he said. It's not too late, there is ketchup. No, it's okay. My doctor says I've to keep off condiments, she said. She handed him the bacon softie, seated on a side-plate. Is there tea ready? he said. Did you want fresh? No, it's okay. It's been stewing a whilie, she said, fine and strong. What time do you open? he said. I work wi the pubs, she said. Open when they shut, shut again as soon as they open. Must be some long night, he said. Nights are long wherever you are, she said, a body has tae get on. Wait till the revolution, he said. Eh? she said. Just wait till the revolution, he said. That'll be ninepence, dear, she said. Oh god, he thought, these are not, wait. Thruppence, a button, a daud of gum, sixpence, that do? he said. That's us square, said the woman, keep a hold of your button and stuff. Thought I was away to scrub pans there, he said. Mind, dinna forget, there is ketchup, she said. Dandy, he said, ravenous.

After the ordering ritual was over, he turned to face the rest of society. The girl in the green midi beckoned him over. Christ, he said, It is you, Iris. What you doing here? Really, she said, I could ask you the same.

He pulled out a tubular chair with a plastic-covered pink-cushioned portion. Psychedelic, eh, in here? he said. He sat down opposite her. She laid aside her book, *The Iron Heel* by Jack London. You do acid? said Iris. Do you? he said. Asked you first, said Iris. Naw, athlete, he said, well, runner. And I'm in trouble enough at school without getting busted, she said. What kinda? With the heidie, the flaming hierarchy. But you were always Goodie-Two-Shoes. There's such a thing as biding your time, replied Iris. Iris, sorry, here's me with tea, do you want? It's okay, I'm floating in tea. This bacon roll's the business, he said. Roon ma hert like a hairy worm. One of his father's phrases.

– Alison's like that, my assistant, my colleague, said Lucy. Always coming out with these strong expressions. Doric.
  – For a laugh?
  – Partly. Never heard her do that one. *Roon ma hert like a hairy worm.* Must ask her if she knows it. *Roon ma hert like a hairy worm.*
  – It's possibly rude, he said.
  – Alison won't mind. Wonder how she's getting on.
  – Going to phone?
  – Don't want to break this.
  – You've been leaning on my thigh for the last I don't know how long. A break won't hurt.
  – Diddums, said Lucy. Don't you like me tampering with your blood supply?

they only believe in change

When she got back upstairs, he was sleeping. She didn't wake him and went back and made another call from the house phone downstairs. She hadn't had a clue what time it was. Then she made brunch, and sat and ate it, ravenous herself, glad of the peace, strangely.

She cleared away her plate and put clingfilm on his. She thought Alison might have phoned her back. It was the first time she had stepped off for ages, into pure life, that limbo. Probably the world went on, but how could you know. It was like stepping off pavementette and going down the Back Wynd Steps during a Spectacle.

She took out some sheets of paper from the printer in the down-stairs study and took them back to the kitchen where it was warm. She wrote down some alphabet and wrote as many names, neat per column, as she could, for each initial, *Andrew, Arthur, Anthony, Bob, Bill, Bert, Colin, Ciaran, Chris,* and so on. She soon ran out of paper, then realised there were three lots sitting blank in the worn folders on the worktop, beside the kettle.

That seemed a very long time ago, the time of her subterfuge.

Whereas January 1st '68 was fresher than yesterday.

He didn't get up for brunch. They ate dinner in the kitchen.

– Did you get through to Alison?

– Eventually.

– How was she?

– Distant.

– Is she the moody sort?

Lucy was absent a second.

– Is she?

– Not usually. Maybe Finlay and her split up.

– Didn't you ask her?

– We didn't get off the subject of work. The meeting I missed today was pretty important. She needed me, she's under pressure. We've lost significant ground.

– Explain.

– Do you want the last tattie?

– No. Let it be.

– It's only like this massive leisure multinational versus a city, said Lucy. The city has half-resisted, then quarter-resisted, but now we're set to lose, big-time. Ready for pud? It's my own blackcurrants.

– At this time of year?

– From the freezer. I've blatted them with ice-cream and yoghurt. Alison told me one thing. You won't believe this. In the middle of all this, they want to change the city's name. Again. Aberdeen for centuries, Uberdeen the last two years. They used to be so tradi-tionalist. Now they only believe in change.

– Right.

– They mooted *Rookton* at first. *Marrdom* even. Now they've picked up my joke suggestion of *Leopardeen*.

– Who cares? It'll make the football scores more interesting. Wolves 1 Leopardeen 2. More like American football.

– Unfortunately, said Lucy, I think that's the general idea.

– I'll do the dishes, he said.

– Dishwasher. Theo made sure I had all that before he died.

– Why didn't you marry after? No ties, good salary, nice big house.

– Don't. Come upstairs. Have you had enough to eat? We might need our strength for the very last bit.

– I hope that's just a single entendre, he said.

They got on the bed.

– If Tam's got this last part properly written, he said, it might propel me through my blanks.

Anyway, eh, what a ding-dong!

– Sorry? he said. You've lost me already.

– I've just started.

– Yes, go back, I've lost the thread.

This bacon roll's the business. Goin roon ma hert like a hairy worm.

– That, yes, of course.

She does them good.

– That's Iris speaking, said Lucy.

Anyway, eh, what a ding-dong!

– That's—?

– You, said Lucy.

What? said Iris. Tonight, the New Year, he said, what a ding-dong. I was going to ask, said Iris. Have you lost weight? Your coat. Yeah, really suddenly. Hey but you look great, the bandana. Don't, she said. What? I look how I look. Plain Iris, the washed-out rainbow. You used to call me *Bapface*. Hell, that was other people, he said. Hell is not always other people, she said. Deep, Iris. Not, she said. Anyway, what are you so hepped-up about? Two things, he said. Just been with this amazing person. Name? Dunno, he said. Person, said Iris. Mabel, Jean, Betty, Angela? Angeline?

– Not even close, said Lucy.

X, he said. She's X to me. No surprise, you didn't even spot me when you came in. And we sat in the same double desk for years. Yeah, that's bad, he said, but that was a wee while back. Whereas X was what, an hour ago? True, he said, but X really exists. As in exist, you know. Yes, said Iris. She's my very own X, he said, and that's all about it. I'd give you my shrink's number, she said, but in that coat you'd probably vanish. Ha, you're good for me, Iris, I spend too much time brooding. Does she? If you can brood at a hundred miles an hour, he said, probably yes. He was silent for a moment.

Iris broke in. Do you want my advice? Sure, he said. Go with it, it may be your chance. But we're no way due to meet again, he said. That does introduce a note of futility, said Iris. Tough, eh? he said. All I can do is develop my own existence, my existingness or something. She thinks I'm a twig, an interloper, some fleeting Mercury. Want to hear about my troubles? she said.

– Nice one, Iris, said Lucy.

Let me get a coupla cuppas, he said. Okay, she said. Lend me a bob, though, could you? he said. These are not my breeks.

– Wandering about in another man's breeks? said Lucy. Tut-tut.
  – I'm another man anyway, he said.

She came with him to the counter. Two teas, Mum, okay? said Iris. That your Mum? he whispered, as Iron Curls disappeared into the back of the premises. She nodded. He glanced at the three old men with faces like scorched ravines. And who are the old farts? he whispered again. These three? she said. Well, Freddie on the right, Freddie Tait, used to let various parties load up free on his tram and out to Woodside to break up Mosley's rallies, '36, '37, that kind of time. He's a good guy, Freddie, but his mind's awander. Then Charlie, him in the middle, his wife's just died, used to have a milk float, Co-opie Milk, and a Clydesdale to pull it, the length of King Street. Rosie he called his mare, he kept her droppings in a bucket and distributed it to gardens. Hector Smith on the left was pretty much straight, a docks shop steward for the T&G. They had their strikes, they maintained conditions, slowly improved them. The old farts stirred themselves, as though they knew they were being talked about. They made a show of peering through the snow-flecked pane.

I see, said Jim. I'm not knocking it, said Iris. I just think the heyday for unions and party stuff is past, as well as for dependable, lovable workers like Charlie there. These struggles were too titanic, too setpiece. We need to take over the actual workplace, large and small, that's where it's at, with workers' councils. You don't develop enough confidence treading a union line. I know, said Jim. Do you? said Iris. There was some commotion or other on the dockside. The door tinged. Iron Curls reappeared. A guy with a scuffed leather jacket and a rakish Lennon cap entered and crossed to the counter. In a hurry, pal, dae ye mind? said the guy. Carry on, said Jim. I've got the rest of existence. Cheers, said the guy. Mina darlin, fit are ye like for biscuits, tea-bags? Ony sugar? Course, Nat. I'm a café, amn't I? Rax us ower a bunch, then. Onything ye can spare. Pit it doon tae the *Spare Me.* Nae accounts, Nat, said Mina. Dinna dae accounts. Young Mr McClung can come in and pay me personal. That'll mak his day, Mina, said Nat. There ye go, said Mina. Abernethies, one packet. Digestives, one packet. Butter biscuits, two packets. Four pund o sugar and four quarters o Lipton's tea. And where's Master McClung headed this fine morning? Tell him I dinna work wi tea-bags. The wild West, said Nat. In that case tell him tae pay me afore he sails. Or I'll hae his guts for garters when he comes back. The three at the window had stirred as far as having a chuckle. It's time ye lot were buyin fresh mugs, said Mina. Ye think ye can jist bide here aa nicht, an sit an ogle.

Jim thought he could see Spermy rumbling about in the dockside shadows. He pulled up his coat collar. Ye cauld? said Nat. Ye fisher? Ye dinna look the type. No – na. Why – fit wey like? said Jim. We're stuck for a coupla men, said Nat, that's fit wey. When are you – fan ye aff like? said Jim. When we're fuelled and watered, an hour at the ootside. Good luck, said Jim.

bitch, said lucy

Jim went back and sat opposite Iris, with the mugs. The good thing, if there was a good thing, about stewed tea, was that it was never too hot. Know who that was? he said to Iris. I've seen him, I don't know him, said Iris. Just some guy off Spermy's boat, topping up supplies. Spermy McClung, he said, there's a name to conjure with. You know I'm working at our old school? she said, Frederick Street. Fredericker, he said, I would have thought you. Oh I had choices, said Iris, but I chose Fredericker. Remember that time Pinners gave three of us a camera? she said. And we went round shipyards, down the docks, and up the Citadel? It was Timmer Market time, said Iris. With me I think it dates back to then. Photographing the occupied faces. That was the day it began to sink in. You're either a tourist in your own place, or you're in deeper.

Christ, Iris, he said, admire that. You're off your tiny rocker working in Fredericker, but yeah, admire that. Since we moved to Northfield, I've got a bit unattached. Or detached, I suppose. From? said Iris. The old haunts, folk, other people's purposes. Varsity lulls you away. Are you still at Varsity? No, building sites. Building sites? she said. But they're nae real, he said, I'm jacking that in. You're not seriously happy, he went on, at Frederick Street School? Not entirely, said Iris. But, fair do's, they're not happy with me. The kids are great, total toe-rags, pretty damn loyal. We've started a big project on Eskimos. You know how a couple came to be washed up, more likely dumped and deposited, in Aberdeen? Still in their kayaks. A couple of centuries back. Well it started from there. Now we're about to build our own. Never had you down as a kayakist, he said. Got an intro at College, said Iris. At Stonehaven, the Summer Isles. In bouncier water a low centre of gravity seems to help.

– So quite big hips? said Lucy.
  – Iris and I— he said.
  – Were just good friends, said Lucy.

It turned out Iris had let herself become influenced by the deschoolers while at College. Nothing of that in the lectures, of course, but you can't keep a good library down. She'd devoured everything from Neill to RF Mackenzie, from Goodman to Ivan Illich. I see the problem in our society as hierarchy, said Iris. I've already had an oral and a written warning. For thinking? he said. For building Eskimo kayaks? For getting too close to the kids. For not accepting that I was getting too close to the kids. And for challenging the heidie. I've got feelers out on a teachers workers' council, she continued. And I was one of the ones who called this meeting tonight, you heard? The solve loveless-ness in a jiffy malarkey? said Jim. Sorry, Group to Unstick Stuckness isn't it? The same, said Iris. GUST. Lots of the potentials said they'd try and come. What about you? Dunno, he said. I was attracted, but it seems a bit forced, a bit put-on. Okay, said Iris, but everything the Left starts up seems awkward at first. It's only since I started teaching I've realised the forces that hold us down, said Iris. We'll never achieve much if we're stuck on our own. Say you'll come? Might, said Jim. Which strand do you represent? Strand? he said. Which group? said Iris. Eh, existentialists, said Jim. Hardline? Very. What's your line on Vietnam? said Iris. Coexist. On stuckness? Get a new life. On loveless-ness? We seem to be still out on that one, said Jim. Anyway, apart from X, you said there was something else, said Iris. *Two things*, you said, wasn't it? Did I? he said.

– Your memory was rubbish even then, said Lucy.

Yes, said Iris. I'll maybe come to it, he said. By the way, X is the daughter of a Commie sculptor. That's about all I was able to pick up. Lucy Legge, said Iris, that's who that'll be. She's a one. Fancies herself culturally, I've been told.

– Bitch, said Lucy, and read on quickly.

The door opened. Master McClung, said Mina, good tae see ye, that'll be four pounds twelve and fourpence. Spermy glowered at the pair nearest the door and ignored her. Seein it's yersel, said Mina, four pounds twelve. I'm nae a grocer boy, said Spermy, I'm a press gang. This twat'll do. He pulled the twat up by the scruff of its coat, and located its scrawny elbow. Let's keep it in the family, eh? Your Da's fishin for ma Ma, so ye're fishin wi me. Let's go. Let him go, said Iris. Fit's in it for me? said Spermy. You'll be lucky, said Iris. Lucky? said Spermy. Iris, doll, I wouldna gie ye typhoid. C'mon, twat. Take proper care, skirled Iris, pair o ye! Be in touch, Jim said, as he was propelled.

very well in

Eventually, at half past eight, the first sun of the year arose, fierce as gold from a forge. Julie gazed across the sea as it vibrated into view. She snapped it.

– Julie again, said Lucy. Going down.
  – That's her business, said Jim.

Then zipped herself into her 8mm neoprene longjohn.

– Sure you don't shag her later?
  – Read on and I'll find out.

She kicked into her second jetfin, spat generously in her mask, bent to the sea and swilled it. There was no substitute for human spit. No proprietary substitute. Even Dow Chemical, who had managed to gel petroleum, couldn't come up with one. Her father, the Lord Provost, had shares in Dow. They'd had a row about that. When she was doing her Masters in Massachusetts, half the demos, more than half, were against Dow, for the napalm. Not that she'd been on one. Then her parents gave her a Calypso Nikkor for Christmas, with Dow lube for the rubber seals. She'd made a show of binning it, then retrieved it. Water in your new camera was not ideal.

She was on a shingle beach. Any stray crab or brittle star would soon be crushed by wave action. She clenched the hard rubber snorkel between her teeth, and waded backwards till she felt resistance against her thighs. She lay back, trusted herself to the water, and was borne up. A chill eel entered her suit at the neck and channelled along her spine. Julie turned on her belly so that she could see the underwater shingle redeemed by bubbles. There were pulses of swell coming from seaward, against a strong riverine ebb pushing her out. Poised between two forces, she felt her own decisive. She exchanged snorkel for demand valve, blew to clear it, checked round quick for boats and beasts, jackknifed her jetfins high, and slid on down.

In the clench of pressure, wheeze of alloyed air, in the flick and drive of her fins, she was in her element. How could you not think we came from the sea? The water was on the murky side. Silver sand eels shimmered into view, sensed her, spun like the snap of a flag, and ribboned away in ragged unison. There was a shard or two on the shifting bottom. She moved her glove to pick one up, and a dissolute cloud of mud rose up and streamed away. The current was getting stronger; she could feel a sting of ice coming down from the hills, she could see the odd rainbow of harbour oil hallucinant on weed. One of the reasons she didn't do drugs. No need. She had visions while she worked.

– Tam seems pretty well into her? said Lucy. Very well in.
  – In his dreams, maybe. Problem—?
  – Oh, no. I quite like Julie, said Lucy. Now she's underwater.

Yet it was wrong, Jamie had kept telling her, her over-responsive approach. Her tutors said isolate, take one variable at a time, form a disprovable thesis and test it rigorously, for scientific peers world-wide. Ahead, in about mid-channel, she saw a big plate of reddish metal, embossed with an acne of juvenile barnacles.

i'd rather be who i am

Spermy in the harbour mouth gripped the spoked wheel with his left hand, while he twiddled with the radar-scale. He'd retained his ex-schoolmate on watch, the rest packed off below, to snore off their binge of dark rum and lager.

– I notice we don't see the name *Jim* so often, said Lucy.
  – Not for a while.
  – Are you really Jim, is that who you are?
  – Interim Jim, maybe. Best keep reading.

There was no booze allowed aboard *Spare Me*; you couldn't become best boat in Scotland by pishing it up against a wall, or thumping into the base of a cliff in a bastard stupor. No clink of cans from the galley, but still drink in the men. Spermy couldn't wait to get back to the grounds, to do what he did best. So many ways you could track herring. Gulls, echo-sounder, a glisk of their oil smoothing the surface. Or a sprachle of bubbles released from their swim-bladders, as they rose at dusk to feed.

In the harbour's jaw the *Spare Me* now. In the very spot. Spermy checked and rechecked the echo-sounder. The *Dépense* would be in smithereens long ago. Wake up, twat. This is far ma Da and them drowned. I ken, I was there, mind, on the pier? said Jim. Ye were just wee then, said Spermy. So were you, you spat on my boot, said Jim. I still get nightmares, said Spermy. Clap yir een on the soonder there. What for? said Jim. Read the traces, said Spermy. Ye'd better look, ye're the expert, said Jim. Why dae ye nae look? Spermy spun the wheel slowly. Scared ye'll see somethin? said Jim.

– Then a spate of *Jims* again, said Lucy. I keep thinking. Would they not still have you on file at the hospital?
  – I'm not going back there. No more ops. I'd rather be who I am.
  – Namely?
  – Don't think the hospital had a clue anyway.

Spare Me circled sunwards. The waters live and scarlet-shimmering. The water was rocking back and fore in the channel. His drowned father never told him stories, not that he often asked. *I come ashore tae forget aboot the sea, loon, nae tae blabber on.* So he followed his father to sea, and made his own story. Just ahead, interrupted, a stream of bubbles rising. It could hardly be herring, this time of day, not this close in.

bubbles

– Julie, said Lucy. Bubbles.

Jim decided not to rise to the bait.

Julie approached the reddish plate. It was waving with weed and knobbled with barnacles. The marine archaeology side didn't concern her. What was under the plate might. A conger laired, with parted snout, ready to slash a diver's finger off with slimy needle teeth. Or a lobster, not red by nature, but perhaps taking on a rouge under this hulk. She poked with a knife. She picked up a vibe, which grew to a vibration. A butterfish pouted and fled. Her quick snap with the Calypso probably missed it. Something heavy was arriving over her, sending a *whop-whop* through the column of water. She held onto the section of wreck with both gloves, and took a buffeting.

She waited till the vessel was on an away path before beginning surfacing, not holding her breath, that was fatal. She was only half-way up when the prop began to throb again. They might do something mad like chuck a stick of dynamite in. Engine hum permeated the waters. They were about to do something. She finned upwards, expelling air in expanding gouts.

Her third snap was of a bronze prop, very close, steadily carving water.

– That's it, I'm afraid. End of third folder. Where's the rest?

    – No more? But none of these so-and-sos has so much as breathed my name. We're no further forward.

– Well, you're on a boat, heading out to sea, or playing about in the harbour mouth, trying to pick up or carve up you-know-who—

– He must have got more on tape than that, Tam, he must have. What was he playing at?

– Did Julie come? said Lucy. I mean come on board. Did she?

– Search me.

– Oh, you getting up now?

– Need a good walk, he said. Blow the webs away.

– Want someone to go with you?

– No. Do you mind? It's a lot to try and digest.

– How long do you feel you'll be?

– Not terribly long.

my sieve's a memory

They called it his *voyage* or *inner voyage* or *trip* but it hadn't helped.

Trip had a double meaning of course.

A specialist in an understated tweed suit had said, Now you were undertaking a nautical trip if my dossier serves.

Sorry?

You had run off to sea.

Had I?

You were all at sea? ventured one, a lady psychiatrist with white earrings like sugary pandrops.

Part of me wasn't, he had replied.

But they needed you to be all at sea, floating on their couch.

When he came back from his latest wander, reeling in invisible wool and stuffing it in his right hand pocket, Lucy was sat in front of the bedroom mirror. She was running her hands up through her hair both sides, running it through her fingers.

– Is *bouffe* a word, would you know?

– *Boof*, he said.

– *Bouffe*, said Lucy.

– Yes, something went *boof*, he said, I seem to remember. Keep saying it.

– *Bouffe. Bouffe,* said Lucy. *Bouffant.*

– Nice pausing.

– I wasn't always a pauser, she said. I went at things full tilt, Tam got it right.

– Why?

– I wanted everything.

Again she ran her fingers, both sides, up through her hair.

– I used to have a beehive, do you remember? Do you remember beehives?

– Like gold wire stuck high with lacquer, he said. They made girls' faces seem smaller, so nobody would think they were too brainy and be put off. Were you too brainy?

– Probably, she said, not quite brainy enough.

She stopped putting her hair up and just elongated her face in the mirror to try and diminish the deepening lines.

She glanced at her eyes, then glanced away.

– I don't know what brainy is, he said. You need to remember a lot of stuff to be brainy. My sieve's a memory. I must have gone to sea in it—

– No, said Lucy. Enough. I want you to tell me straight what happened out there.

– At night. All I know is, it happened at night.

– Just take your time. I put some lobster on earlier, we need to go down and look at that.

– A lobster?

– Some lobster, said Lucy. Bisque.

– Never heard of it.

– Very slow soup.

– When did it come in?

– It's been in a while. Lobster bisque.

making love to the skull

– Let's have a look at that head of yours, said Lucy.

– Being the only one available, worst luck.

– Pull your chair this way a bit. Under the light.

– Then you can interrogate the skull, I've done my stint. What will your weapons be? Apart from light, Lucy?

She tucked a couple of tea towels round his neck. One was a terry towelling identification chart for the more exotic auks and seabirds. Razorbill, albatross and such. The other was of smooth linen and just said, on a green strip, *GLASS*. She went behind him and rattled in a drawer. He could hear the sound of scissors or small shears.

– Your hair, she said.

– Often compared to patches of gorse on a half-burnt hillside, he said. In the traditional love poetry of High Priest Island. I always thought the title of that island was ambiguous.

– Was it nice, apart from the ambiguity?

– I don't remember getting there and I don't remember leaving. I could have been wrecked and then unwrecked, I suppose. Snatches I recall.

– Uninhabited?

– Yes. I breathed and slept, ate and shat there. I wouldn't give myself airs, I didn't go the length of inhabiting it.

– Did you eat well?

– Four species of fish, not counting shellfish, three of berries, plus rose hips—

– You mentioned. Are rose hips not a berry?

– I wasn't washed-up with a nature guide. Two species of root. And one shattered sheep at a cliff base, in a race against decomposition. Which, to be fair, we both entered. The dead sheep and this forked animal.

He had told her all this before. The whole exile thing. Whatever else he had read, she knew he was into *Lear*.

– The next sound you hear is going to be scissors—

– I slept in a cave. A rock-cut tomb—

– So don't move, stay at peace.

– Which had two stone beds, with a passage between them, and a bunch of fern waving at the patio door.

– Yes, said Lucy.

– It must have been hewn out before the day of the priest. A priest isn't allowed to sleep next to anyone, not even in a tomb, in case he has bad thoughts.

She just let him ramble on, not that there was much option.

It was a shock, that combination of repulsion and attraction, to see the skull with its vegetation off. Previously the nearest had been when he was sleek and dripping after the shower. When she first held it in her hands. Now she proposed to massage it. She had a choice of oils.

– What kind of gunge you going to slap on? he said.

– Not gunge, oil. Rosemary, that's for remembrance.

– Sure it's not rue? he said.

After a while she made two cups of tea, and put lemon in them, a squeeze. She placed his on the asbestos mat on the Raeburn. Then rested her fingers on top of the stove a moment. Her hands got colder quicker these days. She was going to try to link the massage up.

It was like making love to the skull.

Now neither spoke.

distant skittles

Alison and Finlay were having a helluva row. And, not many people had seen this, Alison was crying. Finlay took her at face value, the life and soul, a fount of jokes and asides and piss-takes, but she was more than that. Finlay was only just finding this out. And she was insecure. That came as a surprise.

He didn't know how to deal with it, except by means that made it worse.

They had gone out as a foursome to Strike Ten, the bowling arcade. It had only been planned that morning, but by the time evening came, Alison wanted private time with Finlay, and a shoulder to lean on.

Right from the moment Alison's first ball took to the gutter, the evening was on the slide. Finlay was doing his best to keep his team's end up, striking and sparing like one possessed. He showed little understanding that this was not what Alison needed.

The other pair were well matched, both average to useless when it came to tumbling distant skittles with a rotund piece of plastic.

After the second game, while the other couple disappeared off to the loos, Finlay went straight up for drinks, but when he got back, Alison was flushed.

– What is it? Is it that old time of the—? Hell, I don't mind.

He only caught her halfway down the car park. The row surged. Unfortunately it was an otherwise calm night, and every word carried, and carried home.

And especially when Alison said, Bide then, Finlay. Jist ye bide here an play wi yersel. I'm gaain stracht back up the toon tae try an rescue ma dochter.

ill-souled men

– *The first word that Sir Patrick read*, he said.

Lucy just waited.

She didn't want to get back to knockabout mode. Knockabout was very enjoyable, easy on them. Mostly evasive.

> – *The first word that Sir Patrick read,*
> *Sae loud loud lauchit he,*
> *The neist word that Sir Patrick read,*
> *The tear blindit his ee.*

That was all that came. She continued moving her fingers, just playing the white notes, the platelets, still unsure about touching the darker ridges.

> – *O wha is this has done this deed,*
> *And told the king o me,*
> *To send us oot at this time o the year*
> *To sail upon the sea.*

The breakers over the Bar at the mouth of the harbour, that would be bad enough, she imagined, for a boat going out. Even after Davie Dae-Aathing had floated Craig Metallan out of the channel, there was still that further obstacle, further out.

The Bar.

All the grit scoured off mountain crags by frost and ice, all the howffs of granitic sand burgled by floods, all the loam thieved off the sweat-rich fields of Lower Deeside by summer and winter rains, got carried there to build a fatal ridge, where the sea clashed and rumbled, and broke in pieces ill-run ships and ill-souled men.

He carried on singing a few more verses. Some in order, some with a few words altered or missing, but all with the ballad's relentless repetition.

Then it started.

reft

For Alison it had been nothing to do with the ten-pin; how anybody could get into a lather over that predictable clatter escaped her. It was just that she had been out at Huntly earlier in the day, part of an outreach programme from city to county, and after a quick chicken pastie from the excellent baker, she went and visited the castle, then the local kirkyard.

Good to find the courage at last to revisit the place you were brought up in.

Huntly Castle was fine enough, it touched off half-decent memories. Long after her father had first taken her along, rather severely, for a historical introduction, she would flit in and out of the substantial pile at will, with a smile from the young woman curator. She didn't need the printed guide, she knew all her favourite nooks. She would wrink around in the bakehouse, brewhouse, cellars and dungeons. She liked to imagine the different foods seething in compartments of the big black pot: poultry and eggs and onions together, hunks of beef for the laird and the laird's guests, a parcel of bacon, a clootie dumpling with honey and beans.

Then she would go along the passageway, and see the dungeon below, like a stone bottle. Although there was a smell of stone-dust, plaster and clay, she thought there would have been lots more smells when the dungeon was full. All that the poor chained folk down there could likely do was scratch, doze and pee towards the centre, and then, to whichever absent god they'd been led to favour, pray. It was probably a lot worse than you could ever imagine.

How did anyone even begin to have the right to pour your soul into a stone bottle?

This time she went in with a wry grin under the defaced tall frontispiece, a Renaissance confection, with its pierced heart, dragon and griffin. They had been Catholics in Huntly, the ruling class, till the Covenanters bustled in during the 1640s and chipped off the crowning St Michael v. Satan disc. There was always a running battle to redefine the Antichrist.

She went up the tight circular stairs, holding onto the rope, till she was in the earl's bed-chamber. It was wonderfully airy without any earl, you were at tree-top height. Swallows in elegant manic twitter flitted in from the leafy sun to test ledges and alcoves. They made her so lightsome she surprised herself.

She had an hour to spare, so she went to the cemetery outside town.

Her parents had died within months of each other when she was in her late teens, and she hadn't buried them. Going against her aunts' wishes, she had them cremated. She had no truck with religion, that was the thing. And she was sorry about that now and wished she had a place to find them.

Willa, then Jock. Then that infamous night of Jock's funeral, when it got too wild in the Atholl. Waking up about noon, and not on her own. In a way, never on her own again, though her bed-partner emigrated soon enough.

Perhaps she could track some of the rest of the family. She found Andersons, right enough, a potential uncle or two, a blacksmith, a joiner, a small mill-owner, that was some shock, a postman.

Then, to one side of the Anderson slabs, there was a little stone doing its best to keep its head above grass. You could read the surname, it was *Anderson* too, but the lower words were all furred with lichen. It was only a matter of going back to the car to fetch a blunt pencil and an empty white envelope. She tore the envelope open, it was too thick otherwise. She bent over and scoured the blobs of lichen out. Then she knelt on the sappy grass and, with the pencil laid broadside, began the rubbing.

Jean
Who?
Our only daughter
Whose?
Died August 12th 1965, aged three months
Erected by Williamina and John Anderson
The year of our Lord, 1975
Ever in God's Thoughts

She stared at the grey rubbed news of her usurpation. She had to hold the tiny slab by its two shoulders, like shaking a baby. *Williamina and John*. Willa and Jock. She tried to yank it out or push it over, but for all its lack of size, it was deep-rooted.

Our only daughter.

Not a word to her, during their years, that all she, Alison Anderson – Alison Orphaned Bastard Anderson – had ever been was a substitute. Only some bairn reft from god knows where – adopted – never the true Jean.

Our only daughter.

– Oh, Alison, she wept to herself. Alison, Alison.

the famous sea-horse

– We got away from the harbour eventually. Once Spermy had picked up his *fancy science bird*, he called her.

Lucy sought a level of massage that was enough, just enough, now the motor was up and running. It was soon obvious the motor was up for far more than that.

– At first she was just this masked and dripping figure I heaved aboard. Or would have. But she took her snorkel out long enough to say *Ladder*. And in that tone. If we hadn't a ladder lashed to the mast, I'd have had to contrive one. The rest of the crew, with all their skills, were curled in their bunks and far from sober.

We headed north. Whether it was true north or not, it wasn't clear from deck. The sun was broadly behind us. It was having itself a riot before sinking into a cloud. Then I was summoned to take the wheel by Spermy, and he gave me the heading, twelve degrees. *Keep her a berth off the land*. Whatever that meant, jargoneer. He was going down to the cabin to help the diver out of her wetsuit. He was back in two minutes. He was a berth off the land himself, I think.

He had grown to be a volcano.

I gripped hold of the wheel.

I checked the overhead compass so much I was snapped at.

I wandered five degrees west and got bawled at.

I checked the brass clock to the right of the compass and it was still only ten.

The year was ten hours old. No doubt things were happening in Vietnam, Prague and Warsaw, in Paris and London.

The year was unfolding at a frightening rate.

I was right in the middle of all the action. I was part of a film, whirring away, I could feel the sprockets, engaging my ready-made holes. That's it, I could feel the sprockets. Sometimes I was in the projector gate and felt immortal. Sometimes I skated over the screen. And if my mind ever wandered a second, like a mote of dust, nothing was lost; it was still there, my mind, dancing in the beam.

Sir Patrick Spens, locked in his ballad. That Conrad character, in *Youth*.

– Marlow, said Lucy, softly.

– Then Julie appeared in the wheelhouse and I went to the cabin to make three coffees.

When I got down, the crew were lying abandoned in their bunks, some not even under the covers. There was one black knotted shoe sticking out from under a sheet. The smell of sick was worst, but stale beer, whisky, fag reek, farts and the rotten remainder of last year's herring ran it close. Very, very close.

It took time to find all the doings, and to get the kettle under way. By the time I came up with the shoogly tray, the day had clouded, the wind was up, gulls zig-zagged across our wake, and she was giving him a blowjob.

If I'd only known, I could have waited.

How did I feel? I didn't feel anything. It was the kind of film where a rogue reel might slip in. Mainly I thought it was quite a nice touch. He had his right hand on the wheel, with his left flat on the top of her head like he was blessing her. I'd known Spermy since he was ten or eleven. He was a hard man, he wasn't religious.

She faced me as I opened the wheelhouse door. She raised an eyebrow at me, though there was little she could say. I may have looked shocked, so she gave a shake of her head. That seemed to please him; it was just as well something did.

I, being a gentleman, withdrew. I stood outside on the flying bridge, under a machine they called the Triplex. I had drunk two and a half coffees, when the wheelhouse opened again.

Knock, cunt, next time, he said. Na, ye're okay. Come in and say hello tae Julie. Hello, Julie, I said. Hello, Peem, she replied.

Lucy wanted to yell out, break it precisely there, but knew disclosing his name was only part of their purpose. There was the whole head thing to be laid bare, whatever happened there, and to find that out they would have to go on.

– So, everything was nice for a while. The skipper was in a good mood, he had had his rocks off. Julie and me had a bond. We had both been kidnapped and were heading round Scotland together. She asked me what I did; Spermy had only told her my name. I said I was an ex-student, a bit of a poet, a builder and in love.

Lucy wanted to say *Were you really?* but refrained. Her touch now was of the lightest, just enough to keep the hippocampus, the famous sea-horse of memory, swimming through the years.

– She told me she was finishing a PhD, marine biology, specially prawns. Scotland was overfished, so she was off to Sarawak shortly. Out in Sarawak, where headhunters kept their parangs gleaming, she would be an advisor on very big prawns, on how to get the mangrove cleared. *I am completely my own person*, she said.

We went down in the cabin amongst the sozzled. We made dinner, very late dinner, to be consumed after nightfall, Spermy's orders. Much would be mince and peas, the rest tatties. We peeled away side by side in the gathering storm.

As soon as the tatties were on, she led me through to the fish-room and I fucked her standing against the boards. It wasn't love, but it was very, very good. I felt at home on the boat.

Lucy wrestled with herself. Her fingers stopped massaging. Her palms and fingers were spread out over his skull, all ready to press down, all ready to punch through him twenty thousand volts.

– When we came up on deck, it was thinking about getting dark, and the skipper was scowling. Baxter rose, and he took the wheel so we could all get dinner. Around the table there was no grace said. But I think they were grateful for anything hot; they looked peely-wally and some were shivery.

We had come through a wild place, the Pentland Firth, though Julie and me had not noticed the extra bumps. She attempted to talk about moonrise and herring rising, plankton and such. Spermy wasn't in the mood for that. Then she told us she was the Lord Provost's daughter. Nobody seemed amused or even interested. I said I needed to talk to her later. As we came out of the shelter of Orkney, we realised there was a northerly swell running, so dinner was cut short. The cling peaches and condensed milk remained unopened.

I need your help, Julie, I said.

I explained her father's designs, on the source of the city's water, on all the future side-deals from oil. Julie wasn't fazed, *I know what he's like.* Her father bankrolled her many enjoyments. His actions might be in some ways regrettable. He might like to pull some wool over eyes. But, she said. Julie spoke like she fucked. But? I said. Blood is thicker than water. Basic science. Check that sometime.

I spoke to Spermy on his own. Spermy was worse. 77% of the *Spare Me* was owned ashore, by SwinkFoods. Spermy was no more free to act than fly in the air. Spermy was gripped, so no help there.

Never mind that bastard Swink, Spermy said. It's you that better watch oot. And I'm nae referrin tae the fuckin wheelhoose.

'68 was twenty hours old. I was losing my illusions fast, on a pretty high sea with that rum pair.

Lucy made another couple of cups of tea and lemon. She didn't feel like talking. She noticed he had his eyes closed now, and this aid to dwelling in the past profoundly annoyed her.

– The *Spare Me* was a purser. Me, I wouldn't have known a purse-netter from a Botticelli. I sidled up and queried Baxter: Spermy would just have laughed.

Purse, ye're asking? said Baxter. Just a net as deep as the North Sea and as lang as a running track. Drop her ower the boat's arse as she steams in a circle, pick up yir ain end, because naebody's goin to pick it up for ye, whack the twa ends thegither in the hauler, the block, the Triplex, whatever ye want to call it, and heave awa. Thanks, I said. That's when the fun starts, he told me.

Especially if you shot for herring, but only got sprats. Under persuasion, herring would swim in ever-decreasing circles till they were like a ball of silver tight in a purse against the side of the boat.

But sprats, no, not sprats.

Sprats would get it into their tiny heads that they could swim away through the net. They couldn't. Trying to reverse without anyone noticing, they then got trapped by the gills. Not just the odd one or two. A net the size of a running track, a decent mark, ten or twelve million. They had to be shaken out by hand.

I hope we don't get sprats, then, I said to Baxter.

Lucy realised she wasn't massaging any more, and just stood behind him quietly as he spieled. She didn't know how long they had been at this now.

But she wished, sprats or no sprats, that Julie would come to a suitable end.

attachment

Alison stood outside LeopCorp Towers and looked up. She knew there was a surplus of Semtex from the previous Spectacle. She could even get access. But no, she couldn't. For one reason only. Gwen was in there.

She had no sooner come back from the stark, staring shock of the cemetery outside Huntly, than she had been hit with it by email. It wasn't even the email; that was blank. It was the attachment.

The attachment was a thirty minute video file, edited together, apparently secretly taken. Gwen was in it, you could see her face, all sorts of rapt expressions. You could see all of her. And her lover, Bill she presumed. His face more shadowed. So many positions, hard-edited and fiercely rendered.

She had got the ultimatum by quite a different means. A man in the street who spoke behind her in a crowd, and then melted away inside ten seconds. If Alison did not play ball at work, the man said, then the video, exposing her named and only daughter, was going on the Internet.

Given everything else, she was just about ready to kill.

horizontigo

– So that's what we did. We shot at the mouth of Loch Eriboll and steamed in a circle and picked up our end. The purse came taut as the Triplex, massive roller-jawed beast that it was, took its grip and started hauling the net upwards. Spermy was in the wheel-house, Baxter out on the flying bridge. We crew were lodged on the after-deck mostly, beginning to pull down the heavy net from the transporter and make big folds. Then—

Fuckin bastardin shitin cunt! Spratshiters, get tae fuck! We're shaftit noo, Baxter, we might as weel cut awa. Sprats!

Cut awa, is it? Is that whit ye wint? shouted Baxter. Cut awa?

Na, ye daftie! bawled Spermy. We'll try haulin.

Haul awa, is it? Haul awa?

Aye! Come ye an tak ma helm in hand. An let me get oot tae that fuckin Triplex.

He seemed to be in a deeper trance, thought Lucy. Doing all the voices full blast. Probably what it was like in the hospital with Tam.

The sprats were rising like a mass of bristles, silver-shimmering in the tautening net. I heard their scales flying, I felt their screams. I felt the pain of the men as they took hold of the bar-tight net, ranged along the port side, and shook at it and shook – with the strength of their fingers and wrists only – and vibrated the sprats out. The millions of sprats cascaded down and back in the sea like a broken bank – oh, like torn life – like terrible, terrible waste.

Some escaped – oh, but briefly – and were carried up in the dark folds. They were crushed to death between the first and second rollers. They were squashed to oil between the second and third. Oil dripped and slopped on the flying bridge.

The gulls came of course; the gulls were interested in us from when we left port. It was the first of January, after all, no other boat was out that night. We would have the market to ourselves, and sky-high prices. The gulls got sprat enough to sicken them.

Greedy gulls pecked and fought over the same sprat – although there were thousands the same skimmering across the surface within a wing's-length. Blind gulls killed for it. Gorged gulls tried to flap off, but flopped on the water and swam bloated.

I watched their fates probably far too much, and was shouted at to shake harder. I was not the world's best sprat-shaker, that was clear.

Spermy shouted an oath and told me to join him on the flying bridge. Climbing up, I realised the night was growing filthy. What a wind had risen! The boat was giving some right old heaves, as the swell passed underneath. I glanced in at the wheelhouse clock: it was ten to midnight. Come and dae something tae fuckin earn yir pay, said Spermy. That was no way to talk to a kidnappee.

We were wearing ourselves out at the rough end of nowhere trying not to catch these wretched fish. The sky was invisible. The net was making the tiniest progress, then, oiled and slipshod, slipping back. Spermy showed me the red and green control knobs of the Triplex. He showed great faith in my practical powers.

I'm goin doon on deck, tae gee these bastards up, said Spermy. Tak in when ye can.

I had to ask him again.

Pull on the green, ye twat, I only just tellt ye, didn't I? he said. Pull on the fuckin green.

I wished at that moment I had stayed in the city to fight the Provost and Senator. But the battle is always easier on the other side.

I looked down on the men, trying to save the huge net that had been gatecrashed by freeloaders, part of a horrible joke, as bad as any played on Odysseus and his unlucky band. I stood in a swill of oil and scales with nominal charge of red and green knobs, afraid to touch them.

Suddenly the men were absenting themselves from the deck. Julie, we had all forgotten about Julie, Julie had yelled them into the cabin for soup. I felt sick and shouted to her, No, I'll stay on deck, be in the air. *Be in the air*, the crap we speak.

Anyway, our net lay stopped. A hammocky, shroudy section hung close to me, flapping, close to the flying bridge. It was ready to be hauled taut again, steady as fate in the howling wind, up into the maw of the Triplex.

Net lay on the stern, in a fankly pile. Net streamed in a black and silver bow, out to one side. And net no doubt hung deep, weighted by our dying enemies, their swim bladders packed so tight they were packing in. A deep cache of silver, like all the cash you'd ever spend if you lived to be a thousand.

So I looked from the rail of the flying bridge. I was weak with speculation, master of nothing I surveyed. I laid one hand on the red, one on the green, to try and be ready.

And a swell rose from the north and lumped and broke, it washed through machinery, spilled across deck, out through the net, my eyes followed it.

And a swell rose from the north and lumped and broke, it washed through machinery, spilled across deck, out through the net, my eyes followed it.

And a swell—

– You okay? said Lucy.

She saw his head twitch, neither nod nor shake. She didn't want to touch it.

– And I was cycling along the rim of a long curved beach.

And the sea rose and lumped, and spilled and broke, it swashed through my spokes. And the selfsame sea, with one small pause, backwashed the other way.

And the sea rose and lumped, and spilled and broke, it swashed through my spokes. And the selfsame sea, with one small pause, backwashed the other way.

And I was not alone, there were two bikes with me, Lucy on the bike to the right and Julie on the other. Hub to hub, let it go sideways.

And the sea rose and lumped, and spilled and broke, it swashed through my spokes—

O it was horizontigo alright, never described, so never known, horizontigo surely. And the selfsame sea, the selfsame sea— The bridge was oily after all, the kidnappee was dreaming, who pulled on the green and slipped in the net, who was conveyed, and up purveyed, to the gates of hell. His skull but a sprat to burst as a zit!

I thrust my hands between the blocks – I thrust out my palms and rived – life or oblivion – to rive that Triplex apart!

When Peem came out of the bathroom not long after, he found that Lucy's door was locked.

Next morning it was grapefruit. There was no sugar on the table. And eggs. And Lucy, with eyes made up, saying, *I think it's time we entered the real world.*

april 11

elongated, deceptive

Lucy had kept her time off to a minimum, and her reasons for it necessarily false, but by the time she got back to the office she knew that things had shifted and were still shifting.

Alison couldn't brief her – she was busy, there was a Joint Working Group due at ten – so Lucy decided to see what she could find out from Marilyn. Marilyn just talked, however, about a new minimum requirements form that was coming out as regards office space rationalisation. Lucy confessed to not knowing that rationalisation had been decided upon, but Marilyn assured her it was an executive decision and wouldn't therefore have appeared in any minutes.

Marilyn was hovering with her hand over her desk-phone, so Lucy retreated to her office and opened thirty two emails, dumping twenty and attending to none by the time ten to ten came, when she nipped along to the staff toilet.

It was strange, recomposing her own hair after spending so long on Mister Kitoff's head. Peem's head. She would never look at hair again without that X-ray sense of what lay beneath. Memento mori, the elongated, deceptive skull at the bottom of Holbein's *Ambassadors*.

Though not as deceptive as his.

Because of the Julie thing, because of his knee-trembler against the fish-room boards in a gathering storm forty years earlier, on the same day she fell in love and more, she thought of him as – what—? Lucy looked in the bright mirror, and noted her cheekbones.

As a skull on legs.

boohooyoohoo.com

Peem went to the Citizens' Advice Bureau and asked what to do in the case of rediscovered identity. It turned out there wasn't a leaflet on that.

The bloke bust a gut to try and help. He searched the generic list.

If it was a rediscovered *item* like a handbag or mobile, you would of course hand it in to the police.

If it was a rediscovered *march stone* or *burial stone*, then you would phone the City Archaeologist in the first instance.

If it was a rediscovered *work of art*, say a portrait in oils by the local genius Jamesone, then a discreet mention to the Art Gallery's directors might be the thing.

– But when you are neither item, stone, nor work of art, Peem said, what then?

– Your best bet would be Google, the bloke said. *Peem* is not that common a name. I've got a minute, let's have a look. You won't be on MySpot, then?

Peem just looked at him.

They found boohooyoohoo.com, a new site for missing persons, and their search was narrowed to a couple of possibilities in no time.

One Peem was ruled out on account of age, while the other was son of Andrew Endrie and Madge (d. 1956), with two brothers and a sister thrown in.

– That'll be you then, sir, probably, what do you think?

– In all probability, said Peem.

– When did you last see them again? said the man.

– Eh, early '68, I'd say. It's been a while.

– Let me see that name again?

– Andrew Endrie, said Peem. Why, does it ring a bell?

– If it's Andy Endrie, he used to – but then he – no, likely not the same bloke. Anyway, I'd say, better meet up with Clan Reunited Counselling first, sir. There are issues you would need to go through.

– Shock, like?

– Shock would be one issue, sure, I imagine, on both sides. I'll nip through and give the CRC a ring for you. Would you mind signing our wee petition?

The Citizens' Advice Bureau was being moved out of its prime location at the junction of St Nicholas Street and UberStreet to make way for something called GrottoLotto. The new Bureau was to be burrowed in beneath the huge Mounthooly roundabout, with access by underpass. Access to help by long tunnel was not ideal: a mugger's Nirvana, a groper's Eden. The title of the petition was: *Do You Want Underground Advice?*

The CAB man came back off the phone.

– That was the CRC I had on the bell. They've got a counselling slot for you in a couple of weeks, that do? Would that do, sir?

His client had shoved the petition aside, and was rehearsing *Peem Endrie, Peem Endrie,* several times on a scrap of paper. A signature he now appended.

He met Maciek in KostKutters by chance, and introduced himself. Maciek expressed surprise at his appearance, now that he was cleaned up.

– The wheel, Peem said. Spinning again.

– You can come and stay with us, said Maciek, if you don't mind a floor.

the spirit of lottery

Lucy's meeting started at ten. The lack of a pre-meeting with Alison she found unsatisfactory, cagey. She found out why.

– In your absence, began Guy, looking Lucy square in the eye, we asked Alison to chair, and since she's up to speed, the view is that we best continue that way, at least for now.

She was taken aback; Alison had uttered not a word about this.

– The view is? said Lucy.

– Yes, that's the view. And, continued Guy, due to the advent of new global openings, we feel it is an ideal opportunity to look at Spectacle afresh, to seek to renegotiate partnerships and to plot new directions.

Alison said, But we need the views of all the players.

Certain players were not slow to respond. Even the councillors were up for it. They didn't actually speak, but two of them hemmed, and one blew his nose in a hankie.

First Otto, whatever suppurating stone he'd crawled from under, categorised the previous direction of Spectacle – and by implication all of Lucy's, and indeed Alison's, historical and cultural researches – as *not really cutting-edge.*

Lucy said, Chair, can I come in on that?

Alison said, Let Otto finish his point.

Otto said, No, I'm finished.

– Now Guy, you were going to say something? said Alison.

I might as well leave right now, thought Lucy, before I fucking implode.

– And Guy, said Alison, if you can just stick to the fifteen we agreed. Then it'll be you, Lucy. I do want the views of all the players.

What the fuck, thought Lucy, is a *player* all of a sudden?

Guy had fifteen minutes to expound. She felt quite dizzy as his spiel went on. Certain words or phrases buzzed in her mind, so that she got a gist, no more than a gist. A lot got said. She was trying to decode it more than anything.

The bones of it was, it wasn't really for the Joint Working Party to try to devise paltry ideas from month to month, and then impose them on the poor cantonians, most of whom had *day jobs* and *family commitments.* Big Money was now talking, and it was the JWP's central task to transcribe these thoughts.

The collected works of Big Money were quite impressive, and another volume was due to be written. Big Money loved nothing more than Bigger Money, so the whole of Spectacle was going to be *reworked in that light.*

Spectacle would no longer seek to struggle through a blatant series of primary school themes. *Education* and *celebration of the past* both had their place, but not on the streets of a modern city.

Spectacle would be *recast in a new spirit.* The spirit of Lottery.

Lottery, it was to be understood, in society as a whole, had taken over from the *failed narratives* of religion and socialism, which *falsely promised a rich life for all,* here and hereafter, when obviously any pleasure in that would be devalued immediately by its horrible commonness.

Lottery, according to Guy, realigned history by recognising that wealth and high reward were only ever enjoyed by the Few, whether the Few had attained their Fewness by hereditary, military or, as Guy said coyly, in a concession to Lucy perhaps, *less openly nefarious means.*

There was a fit of barking, not by a councillor this time. Lucy saw that Lord Provost William Swink II was at the meeting, sitting along from her in the same row.

The health of Society, continued Guy, could only be restored when proper deference to the values of Chance and Exclusivity was re-established, and the inferior gods of Redistribution and Mass were bidden to remember their place.

– Hear, hear, said Lord Provost William Swink II.

Fucking biscuit brain, thought Lucy. All her thoughts were seething with oaths.

Anyway, a consortium had come in and was going to *underpin the operation.* Because of the consortium's very large commitment, the *balance* within the Joint Working Party would necessarily have to be *adjusted.*

Just as Lucy wondered if it would not be easier to put everything in mental italics from now on, Guy started talking *balls.*

UberStreet's hitherto hidden quality as a street, said Guy, as a long street, a long and very straight street, was its *aptitude as a giant ball alley.*

Alison tried to catch Lucy's eye a moment, pointed to herself and shook her head. She even proffered a pallid smile, which didn't quite make it across the table.

Jesus, Lucy thought, some half-assed private joke absolves her somehow?

Balls in themselves were not the point, continued Guy strongly, sensing the tension between the two women. The existing National Lottery was *a lot of balls,* he cracked, and not much else, and the twice-weekly jiggling of numbered plastic spheres on national TV was growing stale, especially for the fourteen million eternal losers. In a nutshell, he asserted that the National Lottery was too *impersonal,* entirely *bloodless,* and lacked *narrative,* unless fourteen million Cinderellas hanging wistfully round the hearth counted as sufficient tale. It also lacked a *defeat-sweetener—*

Defeat-sweetener, Lucy noted. No greater need for mental italics had ever been.

So, moving on, *balls-with-a-difference* had been sought.

And had been found.

Balls would roll along UberStreet, of a magnificence and significance that had never before been witnessed on our slightly-flattened-at-the-poles planet.

Not golf balls, cricket balls, footballs, cannon balls, regal orbs or, heaven forfend, *polystyrene beads.*

No, these would be balls that Atlas himself would have been proud to heft, at some risk of hernia, on his better shoulder. Guy was getting carried away. All he needed now was a peroration. He summoned up an image of Luna to inspire him.

These were *balls that demanded ballroom,* he said.

These were *balls that carried with them the aspirations of global companies.*

These were *balls.*

– How are they supposed to work? said Lucy. Your *balls*?

It was as though she had farted in the Kirk, shortly after the Reformation. A flush came over her, no one knew why. She remembered asking a similar question of Theo, forty years earlier, about his *Sisyphus* in the winter garden.

But everyone else thought that because she flushed, she was losing her bottle; menopausal. She was, in truth, well past that.

She would take them on. She saw that pitying look in their eyes, in Guy's, in Otto's, in Alison's even, and moved in an instant beyond them.

What did they think she represented? *Lovey-dovey vision*, gone down the tubes? Ah, well, let them bite on this, she thought. Let them bite on this and be fucking-well parched and lost forever in their chosen deserts.

She was no lovey-doveyer, she was no sinking heart. She was sunk heart. Sunk as a plate in Peem's crushed skull. Sunk as Spermy's father's trawler, the *Dépense*.

Sunk as sunk.

She laughed inwardly at boy emperors and global servants soaring their world, like buzzards or bald eagles.

When you were sunk, the good thing was, there was no deeper to go.

– I'm waiting? said Lucy. How are these *balls* supposed to work. Tell me?

Two of them started to speak at once. Alison had to indicate who had priority. This time it wasn't Guy.

– I don't know what Guy Bord was going to say, said the newcomer, who had a soft, impassive face, and a squashed-in nose, like a badly-restored sphinx. But I am sure he would stress at this stage the overriding need for discretion. We would not want to be trumped.

– Who wants to trump you, I wonder? Lucy snapped. And who are you, by the way?

– Oh, said Guy. I thought Alison was going to introduce. This is Mr George Singer, former Chief Executive of NuLot. UbSpec Total, on behalf of LeopCorp, has just bought NuLot out.

a fine additional tring

Lucy knew that she was now officially distrusted. Little of moment was likely to be said in front of her. A sort of housework took place: a cleaning-up of items and details and snags and feedbacks from the one previous Spectacle.

The content of what was coming, apart from the fact that it was centred on an exalted species of universally important balls, was not gone into.

The composition of a new sub-committee was determined. Provost William Swink II would be the sole elected councillor thereon. Alison, the only Council official, would officiate as Chair. To expedite planning issues, and to keep factions apart. Not that there was any sign of those.

Guy Bord and Otto Mobius would be on for UbSpec Total. Mr George Singer would be there, carrying forward in a new context the work of NuLot, within UbSpec Total, on behalf of the Leisure Division of LeopCorp, *in the city as rebranded.*

– Rebranded? said Lucy. It was likely to be her final throw.

– Rebranded, yes, said Lord Provost William Swink II. We've ditched the earlier suggestions. From here on in we're Leopardeen.

– Did I hear you correctly? said Lucy. The Swinks were notorious malapropists, after all. *Leopardeen*?

– Yes, said Swink, you know our coat-of-arms, don't you? It's got a fine additional tring. *The City of Leopardeen.*

He continued to address her.

– We were wondering, Miss Legge, if you could speed the work in ReCSoc of the blue plaque division. To honour the extinguished of the town, now that things are moving on. Leopardeen and Leop-Corp wouldn't want the past of the best to be forgotten, even though it cannot be a patch on what lies ahead.

Or a putsch on what lies behind, thought Lucy.

Swink II had inherited his father's way with words, though some wondered whether it was not a little put on or affected, so as to make him seem fallible and human, and thus disarm critics and detractors.

– Do you mean the *distinguished* of the past, Lord Provost?

There was an indraw of breath from the silent councillors.

– That's what I said.

– A city cannot live by plaques alone, said Lucy. Nor by lottery. Does Mr Marr not realise that? It's a pity the organ grinder isn't here. I do get tired, talking to the monkey.

Alison broke in.

– Lucy, we know you're tired. Some of us know only too well how much you've put in. But everybody should know. Perhaps if I could call on Guy now to propose a vote of thanks. Guy?

cold taps in the ladies

She lay in wait in the bottom corridor, for her former colleague to come down in the lift.

Several others came down first, UbSpec Total LeopCorp people. But they were all UbSpec Total LeopCorp people now. She nodded at some of the councillors, a couple of phased-out genderistas; their star had faded too.

It was as though in a short space of time she had ceased, in effect, to exist.

Guy came down.

– Thanks for the vote of thanks, she said. I'll do the same for you, one of these days.

– Lucy, said Guy. Wise up. Go with the flow.

The lift stayed at the bottom for quite a long while. Alison was probably trying to avoid her.

Then the lift was summoned, up to the third floor, where the Chamber was. It paused. The doorman in sombre civic blue walked across to Lucy and asked if she was alright.

– I'll be okay, just leave me, she said. Thanks.

The man in blue walked back to take charge of the external door.

It was exit time. Nobody needed to come in at five to five.

The lift hadn't made a move.It was up there, suspended.

Then she heard the gate shut. The lift was coming down, with all its antique, slow assurance.

– Bitch, shouted Lucy through the mesh. Bitch! She didn't even let Alison clash open the hand-operated guard-gate. Backstabber!

– Lucy— said Alison, let me oot, so we can spik.

– Spik, said Lucy. Spik! Turncoat minx.

Lucy was anchoring the mesh of the cage, whereas Alison was jerking it sideways. The blue doorman came hastening up.

– Na, na, na, ladies, this will nivver dae. Time ye were hame.

He gave the jerking side of the contest an extra impetus. Lucy lost, and the forfex of the gate flew back.

– See fit happens? said the doorman. Dafties, ye should be ashamed o yirsels. Hame, I tell ye, this is the Toon's Hoose, nae a wrasslin parlour.

But there was some blood, as well as the excruciating pain, and he found himself running a couple of cold taps in the Ladies for crushed fingers, and phoning a taxi to A&E at Foresterhill.

april 15

cripple budgie survives fall

Peem made slow inroads in Torry. It was not a territory that came easy to him, or that he found congenial. It was very much across the river, very much rough Praga to Warsaw's old town; that's how the Poles said they saw it. Peem had never much mixed with Torry loons as a lad, except of course Spermy, and by that time Spermy was ex-Torry and a semi-orphan.

There were some original Torry folk still there: retired boxmakers, redundant filleters, reserve roustabouts and off-rota drivers. But mostly he had the necessity of getting to know Poles. And the scene was changing fast. They had come in by busload, by boatload, from Gdynia and Gdansk. Some of their gangmasters commuted by air, from Uberdeen Airport out at Dyce.

And he had the difficulty of supporting himself. He looked in the window of a newsagent, at the handwritten postcards on display there. They still used that method. Not all immigrants living twelve or fourteen to a room had immediate access to broadband, and – whatever the infinities of the global market – you still had to relate to the folk next to you for most of your goods and services. The cards had duplicates taped to their base, with a red border to flag they were in Polish.

The only unskilled job that might be within his physical compass was Newspaper Distributor. In the old days that would have just been Paper Boy. Then of course, Paper Boy/Girl. But anti-ageist legislation forbade that. And few kids would work nowadays anyway, when the going rate for pocket money was rising faster than Argentinian inflation.

Yes, Newspaper Distributor might be within his physical

compass. Whether it was within his navigational compass was another matter. He went in. He got the job. It would tide him over till his appointment with Clan Reunited Counselling, who were apparently short-staffed and rushed off their feet.

The man gave him a map and a schedule. It was £5 per 100 papers delivered, or 5p a paper. He discovered afterwards the customers were charged 10p, so that made 100% profit on the service alone for the newsagent, on top of the margin on the paper.

The biggest problem he found, apart from the weight of the satchel, which slung from his neck like a feed-bag on a superannuated half-starved stallion, was phone entry. Phone entry tenements seemed to dominate the curved steep scapes of Torry.

You tried the entry phone of the requisite customer. If that failed, you tried the entry phone of somebody else in the building, then of everybody else, in the hope of goodwill. If goodwill was unavailable, you had to take that particular wonderful newspaper away, and come back later in your own time.

But then it was all his own time. He wasn't being paid for his time, which was of no account. He was being paid to deliver newspapers, though if you inspected them, they were more like lurid comics stuffed with gossip about celebs, and stories of utter dross like *Cripple Budgie Survives Fall* and *Udny Man Finds Giant Neep*.

Nobody thought the *Grampian Echo,* the good old *Gecko,* could slip so far, but the signs had always been there.

He delivered some Polish papers too, imported. He picked up an English-Polish primer in Waterstone's, copied out some requisite phrases, and put it back on the shelf again. The Polish-English primers filled a whole bin.

Good evening. Do you wish to receive your newspaper? I have certain goods to give to your neighbour. May I enter? I am not from Social Security. I am not the Police. Thank you.

He thought he'd better not waste time learning basic *Good day.* The Poles had come here, or had been brought here, to work. They would hardly be at home during the day.

Yet he was wrong in that assumption. People were always misjudging immigrants. He found out that there was quite often a Pole, several Poles, at home during the day in these sorts of flats. It was the hot bunk system. The warm, smelly sheet system. One bed between two, shiftwork. But whether any of the current occupants of the twelve or fourteen or sixteen bunkbeds would actually leap with alacrity to answer an entry phone seemed to depend on other factors.

Later, he studied the gangmasters' patterns.

Then he found it easier to be present outside some of the bigger Polish tenements at specific times of pick-up and dump from the dirty vans, whose occupants wended their way to and from the mutton pie process lines and the vegetarian sausage-enhancers; back and fore from doing the lights or serving the pints in *I Hate Mondays, I Loathe Tuesdays, St Vitus* and other nightspots; in and out of the tradesmen's entrances to mortgage boutiques or the back doors to bidet-rich mansions; not to mention urgent attendance to fitting and refitting tasks in the five main malls, stuff-full as they were of retro, metro, and new-wave hetero shops.

He could thus distribute his papers en masse.

He couldn't tell most of the Poles from Adamcek or Eva anyway: he had to take their claimed identities on trust.

But who was he to quarrel about identity, the state he was in?

Lucy had not offered to hem his baggy hand-me-downs.

As for his cracked and shaven brainbox, he kept that item tucked away in a woolly toorie.

So long as the number of papers distributed tallied with the number he set out with in his neck-slung bag, and so long as the complaints recited to him by the newsagent were not overwhelming, with only the odd tenner stopped out of his cash, and so long as he could shoplift bars of chocolate to the value of his stopped wages when the newsagent's back was turned, then all was, if not strictly for the best, at least not sraczka – total diarrhoea.

At Maciek's flat, he got to kip on a much-compressed futon. Lying awake on about the fourth or fifth night, he thought of Lucy an awful lot, but there was no going back.

Sometimes you just knew that. Without knowing a good reason why, you knew there was no going back. You couldn't go back because you had to move on. There was a lack of elastic in that concept.

Lying on a hard mattress, sucking chocolate, trying to snooze, with tired and unemotional Poles tripping over him. Ordinary clumsy tripping.

– You okay there, panie? said Maciek.

– Bardzo, he replied. Bardzo dobrze. Very fine.

Later in the week he was due to go with Maciek's squad on a short-term job, catering support. Swink Stillwater and the Council were jointly hosting an international symposium. *Bottled Water: Your Spring is Your Future.* Evan, Purer, Valvic and the rest were due to be there. Peem was to help in the hall, distributing conference papers, attending to drinks.

He had moved on.

pumping green water

Lucy had been signed off work indefinitely, on account of her left hand. There had been a dislocation, and her ring fingernail was purple and yellow and would probably come off. She was declared unfit for keyboard service.

Alison's explanations as they sat in line at A&E had all been about the pressure she was being put under.

Pressure? Put under? Lucy had said.

Yeah, I canna ging intae detail, that's jist the wey it is, hate me if ye must.

Is it Finlay?

Na, an I'm sayin nae mair, Alison had said, sae jist forget it.

Likely, thought Lucy.

She took to going on long walks. It was a change for her. She often headed out on Countesswells Road. She never knew what *Countesswells* was supposed to mean or refer to, but she spoke it like an empty mantra, and prodded it with her mind, along with so many other things.

Or she walked out towards Hazlehead, but never got there, because she stopped and scrambled up the bank to look into the disused Rubislaw Quarry. They were pumping green water by the ten million gallon, into the street drains and out to sea. Something must be afoot. She sat and watched water being pumped away.

She went back to the big empty house, then went online, gingerly, and booked herself a holiday. Fuck the fucking lot of them, she thought. It wasn't too late in her life to head for Marrakech.

She phoned Marilyn and told her she was taking a month's leave.

– A month? said Marilyn. You'll miss GrottoLotto—

– You think?

one slug from her smoothie

Alison had chosen to stay at work, even though she had a couple of stitches in her split finger. For a full week after her battle with Lucy, she wore an ostentatious leather finger stall strapped across her palm, and garnered some pity while she was at it. She didn't normally give a toss for pity, but when you were in a false and exposed position, your needs were different.

At lunch time she would buy herself a wrap and a smoothie from M&S behind the Town House, then wander up to the Castle-gate, towards LeopCorp Towers.

There were all sorts of works speeding ahead, behind barricades and under awnings. TV positions were springing up, dozens of them it seemed, now that they were going pan-Europe, pan-Asia and Stateside. Indeed, there was much market beyond, if Guy and company were to be believed. GrottoLotto might in time deliver diversion to most watery planets, and serve as a homing signal for the Milky Way.

Universal communication got on her tits. There was only one person she wanted to speak to.

So she hung around the Mercat Cross looking across at North Turret, hoping for that familiar figure to appear at a high window, or emerge.

Gwen had never texted her back. LeopCorp had her daughter, not to put too fine a point on it, by the short and curlies. No matter how much she did their bidding, the blackmail would always be there. She had to deliver but did they?

Gwen, Leopardeen Porno Queen hadn't yet turned up on Alison's searches, or not precisely. But the trouble was this: if you cut it down to *Gwen* and *Porno* as a Google Advanced Search, there were nearly half a million entries. She felt her gorge rise with disgust when she thought of it.

She took one slug from her smoothie and binned it.

She had had plenty time to sound people out. Rookie Marr, she was advised, had had a difficult childhood. Difficult for everyone else that is. Spoiled, pampered, nursed, toyed with by his nurses, he was only ever countered by his father Hubert when he seemed to lack sufficient selfishness, adequate greed, or acceptable levels of lust for power, or when he showed some fevered sign of wanting to share and play with others. Therefore it was only natural and understandable, when he had been afforded such huge rehearsal in human trust, such enormous practice in active teamwork, that his world, his empire, his employees' clothing, his every facility in the Turret and beyond, should bristle invisibly with miniature cameras.

Alison understood perfectly.

She understood why the Leopard was an untrusting recluse.

For were Rookie Marr ever to appear in the Castlegate, or were he to come and attend just one of her meetings, she would not be able to trust herself.

april 20

litany of commodity

The symposium was held in an oval conference room, out past the Bridge of Don. Oval was ideal for conferences: it allowed a measure of face-to-face without being in your face. It fostered the illusion of one world and a common interest. There was also a gap in the oval, on one of the broad sides, for key presentations.

Mineral water originated from volcanic aquifers, or glacier melt filtered through sand, or secretly channelled chalk streams, or reservoirs of rain under granite – apparently. Mineral water springs, when analysed in the lab, were variously rich in sodium, potassium, fluoride, magnesium, calcium, silica, sulphates, bicarbonates, nitrates and chlorides, all of which were deemed to be beneficial to dental longevity, brain tone, skin gleam and other vital signs, in exactly the quantities found – it seemed. Thus to adulterate these quantities would be anathema, and any adulterator would be immediately banned from the bottled water global community – they were warned. For if the odd drugged Olympic sprinter threatened the credibility of an exercise form, one bottle of water with a dash of uranium could threaten empires – was the dire message. Chemicals as such had a poor image, and the only permissible additions to bottled water were zest of lemon, zing of lime or squeeze of orange, all of which spurting citroids were known to be full of sunny stimulation, without a cancerous ion or ageing free radical between them – it was asserted.

The open session was very informative.

Peem moved between the ovalled rows, which were luxuriously spaced, checking that no alien bottle or jug of tap had infiltrated, and making sure that 500ml containers of the main sponsors – Purer, Valvic, Badwasser, Piche, Irrigay, Oosh and Mountain Heart

– were open and available for the hydration and oral satisfaction of each delegate. They were thus revitalised, sip by sip, to focus on the second part of the day, when the symposium went into strictly closed session. Audits, bubble-maintenance. Calories, the eight-glass-day. Gassiness, grassiness. Jeremiahs, kidneys. Pesticide masking, *vichissitudes*, trout. Extrapolations of world shortage.

It seemed to Peem as he listened intently – when he wasn't locked in a death-struggle with some stuck blue bottle-cap – that the litany of commodity barely began to skim the surface of what he cared about.

the girl julie

This time of year, you had to burn serious fuel to find a decent mark of herring. So he had plenty long watches off Barra, the Butt, the Noup and Foula in which to turn things over. But the simple, absolute fact for Spermy was that his shore financier would never let him off the hook. Every seven years or so, Spermy had gone for a faster boat, grander net, bigger block power, vaster capacity. And now a second boat, keeping him company, with his son skippering.

But because, since the outset, 77% had been owned ashore, he could never amass the capital to buy the boats outright himself. Always the profit was being siphoned ashore, as though through a giant straw.

A straw called Swink.

So even well into the new century, when Spermy went for the *Girl Julie*, and his son Finbar took over *Spare Me V* – both built in Finland and fitted out in Denmark, the father's boat 300 feet long, the son's 297 – William Swink II kept the SwinkFoods share of the enterprise at 77%, and kept the vessels' pressure stock licences and vital quota documents in his business office, safe.

Yet it was not as though Spermy and Finbar did not have a very good living, getting the biggest prices when they ran their fish across the North Sea to Skagen, at the north tip of Denmark. And it was not as though their crew, who attended the machinery and monitored the monitors but did very little old style work, were not in clover too. They could gross ten or fifteen thousand pounds per man on an exceptional night, if the market was right; then perhaps a very sustainable nothing for a couple of months.

A very sustainable official nothing.

Covert fishing, circumvention of quotas, and black landings on secluded piers kept the operation ticking over.

He knew his wife approved of the extra blackfish cash in the Swiss account. Julie was sussed. The cash from her own consultancy, BSI, Big Shrimp International, she kept well separate. She still flew out east several times a year, to South-East Asia, helping to make the case for the uprooting of another 100 or 1000 hectares of mangrove, so as to facilitate the meteoric tail-snap of the tiger prawn. The thing was she was a classic pioneer, a bit like him, she had been in at the start.

Greenpeace had targeted her survey boat more than once. The time she fired a rocket flare over their self-righteous heads, she was able to find a powerful enough lawyer to keep her out of jail. The case was tried in Kuching, in the old colonial courthouse of Rajah Brooke. Half way through the first afternoon the air conditioning broke down, but the conditioning of the judge did not.

Self-defence. Not guilty. Case dismissed.

Julie seldom dived these days. Her youthful protests about Dow Chemical had soon faded, and no-one reminded her of them. So? She might have done little to hinder the manufacturers of napalm, but she had opened up, in her own way, much of the coast of Vietnam.

Spermy called up the pair boat on the radiophone. Night was falling.
– Aye, aye, Finbar. Seein muckle?
– Fuckin desert.
– A wee mark jist back a while, I thocht. Nae worth shootin.

birds will do me

Peem was taken aback when he went to see the CAB man the second time. The whole place was being packed into boxes, ready to go into storage until the Mounthooly underpass service could be instated. He had forgotten when his appointment with Clan Reunited Counselling was, so he had missed it, and now there was a two month waiting list.

It seemed, according to the CAB man, that everybody and their granny wanted advice on how to weld bits of a family together again, without splits at the seams arising at the first whiff of sexual wandering, financial insolvency, mental derangement or slight displeasure.

The trouble was, due to TV relationship shows like *Uncle Fesster* – and the Scottish one, *Up Your Close* – the standard for tolerable, liveable, acceptable families seemed to have gone through the roof, and any lightly dysfunctional member risked being adjudged as welcome as—

– As what—? said Peem.

– As a limp prick in a barrel of fannies, said the CAB man.

– Thanks for sharing that concept with me, said Peem.

– My pleasure.

– So what are you going to do? Peem asked him.

– Take a month off. Chance to get a bit of perspective.

– That's always good, I think, said Peem.

– Probably head off somewhere. The Algarve. I think I'll go to the Algarve.

– Do you have people there?

– I don't need people everywhere I go. Bit of a busman's holiday for me, people.

– What then?

– Birds will do me. There's plenty birds on the marsh out there. Do you want to come?

– No dough.

– The fare will be about thirty quid, and you can live for tuppence.

– Wouldn't I count as *people* for you?

– Na, bit of company never hurt. Come on, I'll sub you.

– I've saved up thirteen pounds from my paper round.

– There you go, deposit I call that. Let's go.

– I don't know your name.

– Not that old business. Charles McGinn, Charlie to you. Are you going to say hello to your family first? I'm not saying you should.

– I might drive past. If I knew where they stayed.

– Sounds a bit bloody royal to me, that. Come on, let's go. You'll be in a better state to face them when you come back. Browner anyway.

– It was deep snow when I left the house. They won't expect me to be brown.

– How long ago was that?

– Forty years. Or so.

– People change. They'll make allowances. I wouldn't worry.

– Maybe they're a nest of dysfunctionality, said Peem.

– When they got rid of you, chum, they probably sorted that, said Charlie, and gave a laugh.

an immemorial music

When Lucy landed in Marrakech, dashing in the rain with her driver to the riad's own taxi, parked beyond the masses of Mercs and Audis, driving through the uniform avenues of identical palms and bakebrown villas, gawping at the snowy High Atlas across the plain in the near distance, then swerving through the stone archway into the Medina, the old town, she immediately felt challenged, and at home.

The taxi slowed through the streets, but not much. There were Moroccans standing and squatting everywhere, their scarves and cakes and bread and shoes, pirate discs and cones of spices, spread out the length of the main lanes on luminous prints and rugs.

The taxi couldn't make it up the final alley, narrow, tall, with a scatter of shabby or plain doors along the way. The door of her riad at the very end, though, was broad, prepossessing; oiled, a dark-grained wood, with enough studs to suggest a measure of impregnability. It was not a door Theo would have liked: it was not progressive. But it was the kind of door she needed, at that moment, to be behind.

Inside, round two dim corners, then under the blue of the courtyard sky, a faltering fountain played an immemorial music, splashing under an orange tree.

footprint

While Peem and Charlie were in the air, on the easyJet cheap job out to Lisbon, Charlie asked a question or two. There was no such thing as a free meal on easyJet, and the inflight magazine's offers on perfume and paste jewellery quickly palled.

– So the memory smash-up, said Charlie. How did that come about?

Peem sighed and blew out.

– Head knock.

– Uhuh?

– Head knock.

– Okay, start again. Been to Portugal before?

– Never out of the country overmuch, said Peem. You know the good thing about a scabby memory? Every day seems rich and strange.

– So if we want to cut aviation carbon, all we need do is hit everybody over the head? Ritually, of course – price of a few hammers. Always said this green thing could turn damn quick into a species of fascism.

– This green thing, said Peem, after a longish pause. I've been hearing about it. I think my carbon footprint must have been teenyweeny for years. If you don't have a washing machine or a car or a roof, it seems you're doing great.

– But did you aspire to have them?

– I just aspired to exist, I suppose. All that Lucy asked me to do was *learn to exist*. That's what I did, exist in limbo, here and there, foraging on an island, a futon, a set of outside stairs.

Charlie was quiet for a while.

– You okay? said Peem.

– Yeah. It's just that I make a profession of giving citizens advice.

Maybe you should be doing it. You could come in and do surgeries for us.

– *Dopey Fucker Explains All*, or something? *Ex-Fucker* make that.

– How is your love life? said Charlie.

– Post, said Peem. Post-hope, I would say. You?

– This and that, said Charlie. I meet a lot of vulnerable people. Some of them take advantage of me.

the riad

The owner of the riad, Ingmar, was very impressive. Tall, Swedish, experienced, relaxed, with time for everyone and, if you allowed for a degree of disdain and his charging policy, impeccable manners. She was aware of his presence for a day or so before he engaged her in conversation. He asked whether, now that she seemed settled, she might want to explore.

He suggested she go out and visit the Djemma el Fna no later than early evening, eat at a stall, be firm but never rude with the beggars, and enjoy herself. The huge, lopsided, cobra-packed story-telling square was no longer red and dusty but, even paved, she would find it had endless charm. She should try the freshly-pressed orange juice, avoid the henna tattoo merchants, and when she had picked out the best of the thirty identical stalls, sit down and order a pigeon, raisin and almond tajine.

– Seems quite a show, said Lucy.

– Oh, it's not a show, not by any means, not more than 50%. The stories, for example, they're for the Berbers down from the hills, you won't understand them.

– I'm quite good at not understanding stories. Especially long ones.

– I wish I could come with you. Not that I could translate. But my wife is due back from Casablanca on the last plane.

– Sounds as though there's a story in that?

– Who knows? In Marrakech one never finally knows anything. She is having some dental reconstruction, and prefers her own dentist to have it done. An affair with a prune stone, she told me. Have you been up on the roof much?

– Briefly, said Lucy.

– You know, I think this is the best time. I'll have juice sent up. I have to supervise the plasterer now, he is refurbishing the delicate screens on the old wing.

– Thanks. I appreciate it.

– Perhaps, later in the week, a tour?

Lucy felt cared for but not intruded upon. She felt she almost belonged.

freewheeling

When Peem and Charlie debouched from the Metro, the very clean Metro, they were clearly in a different city. There was a civilised square in front of them, and at least three others promised quite close by.

– That gets me down in Uberdeen sometimes, said Charlie. The lack of a square.

– Nowhere decent to sit in the centre, said Peem. I know what you mean.

– There's Golden Square, of course, said Charlie. Which up till last week had no seats, but was dedicated as a rest home for the motor car. Correction, there were a lot of seats, but they were all locked up inside painted metal boxes. Now, the whole thing's been screened off. UberStreet is becoming a hellhole.

– Where are we staying tonight? said Peem.

– Oh, we're heading off to the Algarve. We have under an hour before we need to catch the Metro again for Oriente.

Peem decided not to demur, though he would have liked to sit all afternoon in the square and listen to the Bolivian band playing, before the sun dipped out of it.

But he didn't say anything. It was extraordinarily easy to fall out with somebody, he had found with Lucy. He wanted to find out if there was a knack of not doing it. Probably self-effacement was the best. It was just as well they were going to Oriente. He was starting to feel quite Eastern about his life.

They went through Rossio and walked down a very straight street grid to the enormous Praça do Comércio.

– They shot a king here, said Charlie.

– Kings come and go, said Peem.

– And they had an earthquake, 250-odd years ago.

– Sometimes an earthquake's not so bad, I think Voltaire said.

– Nothing was left here. It was rebuilt.

– What advice do you think they gave them? said Peem. The Citizens' Advice Bureau of the day?

– Keep well clear of churches, said Charlie. I think that would have been it. It was All Saints' Day and they were half way through morning mass, 9.30 exactly, in their fifty churches, when the first tremors hit. If they weren't crushed by crashing naves and glass and fallen angels, they were burned in a whacking conflagration of toppled candles.

– But they rebuilt the churches?

– Yes, the survivors gave their usual thanks. The perished were less grateful. But I would have pointed out to them one thing, said Charlie.

– What?

– The brothel quarter survived intact.

– The poor whores were probably sleeping, said Peem.

He didn't know if this was what tourists always did. Freewheeling.

All the way south in the train to the Algarve, he stood at the very rear of the train, in the small cabin reserved for smokers. There was a reek about the cabin, but no new smokers came. Only Charlie popped in a couple of times to see how he was doing, and that was okay. The window looked back down the tracks.

He gazed at the glistening rails, balanced on their sleepers, immaculately ballasted, fleeing from him like iron snakes, as from behind his future rushed, or so it seemed, pressed into view on either side – embankments, emptiness, animals, men, stations unstopped at, slopes attacked – until, composing and recomposing, his present flipped round a bend, or zoomed off small, as the irretrievable past.

One field with tall white storky birds. Well, they were white like storks, but elegant like herons. Egrets, said Charlie. It was strange, seeing a brilliant white bird in a field, comporting itself, dipping for bugs amongst cattle legs, then sliding off, dismissed by speed, itself shrinking with everything else, to the palest of specks between dull wedges.

He stood for hours as each brief future rushed on by, swooped into a perfect past.

By the end of that time, he knew.

He knew what perfect had to do with. It wasn't beauty, as you dreamed when young.

It meant it was finished, that was all.

– This green thing, he said, when Charlie came to join him a second time.

– We spoke about it, said Charlie. We dealt with that.

– No, said Peem. But I was at this conference on bottled water.

– Swinkie's Symposium, said Charlie, was that the one?

– 'Fraid so.

– What about it?

– I felt I was drowning amongst these people. You feel so helpless.

april 25

swooping swallows stitched it

She enjoyed Djemma el Fna. But she liked to stay in the riad most of the day. She looked at picture books in the library, she sat across from the fountain, she secluded herself on her loggia, and found herself alone on the roof. There were no tall buildings overlooking, none in all the city, and that seemed to keep the city whole. The swooping swallows stitched it together, with playful vibrant cries, and loop upon loop of invisible thread.

She too, whole, as far as she could be, momentarily whole. It was a great deal to be grateful for, momentary wholeness, after what had happened with Peem, with Alison, even her job. It was not all, but that, of course, was what went wrong in the beginning for her. Wanting it all, yet not being able to give time to, or properly enjoy, the tiniest portion.

Wholeness; all. She turned the two concepts loose to comment on each other, and grazed in the safety of the Marrakech riad, across its patient tiles, from one seclusion to another, a cup of sweet mint tea in hand, under the orange trees.

Then she went back up on the roof, and looked at the High Atlas Mountains, rising frankly, close and beckoning, their browns turning to rose in the late April sun.

routine

They got into a neat routine, Peem and Charlie, and it seemed to suit them fine. They were staying in Charlie's pal's spacious flat, in Lagos, just above a homely piri-piri restaurant, The Firefly. They had no fireflies to light their way, but every day the sun lured them to a different dampish habitat, where the marsh birds sensed the calmness in them, and didn't hurry to hide.

And every night in the smoky restaurant, with endless football dinning on TV, they chose the piri-piri chicken, the salty bacalau, or beer and swordfish.

april 27

i never heard cheep

They had the use of an old blue Mercedes, right-hand drive; people were always donating well-made cars to holiday destinations, where they might be pensioned off and subside. Charlie drove. Every time he pulled out to overtake, Peem was exposed to oncoming drivers who seemed to have reconciled themselves to this being their last moment on earth.

– And I'll tell you another thing, said Charlie, as he noted the whiteness of his companion's knuckles. Never accept a lift or a taxi anywhere unless you have checked one thing.

– What's that? said Peem.

– Whether the driver believes in an afterlife, simple as that. If he's hedging his bets on this life, and is only half-committed, let him drive on.

– Seems like a valuable screening principle. I wonder if it could be applied further.

– Sure, said Charlie. I would include Prime Ministers and Presidents. As soon as they show the slightest hankering to believe in an afterlife, shoot them.

– They could hardly complain. They might even thank you, in a roundabout way, for speeding them to a better place. I take it you would apply this to all fundamentalists?

– What does it mean, this *fundamentalists*? I never heard cheep about them in my young day.

– Fundamentally wrong, I suppose, said Peem. Fundamentally missing the point. I met one or two when I was on my wanders. I can't remember what any of them said, except there was a bad time coming, so better have faith, in as large a dollop as your system could stand. For me and plenty others, the bad time is already with you, or has already been. Say for example your skull's been crushed but you're still dottering along, I mean.

– Yes, said Charlie. Look out for a sign that says *Alvor*, that should be us.

They saw storks, squatting high on nesting posts and making a racket. They saw tall herons, ash-grey herons, miserably conspiratorial, twenty-four of them, standing amongst the reeds. Herons had this marvellous weapon, the long beak. The lightning beak, according to Charlie. But Peem never saw them use it.

They saw three spoonbills swishing their beaks through saltpan shallows. They witnessed the dirty pink grotesqueries of flamingoes. It was no wonder that Alice had so much trouble with one, when she sought to use it as a croquet hammer. The flamingo always tried to twist its head to look at her, when all Alice wanted it to do was propel her hedgehog.

And they saw coots, avocets, godwits and gallinules, satisfied or peckish, brilliant in the sun.

Peem's favourite by far was the black-winged stilt. *Stilt* was the clue. It could stand in two feet of water up to only its knees and fool you. It could pace with monstrous heel-lifting deliberation through cloyings of mud.

Yet as it wafted into the air, looking for another café, it was elegance itself, long parallel legs making a slender wake. The stilt was a stilt. It reminded him of no-one. And there was joy in that too.

films about philosophy

Ingmar had indicated or promised a tour, and he didn't disappoint, though he did not accompany Lucy on her trip over the Atlas, but only found for her *an excellent Berber.* Lucy wondered if there was something patronising about that, or at least patrician. Battened upon daily in her occupation by so much hype and jargon, she jibbed at Ingmar's description. Perhaps she recoiled from the term as though it might be racist.

But he was a Berber, and if he hadn't been, and if he hadn't been excellent, you couldn't have trusted him in these real mountains, up through the twisting steeps, then aslant through the imperfectly ploughed snowdrifts at the swirling top.

Equal opportunities could go so far, but a sense of properness sometimes further. Did you really want a pustular booking clerk from Putney piloting your Landcruiser at 7,000 feet? Did you want an alien Leopard coming in and making his high hide, to slavver over your native city?

She might ask something else. Was it proper for folk to knuckle under, or even, like her, run off to the sun—?

But, when you are in the Atlas, the Atlas have to come first.

The debut of GrottoLotto was set for May Day. She would ask Ingmar in good time where she could go online and rebook her flight back.

The mountain villages were startling, flat, mud-walled, with Sky dishes. There were goat-paths leading down from the road, and up the other side of the river towards them. She wondered if the goatherds and their families would stay in and watch GrottoLotto, and whether they would be able to buy tickets for it, so high up. Did they have broadband and credit cards? She wanted to ask Karim, but it went way beyond her phrase books in Berber and Arabic.

Halting French might do the trick.

– Karim, s'il vous plait. Est-ce que les gens ici ont le broadband, ou le dial-up seulement?

– S'ils ont beaucoups des chèvres, ils ont aussi le broadband.

– Merci. Et, est-ce que les gens ici aiment beaucoup La Loterie?

– La vie, c'est leur loterie. S'ils gagnent trop d'argent, ils doivent demeurer en ville. Les Berbers et la ville sont les bons cousins, mais non les bons voisins.

– But you live in the city, vous demeurez en ville?

– Mais chaque jour je prends l'auto sur les montagnes. Mon âme s'est nourrie et satisfiée par les voyages que je fais, jour par jour.

Lucy cupped two open palms below her heart and then moved them up beyond her cheekbones, and out – beyond.

– Your soul, you mean? Your soul is satisfied?

– Je le crois, said Karim, without taking his eyes from the road.

Once they had dropped on the other side, and into the bony fringes of the Sahara, and across the great, braided, alluvial watercourses with the patches and plots of green vegetables perched on their banks, they came to the vast film studios in Ouarzazate, that Ingmar had half-jokingly mentioned as a possible target for their one-day jaunt.

They turned down left and approached the massive junk lot of clapboard and recycled sets for Egyptian, Arabian, Palestinian and Tibetan films. *Lawrence of Arabia, The Man Who Would Be King, Cleopatra, Kundun, Alexander* and *Kingdom of Heaven* had all been shot there, at least in part. Just about everything of the sandy genre, apart from *The Longest Day, Saving Private Ryan* and *Bhaji on the Beach*. Karim stayed outside to save on fees, to contemplate and – most centrally probably – to avoid boredom.

At the moment there was nothing going on, apart from some desultory tours. There was a plethora of polystyrene pillars, fierce paper Anubises, and artificial palms.

The film-lot guides were young and full of fun and, it being early season, there was one guide between only four of them, plus a tag-along apprentice learning the spiel, the numbing statistics, the film jokes.

– Ah, so you are Alexander the Great! the main young guide said in triumph to one of the other three tourists.

– I am called Zander, said the white-haired gentleman. I wish it to be known that I do not use any *Alex* prefixed to my name.

– Zander the Abbreviated, said the witty lad.

– If you wish, said the man. One cannot achieve greatness merely by length of name.

– How did you achieve it then? said the wit.

– I profess philosophy, said Zander.

– Philosophy, said the guide. We don't see so many films about philosophy these days.

– The fact that there are few films about it is greatly to the credit of philosophy, said Zander.

– Well, said the youngster. Why you out here, Mr Zander, if that's how you feel?

– That is a good, though not insurmountable question, said the philosophy man.

Get on with it, thought Lucy. This was getting to be like one of the more turgid passages in *Icarus '68*, so-called.

– I am from Crete, said Zander, and you will be aware that we have a certain priceless historical monument: a cradle, if not *the* cradle, of European civilisation, at Knossos.

– So you were a Professor in Crete, said Lucy. How interesting.

– I was a Professor of Philosophy in Aberdeen, Scotland, said Zander Petrakis, a part of the neo-Greek world that you are not unfamiliar with, if I am correct in deducing from your slight accent?

The guide turned to the other two.

– What did you think of Aberdeen, Uberdeen? asked Lucy. Or Leopardeen, I should say.

– I am aware of the attempted transmogrifications, said Zander. But a city cannot so easily redefine its spots. I studied these spots, I have suffered from these spots, for the best and worst parts of forty years.

– Were you in Aberdeen in the Sixties then? With long hair?

– I arrived in effect on the last day of 1967. I met the long-haired, the self-deluded, the internally exiled and the desperate.

– And were you none of those yourself?

– A philosopher is required to manage the world's fate, his people's history, and both the peaks and vicissitudes of love.

– A Stoic perhaps is required to. There are philosophies too of the heart, you may be aware.

– We would need longer, I submit, to discuss the contradictions of that fully. Let us progress. I do find it a pleasure to have met you. Now I must assess whether Atlas Studios could host the making of a Knossos film, and save my land and heritage from much ignorant trampling.

Lucy wondered about him briefly as a possible ally in the battle against LeopCorp, UbSpec Total, Swink, Rookie Marr, Guy Bord, and GrottoLotto. Not to mention that turncoat Alison.

– I've never been to Crete, I must confess. But your myth is part of all of us. The labyrinth, the horrible monster at its heart. Daedalus, prisoner and inventor. And Icarus, who tried to fly without listening.

– Thank you for reminding me, Ms—?

– Ms Legge, Lucy Legge.

– But what we will be faced with, Ms Legge, if that film is made, is only labyrinth as folly. Film is the great art form of the last century, but two-dimensional only. A film about Knossos can only be a façade.

The granite is no façade, thought Lucy.

– Now, Lucy, I must prospect further. What is that on the horizon, with so many high walls? he asked the guide.

– *The Kingdom of Heaven.*

– Have they finished with their lot?

– Ouarzazate, what does it mean, Karim? Qu'est ce-que il veut dire? En Berber? said Lucy, as they were driving away west and beginning their climb.

– Ouarzazate. Sans bruit, sans nuisances, sans embrouillement.

– Without noise, without confusion. C'est évidemment un nom ancien, a name given long ago.

april 30

their gift for each other

Peem and Lucy bumped into each other at Leopardeen Airport, at the carousel. There were passengers from about three flights looking glum.

– Hi, said Lucy. Waiting to be reconciled with your baggage?

– Reconciled to waiting, said Peem.

– I think it'll be all over the place. They only changed the name of the airport last week, so not all the airlines will have the Leopardeen labels. And there are no doubt two dozen old Aberdeens, and a dozen mimic Uberdeens scattered across the globe.

– I did not think death had undone so many, Peem said.

– Donne?

– Dante. I am the age I am, and only now coming to the *Inferno*.

– How have you been? Are you reconciled? I was going to get in touch, but you're not on email.

– Never mind me. I've had a nice quiet time looking at birds. How about you?

– Oh, Morocco.

– Lucy, Charlie, I should have introduced, Citizens' Advice man. He's been looking after me.

– Hi Charlie, said Lucy. Full time job, eh? You back specially for tomorrow night? Son of Spectacle? GrottoLotto?

– Charlie thinks my second name's Endrie, said Peem.

– *Dree*, said Lucy. *End-dree?* You know what that means in the old Ewan MacColl song? Endure your fate.

– How does it go again? I think I know it.

– *Work and wait and dree your weird*, sang Lucy.

– *Pin your faith in herrin sales*, said Peem.

– *And oftimes lie awake at nicht*, sang Lucy.

– *In fear and dread o winter gales*, they attempted to sing together.

– Weird for sure, said Charlie.

Some of the other passengers had found good reason to shuffle their way round the carousel.

Lucy and Peem stopped rattling on, and took each other in. The play of a smile. Whatever they'd squandered, they hadn't lost their gift for each other.

They plucked their bags, and spoke even faster for half a minute.

– So if things go bust, Peem, and they may well, said Lucy, forget GrottoLotto, forget Spectacle. Make your way to the beach. See ya.

– Lucy, both of you, do you want to share a taxi? said Charlie.

– Okay, said Peem.

– No, Charlie, said Lucy, got a ton to do. Better head off, thanks. I left my Traveller in the long stay.

the clowns are in it for the long haul

After he had dumped his stuff at Maciek's, Peem asked Charlie to drop him off at the Shack. Still there after all these years, the red corrugated roof, the black door, down at the quayside.

– Come in for a minute, said Peem, with one hand on the passenger door. You must meet Iris.

Charlie steamed around till he spied the last space in a pub car park. *For Patrons Only*, it said. They set off on foot along the waterfront.

– What's Iris like? said Charlie.

– Wait till you meet her.

They found the place was packed. Folk of all ages: lorry drivers, office workers, pensioners. It was tea and sandwiches, bananas, cakes and juice mostly. The place was humming with chat.

– There's no space, said Charlie.

– Wait, said Peem.

There was a steady traffic to and from the toilet. Though more seemed to go than came back. There was no sign of Iris.

– Look, there's a seat, said Peem. You take it. I'll be back.

He went hunting for her. There were three doors in the toilets, *Men*, *Women* and *Staff Only*. He chose the third. In the dark partition between toilets and kitchen, a hand went on his forearm.

– Iris? said Peem.

– No, said the voice.

– I need to see her.

– Forget it.

With that Iris poked her head through, and light from the kitchen fell on his face.

– Oh, said Iris. It's you. I'll see you later. No, put on a mask and come through. But say nothing, unless you have something to say.

– Another Snoopy, she said, when they went through.

– We're just finishing, said a Marge Simpson.

– So when the text comes through, said Darth Vader, pour real fast for five minutes. Spirits. That'll get them excited. No champagne, the corks take too long. Just max the value that hits the floor: rum, voddy, special brandies. And malts, of course.

– If we want to align our action with a Scottish Republic— said Bugs Bunny.

– Okay, said Darth. Agreed, max on the malts.

– No, said Bugs, the opposite, surely!

– Hold it, said Iris, this is not an issue. Each group can pour as they see fit. Get the aisles awash pronto. Alarm the manager, get him phoning for help, but don't harm the staff if they try to restrain you. Encourage other shoppers to join in—

– Tell them it's a stunt for Candid Camera, said Marge Simpson. Or Liver Concern.

– How about just tell them it's the start of a revolution? said Iris. Else it's all part of the general heehaw, and we gain nothing.

– Yeah, yeah, with you— said Marge.

– Spot on, said Bugs.

– Now the clowns, said Iris. The clowns don't want to be compromised. They're fresh from Faslane. The clowns are in it for the long haul.

– Bloody clowns, said Darth Vader.

– What's it about? said Peem, when the others had melted back into the café scene, and Charlie had been invited through to the kitchen.

– Don't completely know, said Iris. None of us has got an overall picture. These three were spokes-persons. Literally, *spokes-persons*, each linking direct to a small group. There's probably thirty groups – within a broad plan, they choose their own targets. I'm one of ten, I think, holes in the hub. Only tomorrow do we roll out the whole wheel. Or try to—

– Sounds great, said Peem.

– All the time, absolutely, we have to keep our lines tight, we're not up against mugs. So what have you two been up to?

a non-love letter

Alison had a thousand things to attend to in the run-up to May 1st. She could have done with a few more reliable colleagues in truth, but she flew around, her mobile red-hot. Otto was being a pain, trying to make out GrottoLotto was named after him. Gwen was still not responding to texts.

Gwen may have felt she was being pestered by her mother, fussed-over, spied-on. Well, the last was true, but from a very different quarter, Alison knew. Though as far as she was aware texts could not be intercepted by the authorities, or by any of those who arrogated authority to themselves, whereas all voice-calls, terrestrial or celestial, terrorist or humdrum, were liable to be tapped, listened to, logged and recorded. And it was unlikely that LeopCorp didn't have access to that kind of stuff.

But from Gwen still, not even a text.

Anyway, take a deep breath, thought Alison. All of the Gwen stuff paled into horrible insignificance – horrible yes, but insignificant – beside what she herself had learned the previous evening.

Sifting at home through a bundle of unopened and tossed-aside correspondence, she had come on a buff envelope. And it wasn't a bill or a circular from the Council, or anything Revenueish.

It was from the Health Board. It was, in effect, though wholly benign on the surface, a non-love letter from the very distant past.

She hadn't stopped weeping till after one o'clock. Her face was still red in the morning.

the queen of newt was blamed and removed

Gwen had taken the job with open eyes. As far as her employer went, she was an Under Information Officer. She was a kind of researcher, with restricted access. She was a species of gofer, but not allowed out. She composed messages, yet was not allowed to send them. Partly because she was not allowed out, she had had to apply together with a partner, who was similarly confined.

Gwen had had little to do, when she was off duty, apart from keep her orange blouses clean and ironed. Bill told her who Luna was. She saw her at the end of a corridor once. Gwen tried to explore. There was a Vision Mixing room, but it seemed to be always locked. She spent her time reading.

She and Bill were given their own accommodation, in a back turret, facing east. It was a one year contract, very good money, with no living expenses, and would enable a couple, if the market remained passably stable, to put together the readies for a 5% deposit on a house. With houses costing a lung or half a liver, their temporary loss of all freedoms was supposed to be worth it.

Bill's job was that of APT, Assistant Principal Taster, and he was ushered into the Leopard's presence nightly, blindfold, and required to sample each meat at the point of the Principal Taster's fork. His interview had been almost entirely silent, apart from the inevitable gnashing Bill made as he chewed his way through two-inch cubes of seared veal, scorched venison and flash-fried seal.

The Leopard mainly just drank during the day, water and juices; the occasional nibble of specially-sourced crisps, salt and emu, gnu and onion. Bill had to taste these too. The main meal was eaten at night. The Leopard had lived in many uncongenial places – Australia, Chicago, Singapore, Kampala – at his father's behest, and had dined exclusively on local meats.

There was a mobile barbecue always available for North Turret, with a self-filtering cowl. After darkness had fallen, the barbecue was taken up to the Fastness in the lift, already fired. Whatever the plat de la nuit might be, its choicest chunks would be barely introduced to the glowing embers.

At meat-time, the Leopard was at his most charming. He would pace round the room stroking the fangs and snouts of the dozen leopard heads mounted on the walls.

Tonight the starter was Capercaillie and Blackcock Kidneys. With kidneys, Bill knew, there was always the strong chance of a dash of piss. Piss the Leopard might not like. Piss he might associate with poison. Bill gave the kidneys the thumbs-down. They were flung out the lower half of the slit window, to bounce amongst the pie-dogs of Leopardeen's Castlegate.

The alternative starter was announced as Urban Fox. A lot of foxes ran about the Links these days, not far from the sea, between the HyperMall and Jumbo Arcade. Bill was afraid they might taste over-poweringly of Kentucky fried chicken, but there was barely a nuance. He passed the Urban Fox, and the Leopard was soon munching in.

Entrée was Cairngorm Reindeer. There was never much fat on one of these, roaming the plateaux, choosing their moss, tinkling their bells obligingly so the harvester's rifle could zero in. Bill chewed and chewed. The Leopard was mainly afraid of quick and violent poisons. After ten minutes of Bill's chomping, the Leopard got torn in too.

Dessert in Australia had often been platypus, in Singapore, snake, and in Kampala, chimp, but here in northern clime the Leopard was reduced to Queen of Newt Pudding. Bill was prepared to find the taste of newt dull, but, as he prised his slightly rubbery portion off the fork, he was pleasantly surprised.

He was less pleasantly surprised when his blindfold slipped a little. He blinked at the nine flickering monitors, over the hunched and munching Leopard's shoulder.

Particularly one monitor. He could see a woman, in her bedroom, thick hair wild across the pillow. It was their bedroom, and Gwen was reading late, the latest Rosa Luxemburg tome, waiting for him. Then she got up for a snack or a leak, and stretched her legs towards the camera. It was abundantly clear she had nothing on. Towards just one of the cameras. There was a clutch of screens, displaying their sweet pre-marital bed ambushed from a splay of angles.

Bill spat out.

The Queen of Newt was blamed and removed. They had to open a tin of monkey.

freedom is always the freedom of dissenters

Gwen was reading one of her favourite passages from her favourite revolutionary.

Freedom only for the members of the government, only for the members of the Party, is no freedom at all. Freedom is always the freedom of dissenters. The essence of political freedom depends not on the fanatics of justice, but rather on all the invigorating, beneficial, and deterrent effects of dissenters. If freedom becomes synonomous with privilege, the workings of political freedom are broken.

Bill came in the bedroom door, looked round their room swift and strange, came across and whispered, and told her what he had seen.

ocean roulette

So, year by year, from bigger and bigger wheelhouses, set on higher and higher bridges, Spermy had looked out with his searchlight over wider and wider undulant rings of coloured buoys, marking the utmost perimeter of his net. White buoys marked the wide wings of the net, pink marked smaller mesh, while between the two red buoys hung the dense, black mesh of the reinforced bag, the heart of the purse. Here the herring or mackerel would be corralled and held in not too agitated readiness to be vacuumed aboard into chilled tanks of brine.

As Spermy watched, from the canted window of the high wheel-house, and as the purse block began its inexorable work of tautening and retrieving the net, here and there a buoy would twitch or duck as a sweep of anxious, panicking herring sought to find gaps in the shuttling curtain. None existed. And as Spermy observed, and as he considered the information relayed by sensors, he was privileged to be able to adjust his effort to baffle the blind, collective dash of the fish. These days there was no risk of a wrongful encirclement of some clogging, time-wasting species like spurdog or sprat. The modern sonar could pick out a single fish at 200 fathoms, declare the species, its likely size and probable birthday. No longer was fishing a dicey do, ocean roulette. And the good thing was, his son was sitting in the pair boat a hundred yards off, nothing but nav lights on, heaving up and down, waiting to take his share of the load.

Because with all the different information, and differential pull, adjusted for the swell of sea in its larger motion, and for lurching peaks and sudden holes in a cross sea, it was a pretty sure thing, heavy odds, a dead cert, that soon it would not just be a kaleido-scope of buoys bobbing on the surface. Nor would it be only the standard choleric jostlement of gulls. Nor merely a submarine impatience of larger snouts and jaws. There would be a kything, a serious agitation. Then the first fish would break the surface and – thrashing its tail – freak out. Two hours later the *Girl Julie* and the *Spare Me V* would be full to the brim. A further million or two herring, mad on adrenalin, scaling themselves and prone to disease, might have to be released, twindling through the water column in spasm and shock.

It was on exactly such a night, when both fine boats were full – nudging deep noses a mile apart through an oily pleasant sea, nearing the market in Skagen – that the bombshell was released.

core business

Spermy was never a hesitater. He was not known to vacillate. No shadow fell across his decision-making. If he ever had an Oxford Dictionary in any of his series of six cabins or staterooms, propping one end of his diligent collection of scud DVDs, then the word *procrastination* might as well have been Tipp-Exed out.

Close as he was to the market in Skagen, as soon as he was radioed by his wife with the news he had been shafted by Rookie Marr, Spermy swung the head of the *Girl Julie* for Leopardeen. *Spare Me V*, after a fierce harangue on Channel 12, went hard over on her rudder and, gunwales streaming, followed suit. It was a minute past midnight. Spermy made rapid calculations.

Not that there was a herring market at all in Leopardeen; there was hardly even an outlet for white fish these days. *Nae fish market worth a docken*, as the grizzled locals, the pierhead parliament, the weary bodachs in the Shack, proclaimed. It was all oil now, the Harbour, and oil boats, with bluff noses and flat arses, for portering mud and pipes.

Spermy phoned up Frankie Leiper of Leiper Lorries.

– Fit kind o time's this tae phone a man? said Frankie.

– Aabody doesna sit on their dowp aa day, Frankie. I'm needin lorries aff ye.

– Thocht ye were landin in Denmark?

– Aye, weel ye ken fit thocht did. Damn little, an never got peyed.

– I can gie ye fower, six at maist. I'm oot on contract.

– Mak it a coupla dizzen an we're talkin, Frankie. Nivver mind if yir ither jobs get shoved tae the side. These fish o mine are specials. But they winna be gaain nae distance, dinna fret. Yir drivers will be hame an hosed inside the hour.

    – Ye're some fuckin boy, Jed. A coupla dizzen lorries oot o thin air?

    – That's it, said Spermy. Five on the nail.

    – Fifteen, said Frankie.

    – Ten in yir haun, said Spermy.

    – Grand?

    – Fit in hell else? said Spermy.

    – Grand, said Frankie.

    – Mak sure that it is, said Spermy. I'm oot aff Denmark. I'll be in at ten o the nicht.

It was easier for Spermy when the Swinks had pitched their long-held fishing-boat portfolio over to LeopCorp. Otherwise there had always been that scunnersome family complication with Julie, William II being her only brother.

    The Swinks had sold on. But now so had LeopCorp, sold him out straight, sold the boat from under him. Streamlining the core business was LeopCorp's story.

    If Spermy and son were to try to land in Denmark, both boats would be impounded.

He was nothing to LeopCorp. Fair enough, LeopCorp was nothing to him.

    And Rookie Marr was as good as finished.

an equal opportunities selection

Lucy spent the early part of May Day supervising the putting-up of memorials. There were at least two aspects that needed careful handling.

    One was that not everyone gladly consented to having a blue plaque mounted proud on their house wall. There could be ticklish conflicts of belief and prejudice.

    The other was the wording on the plaque itself. You could get very few words on a round blue plaque, bearing in mind the need for the name, plus the start and stop dates of the celebrated one. There had been trouble before when one former Communist activist and Spanish Civil War International Brigade veteran was labelled simply *Radical.* Granted that pruned the number of letters somewhat but, after all, a radical could be a mixture of mercies. Good grief, thought Lucy, the Leopard is hardly conservative in his approach.

As she travelled about the town, in the areas that weren't newly no-go, Lucy could sense it coming. Down in Union Terrace Gardens, the civic grass had been turned into a police horse paddock. The horses were tail-swishing, skittish, one was skittery. They knew there was something up.

Up above the paddock, just below His Majesty's Theatre and along from the William Wallace statue, was the famous civic coat-of-arms, displayed on a steep bank. The coat-of-arms with the leopards. It was done in heraldic grade geraniums, pelargoniums and small French marigolds.

And, of necessity, it was being adjusted slightly.

A pair of leopards rampant – dexter, sinister – had always been what were technically called supporters on the coat-of-arms. In Crusader days it was believed that while Muslim and Christian were mutually exclusive species, Lion and Leopard were both so fierce, proud, dominant, they were basically the same beast. The Leopard's intrinsic spottiness, though, might have been the basis of a knockdown offer. So the old heraldic beasts were ideal for Leopardeen, their wavy tongues thrust out at the public. Swink handled dexter. Rookie was more the sinister side.

Only the associated motto presented a problem.

When the city was still grinding along as Aberdeen, Uberdeen even, fair enough, the motto *Bon Accord* was an understandable aspiration. But now that it was Leopardeen, things had to change.

Bon Accord was also the name of a major mall, so there was *no level plaza*, as Swink succinctly remarked. As regards motto, therefore, they had to institute an annual toss-up, between the five malls.

Bon Accord. St Nicholas. Trinity. HyperMall. Sonsy Quines.

The duty squad of three gardeners for Union Terrace Gardens had been instructed as to the result, and were now tossing flowers off the back of a lorry, hoicking last-minute plastic trays from the Hazlehead nursery down the brae, and bending to trowel them in. The winning motto was being embellished in an equal opportunities selection of white, pink and yellow petunias, and chocolate pansies.

Sonsy Quines. Not many folk knew the meaning, Lucy guessed. Though she knew a woman who would.

destiny in the air

The day before, Peem had gone back to Maciek's flat after the masked encounter in the Shack, but the Poles were up to something, and he had to hunt half of Torry to find him. Hunting half of Torry, he noted plenty other activity, definitely a buzz. He had seen black bags being bundled into tenements, with coloured garments sticking out, feathery boas trailing. He had seen vanloads of long, sawn sticks of wood. There were young sentries at the corners of streets, casual, never off their phones, and police cars cruising.

And now this morning, he'd witnessed a couple of brutal arrests. A bloke with his arm twisted right up his back, thrown into the back of a van. A woman in flip-flops being dragged along the pavement just outside his pad, on her bare heels. It was getting tense.

As someone who had cultivated an ability to be at the arse end of nowhere during world events, who had been holed up in a clinic during the Tet offensive, had stumbled about in dank groves rather than march on Grosvenor Square, had been intimated his classification as soft-in-the-head at the heights of the Sorbonne, and had done sod-all in the slightest to hinder Swink and Co, Peem had a sense of the long-awaited, the long-avoided; a moment in the stream of history, destiny in the air.

the electrical impulses

Everyone thought that the first running of GrottoLotto, due to be broadcast that night worldwide – or if not broadcast to certain countries, beamed, or if not beamed to the other side of the world, streamed on-line, and in high-tariff locations cabled – would be pretty momentous, though nobody guessed just how momentous it would be.

There had been other golden dates in the history of communication, and the basic principle of *nation shall speak unto nation* was the foundation. The BBC's triad of intentions – *inform, educate, entertain* – was pretty impressive, and had taken the airwaves, and electrical impulses generally, amazingly far.

But never before – and Rookie Marr was sure, and in that visionary's wake the Guy Bords and William Swinks of this world, the able retainers and public pickpockets, were also sure – never before had one billion, potentially two billion, perhaps three billion viewers and rising, been offered the simultaneous chance – as Rookie put it – *to be entertained, to save the world, and to become rich.*

Without indulging in even a nano-smidgeon of hype, it seemed for all money an unstoppable combination.

naked pushees?

You had to be in Golden Square to see it all take final shape. Beyond the high architrave and Ionic pillars and massiveness of Leopardeen's Music Hall, behind acrylic translucent screens as lofty as its sonorous roof, pre-preparation, and preparation proper, had taken place.

Is global capital present?
Yes. The top 21 listed companies in the world, as determined on the New York Stock Exchange.

Are the companies in playful mood?
Very playful, and deadly serious.

What do they have in common?

Each has invested hope and reputation in a soft plastic transparent LottoBall, five metres in diameter, branded with their logo, and also numbered according to their position on the New York Exchange, as at 17th April, from 1 to 21.

Some pretty famous names then?

GoPlut, Cyklops, Tosh, KUM, Sushi MacBun, Ciel, Shriv, OediBus, Colonel Motors, Sexxon. Need I go on?

Yes.

Plus, Shall, UCKU, Next Butt One.

Fourteen.

Dot, Pi, Lug, Gold, Havakama Parang, Jeremy Futures. Finally, Imperial Wallhole, who just squeezed in, relegating Random Virgin Extra Holdings to 22nd spot as first reserve.

And who is No. 1?

GoPlut, the energy giant.

Anything special about each ball?

Each ball will have nine beautiful young people lodged within, four or five men, and five or four women. These are the Pushees.

How were potential Pushees first identified?

From last month's pages of *Hiya!* and *Kool!* magazines.

Are they distinguished in any way?

They have all come through a rigorous selection process, based on personality in the widest sense, balance and agility. They are all well fit. They have had to demonstrate preternaturally low levels of claustrophobia and high willy-nilliness resistance.

Willy-nilliness resistance?

The balls will be rolling and colliding with considerable velocity at times. Each of the Pushees will be standing with his or her feet braced against the small balance ball in the centre, with their arms outstretched and their hands pressed firmly against the inside of the giant sphere. They may feel dizzy and be dislodged, and land up tumbling like dolls in an industrial dryer. Whatever happens, willy-nilly they must be up for it, and able to roll till they drop, collectively of course, into the Grotto or Hole. Each of the Pushees will be naked.

Why?
  Why not?

Naked Pushees?
  That's correct.

Is a nude show likely to be permissible on global TV?
  Several nations have indeed an advisory watershed, or else their main religion, or potent sub-religion, holds that the female form should at all times be totally clad. But the World Open Trade and Transport Organisation, WOTTO, has argued that such rulings act as *restraint of intercourse,* and two injunctions, firstly contra *advice,* and secondly contra *religion,* as *ultra vires* have been successfully sought at the Hague.

When is the event due to start?
  At first darkness.

What is the goal or object?
  The goal or object is to propel each ball as fast as possible, from the Music Hall towards LeopCorp Towers, and plop it down the Hole or Grotto, under the Market Cross.

With what ulterior motive?
  The order of the balls' arrival will determine the global winner, the GrottoLotto winning ticket.

Example?
  7, 1, 20, 17, 9, 3, 6, 8, 13, 15, 21, 4, 10, 19, 2, 16, 18, 11, 5, 12, 14.

What are the odds of winning GrottoLotto?

It will be appreciated that, because the first prize is vast, in the teens of millions, the odds are quite significant.

How is it proposed to propel the balls?

By means of squads of sports players, the Pushers, also nine per team.

How were the Pushers chosen?

A fit player nominated by each and every nation on earth will wear their nation's flag as leotard, as well as their sponsor's logo and sponsor's number on mask, shoes and bib.

Why one Pusher from every nation?

The winning ball's nine propelling countries will each receive an SPP, a Sustainable Planet Prize.

Like what?

A bespoke GrottoLotto windmill will be set in place by US Marine Chinook helicopter on their highest hill.

How big?

Half a Meg. Enough to power the mobile phone chargers in an average village.

189 countries taking part? 21 times 9?

Correct.

But are there not 192 countries in the United Nations, give or take Taiwan?

GrottoLotto has dealt with the arithmetic head-on.

Is ball interference to be permitted?

No. GrottoLotto seeks to set the highest standards, and to influence the behaviour of the young everywhere.

What will happen in the event of foul play?

The nine Pushers concerned, and, by inevitable implication, the nine Pushees, will have to retrace and reroll their path, and start from the Music Hall again.

Will the game not be over very quickly?
No, the pavementette will be switched on in reverse. All teams will have to contend against a broad band of high-tensile pavementette rolling *away* from the direction of striving.

Where can one get a GrottoLotto ticket?
Tickets at 1 dollar are available at 10,000 global outlets, and online. Any more questions?

No, that's about it for now. Just one last.
Yes?

I have just worked something out.
What?

The odds against purchasing a winning lottery line would seem to be 21 times 20 times 19 times 18 times 17 times 16 times 15 times 14 times 13 times 12 times 11 times 10 times 9 times 8 times 7 times 6 times 5 times 4 times 3 times 2. Times 1 if you can be bothered.
And your point is?

Never mind people for the moment. Are there in this world five thousand million billion anything, apart from flies and grains of sand?
I'm sorry, sir, that's not in our briefing pack. Perhaps if you could call and see our Operations Director, Mr Bord. Mr Bord is on Balcony A. I'm sure he'll deal with any query.

Thank you, I may do so.
Have a nice GrottoLotto.

As afternoon wore into evening, Rookie Marr became more and more animated. Even a motivator who had achieved the gratitude of fifty councillors, the participation of three hundred staff, the exploitation of a thousand workers, the channel-flicking attention of a billion viewers, even a godlike figure who had broadened the horizons of the media beyond belief, even a backhand shanker who needed streaming porn in his penthouse to raise a flutter—

Even such a man was excited now.

He was tempted by three choices of viewing platform.

One. In the Fastness, the Leopard's lair.

Two. On the gold throne on a raised dais on Balcony A, in public view, where he might be seen justly as a contemporary emperor, might adjudge the quality of play in the GrottoLotto arena, and direct cheats back to the Music Hall with a peremptory flick of a horizontal thumb.

Three. Down the Hole, where each ball must fall and roll along the rail, and where all hopes, and many cameras, lay focussed. There, on his second-best throne, he might quaff from the silver-chased cup, engraved *Bon Accord,* that had been presented to him personally just last week, to mark the demise of the old city, and the birth of the new.

Guy Bord was updating him on security, at his request. There were all sorts of last minute rumours. The old G8 Gleneagles protestors had been heard on the waves, blithering on about *GL9.* The Faslane clowns were sniffing north for anything nuclear.

– Mounted police? queried Rookie Marr.
  – Mounted, replied Guy Bord.
  – Plainclothes security?
  – Roger.
  – Aerial surveillance?
  – Lynxes warm, turning over, ready to hover.
  – Tanks?
  – Tanks shouldn't be necessary.

– Tanks? repeated Rookie Marr.

– The Highland Light Desert are in reserve. A local regiment, they command affection.

– Good work, Guy. This won't be forgotten. Oh, I have a picture of you with Luna you should see sometime. I know you like her.

Guy Bord, at the other end, missed a beat, missed Luna, missed another beat, and missed Lucy in that sudden moment. Her doughty deconstruction and reconstruction of sentences. *This won't be forgotten.*

Unfortunately for you, Lucy would have added. It all piled up now, it had been piling up for weeks in Guy's mind.

It was no mean feat to coordinate such Spectacle.

The battle over which three nations should be omitted as Pusher-suppliers had strung him out. They had tried a blind draw, but somebody hadn't mixed the folded squares of paper properly, and it was *Uganda, UK,* and finally *USA* they landed up picking.

Lottery having its limitations, they tried reason. Alison suggested some of the former Russian states might want to reamalgamate. Or a few Balkans. She was in a dangerous kind of mood.

It came down to Otto's brainwave. They picked out three infinitesimal countries with probably very bumpy airstrips, that would struggle to fly an athlete out to Leopardeen in a month of Sundays. Palau, Nauru, Burkina Faso.

The setting of the closing date for company qualification had been another bummer for him to handle.

When GrottoLotto's entry conditions were first announced, there was some desperate trading on the exchanges, as companies tried to squeeze into the top twenty-one. Tokyo and the Hang Seng went bull, which was rare enough these days, and Frankfurt, the Footsie and Wall Street soon followed suit. The masses of action TV, free publicity, and universal pump-out were unrepeatable, short of the Olympics or World Cup. But those lofty spectacles appeared infrequently, once every four years, a marketing nightmare. Grotto-Lotto would be every month, soon every fortnight – perhaps, when geared up, once a week.

Guy Bord pushed through a deadline of two weeks in advance, for company qualifying. Thus April 17th was the cut-off date for the May 1st opener. Even then, there were bitter complaints. A fortnight was a long time in business, an infinity in volatile trading. A company might be top whack on April 17th, but then by May Day be totally bust.

So Guy was not short of potentially runaway horses. He wished Alison would arrive and juggle a rein or two.

the supremo

Where to position himself was still a toss-up, but since Guy was getting to be too much the supremo on Balcony A, and because it would be inconvenient tonight to sack him, and because the Hole was too much out of it, except at the end, then Rookie Marr tended to think that it had it best be the Fastness for him. Security had demanded he choose at the last moment anyway.

In the meantime he had brought his main meal forward, and had ordered barbecue-firers and tasters to present themselves in good time.

an orb with a pulse

The moment for GrottoLotto had almost arrived.

From Golden Square, from its fresh-marked grid, shortly would be released the Top Twenty-One. Transparent, strong, soft, sac-like, these were balls almost like human eyes. Eyes like something out of Bosch; eyes with people climbing in. In the membrane of each ball there were nine sealable lids. The lids were as wide as naked shoulders, with tubs of grease on hand to ease ingress for the big-hipped, the better-endowed.

Within each sac-like eye, eighteen bare feet now locked into position, soles curved in dynamic tension against the central balance ball, while eighteen palms pattered about till they found their optimum position and braced outwards, against the membrane. Like Barbarella plural plus attendant Orcs, like an UberEye strutted with flesh, like an orb with a pulse, within the strong, soft sacs now stood the tantalisation and transfiguration of Lottery; the beautiful Pushees. One hundred and eighty nine of them.

Shortly all hundred and eighty nine Pushers would move into their positions too.

Shortly all the banks of red lights in UberStreet would flick to green.

Shortly all three hundred and seventy eight Tiger Cub Supershoes would be driven, against the considerable friction of adverse pavementette.

And shortly, the naked Pushees, all of a whirl, on to the public concourse would be impelled.

– What will shake will shake, said Guy to the acolytes, come the hurly-burly.

He realised that Luna had exited his mind, what with the Leopard's veiled threat, what with the bevies of naked beauties. He wished that Lucy was beside him, and Alison. There he was in the middle of history, a situation he had midwifed, practically single-handedly, and his words were thrown away.

What will shake will shake, he spoke to himself, *come the hurly-burly*.

some trust or faith

Ludwig was an ex-POW, and though he had worked in Scotland during his incarceration and ever since, he did not qualify for much in the way of pension. Amande, his partner, was an immigrant, multi-jobbed, probably unemployable now, being seventy-odd, and with few insurance stamps accrued. Andy, their next-door neighbour, got his state basic, plus bits and bobs, and, being the man he was, he divvied it in three.

These straitened circumstances explained why they were headed downtown now. Ludwig piloting the motorbike. Amande with her lined cheek laid to his cracked leather shoulder-blade, and tugging at his waist. Andy Endrie in the sidecar, neck and spine taut.

And their chestnut-roasting stall, squat and stainless, 3,000 chestnuts aboard, bouncing along on a ball-hitch, swivelling behind. It was like a remake of Jarry's *Supermale*, only it wasn't. For of late they had supped but little of nectar, ambrosia, perpetual love food: some trust or faith must have pickled them, for three to have come so far.

how's your pavementette?

Guy decided to see if he still had Lucy's name in his phone.

– What's that, is that you Guy? she said. You serious, who do you think I am? Come where?

– I'll throw you down a security badge.

– What's got into you, I'm not even dressed.

– I'll think you'll find that fits the spirit of the evening, Guy replied.

– I won't know anybody, will Alison be there?

– Oh, sure. You know her. Sometime.

– Good, because we have a distance to make up, said Lucy.

She suddenly felt almost jolly, caught up in something bigger, conscience quietened, if not stilled.

– How's your pavementette these days? she said.

– As yet unmarked. But this is the test.

the one is valued who is the same

Bing Qing had always had the same weakness; it was the secret of her success. She did not delegate. Tonight's catering for the special guests would be the pinnacle of her career in Scotland. It was indeed strange. She had left China to flee a Cultural Revolution. Forty years on she found herself, in this most stable of cities, in this most traditional of countries, in the middle of yet another. She did not know what to think; she did not have time to. Her string of restaurants, inherited from her uncle, spoke of a care for quality, a care for the customer, that was in her both cultured and innate.

When you make each small thing good, there is great profit, her uncle used to say. As well as the obvious surface meaning, he intended that as advice for a whole path in life, a path she followed. *In the middle of revolution, the one is valued who is the same,* was a saying which she had more recently composed.

And even though her sayings would never be published, and her poems on sand perished away, they guided her. All her children and grandchildren were enslaved by the TV. A set sat high in each take-away, and in a corner of each kitchen. Vexation.

Tonight was GrottoLotto. Lesser guests on Balconies E to Z were being hosted by Proof Positive, the alcohol provider, and Hints, the luxury ice-cream. But Bing Qing had gained the contract to cater fully on Balconies A, B, C and D for distinguished guests.

A street can be a dangerous place. She would stay behind the curtain. She would not watch it.

it takes a long fork

For Rookie Marr, the tasting of his meats was more than short-term precaution, it was part of a deeper ritual.

Given the envies that pertain against the successful, it was not beyond the bounds of reason that some slow poison was being administered to him. Nevertheless, by keeping the same person in post, the cumulative effects of any longer-term venomous addition to his meats would affect the Assistant Principal Taster too.

But even the standard taster stratagem might not signal quickly enough any vile intention of the envious. He had thought of that too. Therefore it came about that he required his taster every night to eat twice the size of portion that he, Rookie Marr, had appetite for and could consume. It required a taster who was practically starved the rest of the day to do full justice to his prophylactic role.

The Assistant Principal Taster, by keeping his stomach otherwise empty, seemed to fulfil this, and the truth was, as Rookie Marr knew by diligent DVD recording, that whether he was weak through irregular aliment, or fatigued by the antics of fleshly labour, his Assistant Principal Taster spent much of the day in bed.

All for the best. The matter of the CCTV was good too. The taster man and the Gwen woman could have no knowledge of it, and constraint was placed only on the mother, the Alison woman. It was ideal to have a hostage on the Council, so that nothing arose from that quarter to disturb his plans for world entertainment.

Except that, on the previous evening, the Bill man had spat his newt, and had gone purple, indicating he could eat, or would eat, no more.

Thus he had a crisis, one that could not readily be solved by asking the Principal Taster to abandon his administrative role and munch for him again. Such a stratagem would set his scheme for detecting long-term, cumulative poisons at naught, and if there was one thing that Rookie Marr prided himself with knowledge of, beyond the global leisure market, it was long-term poisons.

He required that his Assistant Principal Taster come round to a better way of behaving. To expel his food in the company of The Leopard was not becoming. But it might have been, however abhorrent, a one-off aberration. He would give him another chance.

Bill now entered, preceded by the Principal Taster and followed by a couple of flunkeys, each with platters of raw, chopped, locally-sourced ostrich, and two more hauling the special barbecue, already radiant.

The Principal Taster went to open the slit window, so the ritual could begin.

While the PT's back was turned, Bill snatched up the serving fork and fell on the Leopard. The Leopard saw him coming and rotated in his chair, so that the fiercely downthrust serving fork quivered in his shoulder and stuck there.

That's for Gwen—! said Bill.

The Leopard roared and, seizing the weapon that lay to hand at all times, pistolled Bill through belly and guts the maximum number of times. Transcending his sedentary and pampered lifestyle, he dragged the limp lump that was Bill to the open window, and as one groaned and the other gasped, tough to tell which in the shock that prevailed, levered him up and out. Plucking the implement at the third attempt from his shoulder, the Leopard was satisfied.

– It takes a long fork to sup with a Leopard!

Below in the Castlegate, the crowd, spattered with gore and brains, stood shocked, pressing in and backing out, saying *Oh, Gad's! Fit's gaain on? Far's the bobbies?*

Three minutes later, Gwen's lover's body went screeching out of the Castlegate, hard right, and away down Justice Street.

Perhaps he was going to A&E. Redundant. Perhaps he was going to incriminate himself at the Police HQ in Queen Street. Unwilling to talk. Perhaps he was off to lie in state at a funeral home. Unlikely.

Whoever was giving the orders would determine Bill's last fate.

a speck on his brow

Three intrepid pension-sharers and their chestnut stall were roaring up through the cavern of West North Street, a rusted exhaust amplifying their progress, when Ludwig jammed anchors and Amande whacked into his back and Andy just gawped as usual, as a dirty white van cut clean across, veering at the junction.

The van was on two wheels as it screeched out of East North Street, and hammered off down King Street towards the Bridge of Don.

If the eyes of Ludwig and Co. were not so ancient, they might have spotted a thin arc, an aerosol of red, come spraying up from the van's rear door. Andy caught a speck on his brow, no more, and it felt to him like warmish rain.

Ludwig was never a one to swear, but even if he had, it would have been inaudible above the kicks he gave his stalled engine, as he kicked, and kicked again. They had not gone a furlong more when they hit the roundabout at the top of the Boulevard and again had to wait, to sit and wait, throbbing like crazy this time and heating up.

Leiper Lorry after Leiper Lorry was taking precedence on the roundabout as they nose-to-tailed it and curved away down Commerce Street and off to the harbour. They were all pantechnicons, the kind fitted with onboard chillers; there must have been about twenty of them. Ludwig still did not swear. He put his elbow on the handlebars, his gloved artificial hand bunched and pressed against the side of his forehead, as he looked across at Andy. In former days Andy might have laughed at that classic pose and said *Aye, aye, Ludwig, a good think never hurt a man.*

But Andy was not even aware Ludwig was looking at him. Andy Endrie was staring at the electric night sky, his Adam's crab-apple protruding, his mouth gagged from the speeding air by a wool scarf of Amande's. She had offered him mohair, but, with his strained throat, he sensed fluff as a life-threat.

Andy's thoughts ranged, as always, over the best part of the previous century. There was a best part too. There had been peaks, there was a reasonable plateau, as well as four desperate chasms. The war, the loss of Communism, the early death of his wife, Madge, and the senseless disappearance of a son. He kept trying to think it through, so that chasm might not become abysm. But once he contracted spondylitis, he looked more and more the baboon, howling at the moon, and sometimes felt so.

He wasn't just the Leopard, he was Rookie Marr, and it left an unpleasant taste in his mouth once the rage was gone. It soured the evening. Not that it could be cancelled now. He was a puppet of fate as much as ringmaster, he acknowledged to himself.

GrottoLotto was bigger than him, than any Marr perhaps, potentially bigger than LeopCorp could handle, and to market it fully, once the momentum upped, they might need to bring in Chinese money. They had already liquidised a lot of assets, the food sector and such.

Anyway all that could wait.

His immediate decision was that the Fastness had been contaminated by a traitor and was unsuitable for vantage, at least tonight. He turned to betake himself to the Hole.

Something shook him then, shook the whole room, and made plaster dust tumble like ancient snuff on the wall-leopards' noses –

The cannon had blasted on the battlements, just above his head. Somebody, somebody premature, had given the baroque signal for GrottoLotto to commence—

– Traitors, more traitors!

In a feline rage, he shouted to retainers to freshen the room – he had decided instantly to hold tight in the Fastness – and leapt into his chair. As retainers flew with mop and bucket, and as he spun and spun in his furry chair, all the orange leopard heads, at dado height, merged into one bright blur.

He came to his senses, and put his foot down, so that the chair stopped spinning. He slid the chair on its castors to the slit window, and reached high for his digigun.

He breathed more easily at last.

He breathed on the lenses.

Alert, steadied – in the zone – out of the window he poked his gun.

in mid-whet

Alison had just made it onto Balcony A, beside Guy. She couldn't give tuppence for the whole jing-bang, the way she felt now.

But Guy went up to high doh the moment the cannon went off.

– What the bejesus!

Similar ejaculations filled the air the length, breadth, and depth of the GrottoLotto arena. A hundred TV stations were in mid-ad. Worldwide appetites were in mid-whet for plutonium futures, toilet tissue, direct insurance, funbar cereal. Decisions had to be made on the hoof.

Spilling up North Silver Street, the 189 Pushers had been limbering, bantering. They were no way ready to push when the premature cannon-call came. The maddest scramble now, to get back into Golden Square, to man the balls, to shove for glory.

bhuggi awf!

There was a bit of a scramble too for the three chestnuteers.

They had been allocated a stance on the Plainstanes, just off the Castlegate, in full view of LeopCorp Towers, and the chance for a decent sale was there, though hardly a killing. Folk had many choices these days when it came to stuffing their face, and chestnuts were seen as primitive, a choke-risk if you were busy, and bare of all the fast food comforts of sugar, salt, grease, oil, vinegar and spice.

Ludwig had employed a bottle of meths to get the coals glowing, and the first rows of nuts were set to roast. Amande was arranging the scoop and the bags. Andy could do no more than stand by.

A boy came up and spoke at Amande.

– Het yet, nup—?

– Wait, said Amande.

His pal piled in.

– See's a sample—

– Go away, said Amande.

– The only right nut here, said the first, is that gowk—

He flicked his thumb at Andy Endrie.

– Ughi bhuggiz, said Andy Endrie, not seeing their small faces.

– Is he wi you? said the second one to Amande. The muckle daftie—?

– Bhuggi awf! said Andy.

– Bhuggi awf yirsel, said the lad.

Ludwig brandished the scoop at the brats, and the brats scarpered.

Andy just stood there, with his mouth open. The scarf over his mouth had slipped.

– To move him a little sideways, peut-être, is one idea? said Amande quietly. For better sales?

Ludwig was coaxing his coals. He used tongs, clenched in his artificial hand.

– For the good of all? said Amande.

Ludwig didn't answer. The heat went into his wrist.

– Un petit peu to move him?

– You can put mair chestnuts on now, Amande, said Ludwig.

streetwise

Guy Bord had the job of refereeing and ensuring fair play in Grot-toLotto, now that The Leopard had chosen to sulk in the Fastness. Guy had a team of ballsmen along the course, marshalled by Otto, but final sanction, based on online playback of any underhand incident, was his. If he couldn't guarantee fair play, there might be all sorts of repercussions.

As twenty-one LottoBalls stampeded out of Golden Square it was like lowsing-time at the Tower of Babel, a wild cacophony of slogans, gee-ups, hortation and abuse, in a hundred major tongues and dialects.

GoPlut had a Barbados bobsleigh champ and a Kiribati strong-man shoving for them. A French World Cup defender from Dominique. An anabolic sprinter from Azerbaijan. The New Year's Day winner from that grandpappy of all streetwise ball-shuffling contests, the Orkney Kirkwall Ba. A quarterback from the New York Patriots. A Namibian shotputter. A Mongolian Sumo wrestler, like a LottoBall himself, with stubby limbs. A recent Mr Universe from the Ukraine. GoPlut had clout, they were full of themselves. They were favourites.

Yet, shame of shames for that hard battalion, it was Sushi MacBun who took the lead. Because Sushi MacBun's Pushers had got a chant going, in a funky Esperanto.

Allez Sushi Drive! Allez Sushi Vamos! Allez Sushi Drive! Allez Sushi Zou-Zou!!

Their ball was whirling along. Their Pushees, naked, blurred and anonymous, were even taking the odd hand off to wave up at the indistinguishable guests on the balconies.

Soft on their heels came shoving the balls of Colonel Motors, UCKU, Sexxon, Ciel, Cyklops, GoPlut, and so on.

But *Allez Sushi Zou-Zou!!* was winning the day.

plutonium's representatives on earth

The rolling vanguard of this huge bright scrimmage was approaching Balcony A, with GoPlut trying to mount a sprint, when Guy spotted Lucy in the crowd below him, waving. He got a spare security badge from Otto and threw it down as promised.

Guy spotted something.

Odd clowns here and there had ducked under the police cordon and formed a posse. They were now obstructing GoPlut to the extent of being bowled backwards – hats and orange wigs and sticks flying – bouncing their heads off the pavementette, and being rucked, trodden and squashed. This diversion was concerted, it was confusing, and he didn't know how to intervene.

Guy mopped his brow.

The hefty GoPlut Pushers were screaming abuse, kicking the clowns and flailing their fists. Their massive promised bonus was on the line. More clowns came piling in.

Guy mopped his lips.

There would be hell to pay. For if plutonium's representatives on earth were unable to move one ball less than a mile, they were hardly the answer to an energy crisis.

totally love it

From his higher vantage, The Leopard saw much more of the badness.

The heaving mass of costumes and spheres was careering down the street towards the Hole. Heaving, bouncing, barging, skidding, grappling and interfering, they had spread the full width of the pavementette. The pavementette was itself moving swiftly in the opposite direction, back past the Music Hall, freighted with the mashed and broken, sauced with fluids, garnished with bits of ripped-off mask. The aftermath of failure was not for the global viewer.

Through the telesight on his digigun, the Leopard zoomed in on a single LottoBall. It was Cyklops, Cyklops who made their fortune from DVDs. He saw their Pushees change the rules as they went along. One moment they were braced hand and foot, whirling like gyroscopes. The next, as if by collective signal, they turned inwards, and collapsed into a whirligig of overlapping limbs, balls, boobs, eccentric body parts, really wild hair. This was a breach of the Pushees' contract. Why?

A lance—? A bird, a ten foot bird, had stridden across his view, all pink feathers and very stiff legs, and pierced straight in. Cyklops was skewered!

– Oh, yes! shouted the Leopard. Get in!

He'd heard his barbecue people use this yelp when they managed to slice the tougher fibres.

Before he had time to focus his scope, there were more tall birds, strutting and boarding the pavementette. Yellow feathers, scarlet, blue, white and grey and black. They were going berserk, jerking their beaks high, skewering.

    – Guy! he shouted. Guy, what is this? Do something!

    – I've no idea, said Guy to his lapel.

    – I'm going to shoot!

    – You can't shoot, we're on world TV.

    – Guy, I'll shoot—!

– Great, said Alison, as a second, third and fourth bird plunged home, leaving Pushees squirming behind each other, pierced in their punctured cell.

    – Go down and check it out pronto, said Guy. I'm calling for horses and Tasers. TV will work flat-out to edit—

    – TV will love this, thought Alison as she came off the balcony, totally love it.

    And banged straight into Lucy arriving.

safesburg

Peem was surprised to find, as he reached the top of the Shiprow, knots of police unravelling in four directions, crossing each other. They were jabbering about AllMart, Safesburg, Bestco. Some booze heist was on. Dozens of police went hurrying off to the city fringes to protect the super and the hypermarkets.

    Cheers! thought Peem. He toasted his masked acquaintances of the day before. He imagined shop floors flooding, the expensive fumes rising.

Plenty commotion now as he came full out on the Plainstanes and smelled chestnuts, the same savour that was wafting in Oriente the day before, on their way home.

    Folk were pressing all round him for a better view of the shambles developing. Few had patience to queue for chestnuts.

    There was a tallish guy, he stood behind him.

– Fit the *fuck* ye daein here—?

    – Alison, Alison love, said Lucy. I'm over all that, I've gone beyond.

    – Fit! Ower aa fit? screamed Alison. We havena even startit yet, fuckin mither!

Bing Qing looked across her spring roll and salad table, and felt quite sad.

kamikaze

None of this was according to script, the Leopard knew. So the Leopard decided he would act. Nobody had a better view. If Guy, that pervert, was determined to frustrate him, he would take Guy out; these birds could not be allowed to foul things up.

    – Tricksters, infiltrators, these birds are shits! he screamed. Where are the tanks, when you've paid good money for them?

    Nobody reminded him he paid no tax. The Principal Taster, a taxpayer, kept his head down and left the room, without even asking. He was the last to go.

Even from on high, with the best of scopes, from his slit window, the Leopard could not zero in on Guy's head, because of all the flap around him. He focussed, piece by piece, on the chaos below, without comprehending.

Burst balls, or balls where the flesh was huddled in bloody fear, were becoming impossible to push, so lumpen. A few, far too few, police were deploying, trying to tackle stilted birds round their non-existent knees. Some were successful with their Tasers, and got showered in feathers, and one got skewered too.

    The mounties arrived. The mounties did what they did best, they multiplied the panic. You needed no great insight to realise that a steel-shod stallion and a Montenegran handball player would not be evenly matched.

    The balconies went rogue too. There would be no cobble-throwing, this was no Paris. The street had been torn up months ago, to make way for pavementette. Instead they were lobbing lumps and blobs of complimentary icecream. Hint of Mint and Hint of Mango and Hint of Pistachio were running off the flanks of horses, down sponsors' bibs, smearing the membrane of the balls, and further stickying the bloody bills of attack storks and kamikaze flamingoes.

The fact of panic was bad enough. The result was worse, for The Leopard.

Not a single LottoBall had yet reached its allotted destination. His world was on hold, the world itself on a massive loser. He stopped the pavementette with his remote. He reversed its direction, to give any surviving balls a sporting chance of reaching the Hole. A heaving mass of débris, squashed horseshit and bright detritus began to move forward, into the world's view.

A hundred yards away or less, the Leopard saw a face laugh up at him, laugh directly at him, throwing his head back to give one big guffaw. That man had a half-mask on earlier, a scarf, he'd noted that, but the mask had slipped.

A sneering ringleader if ever he saw one.

Rookie Marr swung and drew a bead with the SAD 3 on the ring-leader, the forehead. He steadied, and let rip.

coincidence, by fuck

– Total cunt, said Alison. Ye kent aa alang ye were ma mither.

– What! What? What you on?

– Aa these years, aa these years. Fit did ye dae, sell me aff, or rent me oot? Yir ain dochter, ye absolute cunt!

– What! said Lucy. Where you getting all this?

– Oh, there's sicna thing as DNA. There's sicna thing as A&E, div ye nae mind? Yir bleed, ma bleed – the same bloody bleed! They askit if I kent aboot a *coincidence*. *Come and see what we found*, they said. *Coincidence*, by fuck! Div ye nae mind, mither—?

Lucy was groping for a chair when Bing Qing slid one in below her.

nicht mehr

– I'm saying it, listen, listen, écoutes! said Amande. He is— Help him, he's Andy.

Peem sank to his haunches and began panting. The body had struck across him as it fell; the blood was on him.

– What, what—?

He could hardly hear himself speak for all the commotion in the street.

– Shut up, everybody! he screamed. Just shurrup! What did you say?

– I know you, Peem, said Amande. Oh, so awful. Terrible, terrible.

It was the accents, still strong, that brought him to his senses.

– It is your own father, loon, said Ludwig. Oh, loon, it is Andy there.

– Da, said Peem, as hoarse as anything.

– Speak to him, said Amande. He's listening for you.

Peem knelt to whisper in his father's lug.

– Na, na, Da, na – Da, ye canna go, I luve ye. Dad—

– He can nicht mehr, said Ludwig.

He couldna see for the weet in his een for lang eneuch.

When he saa, he saa there was a sma, sma merk, aboot the bigness o an auld farthin, drillit in ees faither's broo. The aft side o his heid wis smush.

– Has naebuddy gotten a tissue, naeboddy gotten a tissue handy? he said, tendin.

It wasna a tissue they brocht in the end. He liftit and laid his faither's heid on a foldit coat that somebody brung and offert.

Hunkered doon, he strokit his faither's chowk till it lossit the warmth that had aye been there, an startit tae grow cauld.

Bye an bye he spread anither gift o a jeckit ower the strange, estranged, auld familiar face.

Bye an bye he stude up.

An there wis Amande staundin aside him, weel on in years, a bonny time tae be meetin her. She needit every last tissue tae hersel. Trusty auld Ludwig wis in aboot as weel, wi a gey shak o ees heid. His ayebidin, communistic heid. Nae folk tae greet that muckle, Ludwig and Amande, in the usual wey o things. But greetin noo.

An here wis an angert young chiel he didna ken, ees finger poke-pokin at North Turret, ettlin tae tell him somethin—
– Fae up abeen cam the shot. I saa the glint. It cam fae up there.

sweat, blood, and free ice-cream

Rookie Marr guessed the line of the shot would be traced and there might be a question or two, so, hoping to publicly shepherd a few surviving GrottoLotto balls into the Hole or Grotto, he made his way down.

The Leopard left the building, not by the front door, but through the bowels. Having passed, smoother than peristalsis, down the stainless steel oesophagus of his private lift, he was handed in by a guard to a silver capsule, and slung through a new-tiled tunnel on monorail.

Dismounting the Leopmobile, Rookie Marr took three steps and attained his underground throne. Luna he left behind in her plasma zone.

He beckoned for the cup of *Bon Accord* he had been gifted. He would have the best view possible of the giant balls, as they dropped like fate into the crevasse and funnelled into their final placings.

The first three now struggled to the lip, and toppled in short order, jolting and juddering their cargo, the beautiful, bruised Pushees. It was Tosh, Ciel and UCKU, smeared and asymmetric. They had to snip with giant snips from lid-hole to lid-hole to free the Pushees lumped within.

Three balls only.

Every ball else had slid backwards and forwards to no effect – going nowhere on a pavementette slick with sweat, blood, and free ice-cream.

The Leopard waited. No more balls hove into view. So it looked like no gold bonanza from GrottoLotto for a global winner anywhere tonight. Just a trickledown of tinsel in prospect now.

Then the Leopard heard and felt the beginnings of a rumble, not just a rumble, something seismic—
He looked up from the Hole, and, from the comfort of his trap, stared up towards the surface for what might soon befall. He could see one building, a bank, with four vibrating pillars. He feared them. He saw a blue-cloaked statue, high on the shuddering architrave of the same building. He thought it was Britannia, a horn of victory under her arm. In one corner of his stunned eye, service staff and Pushees were fleeing up a stair.

It wasn't Britannia, it was Ceres. She clasped no horn of imperial victory, but a tipping, low-slung, cornucopia. From Rookie's angle he couldn't see the round-cheeked apples, stopped by art in mid-roll, and the other bulges of spilling goodness.
The rumble gripped the city deeper, and shook him in his crevasse.

up justice street

From quite another angle or airt, from deeper-down, from the new oil harbour, rolling not on spheres but on wheels, had begun to throb a score of dark pantechnicons. They had no carnivalia nor masks, neither costumed driver nor painted number. Even where *Leiper Lorries* would normally be illumined, above the cab, they were, for tonight, specially dark. No-one could tell whether they were the lorries from hell or had any sponsors.

Bumper-to-bumper, on double axles, trailing lines of fluid as they climbed, on came the twelve-wheelers. Along Market Street, Virginia

Street, the continuation of Commerce Street, then sharp first left up Justice Street, Leiper's lorries came. There were barriers, cullises, all along the route. The lorries broke through them like lollipop sticks. At Virginia Street, the road patrol radioed Command in North Turret, but only a strange girl answered. At Commerce Street a team of police tried to deploy a Viper, an arthritic, steel, cross-road snake, mediaeval with spikes. It was soon as flat as a strip of tin.

On the wide roundabout, saucer-eyed guards looked up at the darkened, remorseless cabs, and wisely forgot to draw their pistols.

off, blundering

Peem hugged Amande and Ludwig both, a good long hug, and was off, blundering.

He was spraying *sorry, sorry,* and *I'm affa sorry* as people parted in front of him, they must know what he was about, he was taking on their burden at last, they need not doubt it. He would get whoever or whatever was in North Turret, if he did nothing else.

There was heavy revving, arriving, leaving, all round him. Smells assaulted his nose, slitherings assailed his shins.

For centuries there been fish-hawkers there in the Castlegate, each ekeing a living from a wicker creel on a bent, unmendable back.

Now it had come to this. A pure mass of fish was piling around Rookie's crevasse – unstable, toppling, and sliding in. A score and more of lorries were opening their doors remotely, and pulling away in low gear, to let the herring outspew. Spermy had vowed, since he got the news, *Tae gie The Leopard his due. I'll bury that bastard.* Cascades of carcases, a heavy chute, a great rasp of scales, came silvering out of each Leiper lorry and into the Leopardeen night.

you have no others

He was in an agility of fish. The first downsweep carried him into a hall already combed with waves of buckling, bucking, bright, mortified herring. As he felt his wellies slotting full, he flicked and kicked them off. Just as the second wellington loosened, another massive wave of dead fish poured in.

Whummled, bouleversé, nigh-on kaput, he tried to swim upwards, with the spading hands and frogging legs of consummate panic.

He gasped up clear. He was six feet away from two beady eyes. There was nothing liquid in a beady eye, nothing to melt, or be receptive. The two beads made a triangle inverted on the business end of a small black pistol. Much of the rest of Rookie Marr was concealed. Because, pinned against the back of his throne, he was up to his neck.

Maybe it was the intonation, probably just the words—

– Save me, said Rookie Marr, or I'll shoot.

Peem stared back at him, offering nothing, perfecting the while the steadiness of his breast-stroke.

– So that's what you killed him with?

– No.

– The man you shot was my father.

– Been here, said Marr. Down here. All the time.

– Who was up in the Turret, then?

– Nobody. The others.

Peem put in a couple of amphibious leg thrusts. Now he was three feet away.

– You, he said. You have no *others*. If truth be told, you've none of those.

Dead herring rippled past, just under Rookie's lower lip.

– A million, he said, I'll give you a million.

– Two, said Peem.

– Two, said Marr.

– A hundred, said Peem. A hundred million.

– I'll give you a hundred, said Marr.

– Million, said Peem.

– Million, said Marr.

– How does dirt like you get so much money?

– I work for every penny.

– Show me your hands.

– Not falling for that, said Marr, brandishing his pistol like a fevered boy shrinking under the covers.

– You did enough work for a hundred million?

– Everything I made I invested. My father taught me to invest solidly.

– And here's useless old me going round begging. For change.

He swept a mini-tsunami of herring across Marr's face.

– You're not useless, said Marr. If you get me out.

– I'll get the *others* to help you.

– There's no time.

– Time? said Peem. Try buying some. Tell me why you shot my father.

He put his red palm in front of Marr's face, resting his gory cuff on the oscillating herring. Like *Gun v. Hand* suddenly.

– He was the ringleader, said Rookie Marr. That's what it was.

– Of course, said Peem. My Dad. Total ringleader. That's why we never got on. Andy Endrie, king of the ringleaders. And do you know why? He had more guts and more integrity in his pinkie finger than you have in your whole thieving arse.

– There's no dime for this, said Rookie Marr, his chin was hampered. Nod now.

– Not now, said Peem. Not ever.

– Fibe hundred, said Marr.

– Round it, said Peem.

– Am billion, said the man with a droopy herring for a moustache.

– Speak up, said Peem. I didn't quite get that.

Rookie Marr's eyes were rolling, beseeching.

– Mpillion, said the man with scything fins making his eyeballs water.

– Louder! said Peem.

– Umbillion! said Herring Man. It was finally all too much for him; the fish closed over his head and he disappeared. Only his hand on the pistol visible now.

Rookie made two mistakes.

One: he pulled the trigger.
　　Two: he fired till the mag was empty, but missed.

It would have been easy for Peem then, bearing in mind so much offence.

Cold as charity, beyond easy, he reached down with his bloody right hand.
　　He grabbed the creature by the orange tie, and shouted up at spectators crowding the lip.
　　One of them jumped down beside him.

– Grab his tie, said Peem. I canna haud him.
　　– Naebuddy tells me tae grab things, said the newcomer.
　　He recognised the voice: coarse, peremptory.
　　– Christ, Spermy, said Peem. Trust you tae be mixed-up in this. It's me, Peem. Tak his gun.
　　– Whaur in hell did you spring fae? said Spermy. We put ye in an ambulance at Kinlochbervie and that was the last we heard. That was a while ago, if truth be tellt. Ye're supposed tae be deid.
　　– Thanks, said Peem.
　　– It was too wild for the chopper that nicht, said Spermy.
　　– So an ambulance, was it?
　　– We heard it cam aff the road at Garve on the ice an hit a tree. When the rescue found it, the medics were baith snuffed-it, an the patient had done a runner.
　　A runner, thought Peem.
　　– There was still heavy snaa faain like, they couldna follow yir tracks. They reckoned eftir a while ye must be a goner. I've wondert whiles far yir banes were lyin.
　　– Oh, sure. Thanks!
　　– Ach, it was me that savit yir life, ye scunner, said Spermy. It was me that cam on deck, an rammit thon Triplex in reverse.
　　– Was it? Why did ye come back?
　　– I kent ye'd mak a fuck-up o it.

– That maks sense. I've often wondered where ma strength cam from.

– Strength? said Spermy. Ye were never namely for that. Dump that guy.

– Grab his tie.

– Dump him, I tell ye. He isna worth the shite on yir shoe.

– He says he's worth infinitely mair than that.

– Weel, haul the bugger up then—

may 2

dropdown lifestyle solutions

After what Alison said, she was coming apart. The sun was just coming up when she drove to the dump. A herring gull whanged on her roof, so hard it bellied it. The gull's bulk, making an inwards belly in the roof. That was all she needed.

It wasn't a 4x4, it was only a Morris Traveller.

Lucy nosed out on a ramp of cinders. The front wheels crunched and the rear recrunched, bringing her near the edge.

There was ash, smoke, void, there was allsorts.

She yarked the hand-brake so that she slewed, and the gull came walloping down her screen like a cudgelled angel.

After what Alison said, she was coming apart.

She remembered Dante. As you do at a pit, as you do round a smoking rim.

Go Plut, Cyklops, Tosh,
KUM, Sushi MacBun,
Ciel, Shiv, OediBus,
Colonel Motors, Sexxon.
All the dropdown lifestyle solutions, of mythic power.
Plus, Shall, UCKU,
Next Butt One.
Most of the masks had already done so.
Hers too—

Dropped.

Down.

Close by, a lorry was tipping box upon cardboard box of tashed bibs and torn leotards.

At the far side, another upended loads of soft, burst, giant spheres and smashed up backdrops. Spears of acrylic broke away, and flashed in the air, as the load went rattling down the deep quarry.

What did he say? *Who knew wealth had undone so many?*

Deepest Manmade Hole in Europe. Now the old Rubislaw quarry was being filled in. Reverberating, issuing ash.

The gull, prising an edible clot from Go Plut, flapped, off.

Lucy hung on, thinking of Alison.

There was no getting away from it. She had lost her own and only daughter.

Loser.

A new lorry arrived and parped at her, twice.

She jumped at that.

She depressed the clutch with her left foot, and slotted the stick of the Traveller in reverse.

She remembered what she'd said to her man. *If the worst comes to the worst, she'd said, forget GrottoLotto, forget Spectacle. Make your way to the beach.*

lovely and bright

Half of the Shack was a clearing station for the walking and hirpling wounded. Half was a café still. The astringency of Dettol fought for the air with the scent of hot sweet tea.

– Hi, he said. How's you?

– No time for that. Lend a hand, said Iris.

Peem poured tea and refilled mugs from a large black kettle.

There was a thistledown of dried scales fluttering from him still, but nobody noticed, or if they did, nobody said. The immediate wake of a revolution is rarely a fashion parade. He had to use an old stained spoon to bail a smelly herring scale out of somebody's tea.

The guy with the tea, Alfie, a docker, was sitting with his leg across a plastic-cushioned chair, waiting for attention. He was the worse of a horse kick to the shin. Though the mounties had been withdrawn not long after they arrived. By order of Lord Provost William Swink II, when he'd seen the almighty muck-up Rookie Marr had made.

A leopard in a pit should quit from clawing, Swink had apparently said to the blue doorman at the Town House, just as he was leaving.

Swink himself was being airlifted to his *peed-a-terre,* his Mountain Heart HQ at the summit of Braeriach. *To see how things pan out, you ken. I shouldn't be watching shenanigans like this from too close up. In case I have an apocalyptic fit.*

A fit? said the doorman.

And I'll give you a tip, Swink had continued. *If I was you, I'd get out too. More tanks are coming, and we folks in the toon have but small power over the likes of them.*

– Oh, and anither thing I heard, said Alfie, the docker. Aboot thon wife Julie, Julie ye ken. Weel she wis the ane that radioed Spermy wi news o their twa boats bein selled oot. I never heard him so livid, said Julie, and she's nae doot seen her share o Spermy's ragins ower the years. Spermy's got a haud o the Leopard.

– I ken, said Peem.

– An he's threatenin tae maroon him oot on Rockall. *On Rockall wi fuck-all,* was the words Spermy said.

– Marooned? Wi fuck-all? Marr, he'll never be that.

– Why nae? said Alfie, I dinna get ye.

– I daresay he's got offshore investments, said Peem.

Julie, eh—?

He heard the clack of the fish-room boards, the old fleshly percussion. He was back in the old now of Eriboll, the now of the Shack. He felt the spirit of Mina prevailing, the way she tended bits of black pudding.

– Peem, get a move on with that tea! Iris shouted.

As he went round with the dribbling spout, some of them were giving a groan, but most were glued to TV. Somebody must have put some life in Echo TV, or taken them over, because they had a presenter out in the street already.

She was some woman; resolute, straight down the line, revelling in it.

She had on an orange blouse, smart, like a livery. She unbuttoned the blouse deftly, and took it off. She had a slip on, she was only a slip herself. She held the blouse high to the crowd and lit the tail with somebody's lighter. The blouse went up in a harsh frazzle and she dropped it, like a piece of flaming shit, into the gutter.

That was an image that would endure.

– For Bill, she said, straight to lens. She grabbed somebody's jacket, and moved determinedly on.

– C'mon, Luna, she could be heard adding. Time to get a grip.

A woman in a silver dress was carrying a mike in and out of shot, unsteadily on a boom.

– Wait for me, Gwen.

Doing interviews and pieces to camera, Gwen opened up aspects most folk never knew.

It wasn't just the folks he knew then. In the old days outside Swink's villa, it had seemed for a moment it might be only him. And then, swifter than swift, as he was swept into bed and off to sea, not even him.

But now there was a whole movement, a movement of movements had come in, to divert and disrupt GrottoLotto. It was like the best of the G8, really. No strict leader, so none had bossed. The young got tuned, their mobiles pealing, like small bells in a siege. They could see what needed doing, and *up and off and did it*, that was the story.

You could only gradually piece it together, from the interviews by the woman; Gwen she was called. But it was clear the stilted Ballbusters, the clown birds, were only part of it. Though they were the initial shock-troops, the natural world guising in and taking the nonsense on. Feathers everywhere, concealing their sharper purpose. The Boozebusters had played a key role too, rubbishing the supermarkets and luring police away.

The Poles had been great. Poles in unassuming clothes had evicted balcony parties right along the street, using the night's confusion to set up possible squats.

On Balcony A in the morning, Bing Qing had fed them won ton soup, packed with pork, shrimp, water chestnuts and ginger. One of the Poles told Gwen they now proposed inviting Bing Qing and her kitchen workers to a reciprocal feast, dzik z Zubrowka, whole roast boar with fragrant bison grass vodka. Now that they'd liberated some fancy malls.

Over the street, one bright bunch had hijacked a mobile crane. They had prised William Wallace from his plinth tucked well away from UberStreet, along by His Majesty's Theatre.

A second yellow crane was uplifting ponderous Edward VII from his domain on UberStreet. *That fat clort* as the poet Alistair Mackie once called him. They were crawling him down to the seaside at dead low tide. Out in the shallows, given a season's weed, the stone king could become a haven for blennies, a Red Green spokesman was saying. A lee for idle eels, he enthused, a living Eddy! A far, far nobler thing than being doodled on by doos for centuries, and shat upon by pigeons.

Everything Gwen – and Luna – picked up on seemed vital, funny, outrageous, vibrant. As somebody said, *I aye thocht the toon could dae wi a makower. But I nivver thocht it wid be like this!*

Back they switched to the first group, teetering with Wallace stropped on the end of a cable, along Union Terrace. Revellers were dancing close, reining themselves in to suit the swing of the crane by complex convolutions of their conga. Wallace was going where King Edward had been, the ample gap-site.

The crane stopped. Wallace's mailed left arm gradually reduced its arc and was indicating. Even after seven centuries, even after they had killed his body, he still had command of his reason. The camera followed the line of his expressive cupped palm, upthrust above the battlefield of UberStreet. What were the young doing, hanging out of windows on opposite sides of the street? Pulling on a long rope to raise their white banner. Every letter a different colour, the paint still running, lovely and bright—

Republican Road.

you are me

There were plenty more sights.

Outside the Town House, the bulk of a khaki camouflage tank had vanished, with only the barrel of its cannon jutting vertically, as though the commander had ODed on erection enhancer. The Highland Light Desert's shells must have clattered into the granite, as they sought to intimidate Maciek's guerillas. But when the dust of chips, mica and depleted uranium wafted and fell clear, it was revealed how laughable the effect. The tank's successive, concussive recoils had made good inroads, punching through its naïve stance on Guy Bord's pavementette. The top layer had dented, weakened, and ripped: the tank's arse must be resting on the return strip below.

Pawel spoke to camera, We drive them out. We drive them into Kanal.

From the Town House clocktower, a red and white flag jutted and flew.

Iris's husband, Tam, was being interviewed now. No, it's great, he said. You look at statues half your life, they sink into your soul. But really, man, if you can't stand them, move them on! said Tam.

Tam had white hair, as near as dammit, swept back, quiffed, luxuriant. And Tam expressed it perfectly. Those who were hurt, those who were shot by Marr's forces, we salute. All we are saying is give peace a chance.

– Are you technical? said Gwen.

– Sure, said Tam.

– This feed will go, said Gwen. They'll cut us off. Get us up and streaming on Internet. Get who you need. Do what it takes.

– Right, said Tam. Do ma best.

– Hold this, she said to Luna.

Luna put down her boom and held up a web address on card to the camera.

– Iris, babe, gotta go, Peem said. It's early days.

She was slitting bap after bap open, for bacon rolls.

– I admire you, Iris. I'm glad that you and Tam—

– We never had family, though, said Iris, you know that. That was our sadness. That's why I kept on at the teaching so long. And various actions, of course. Now this. Did you ever track yours?

– Track—? he said. He was thinking of tanks. Everybody knew the rest of the tanks lay out beyond, barracked at Bridge of Don.

– Your family—?

– Mislaid them, quite a bit, he said, and knew the tears would well.

He planted a kiss on her floury cheek.

– Must dash, Iris. Ciao. Keep fighting.

– See you, Peem.

He left the Shack and there at the dockside was the *Girl Julie* loading up. A pinioned figure with a bag over his head was being hurried on. He saw a chopper swoop low over the harbour and guessed they didn't have long.

He walked up Marischal Street to the Mercat Cross. A mountain of free fish was being mined in buckets by a tatterdemalion army of young revolutionaries, casual minkers, Omega-3 addicts and sledz-loving Slavs.

One wag had clambered up on top of the ancient execution site, and then shinned up the long pedestal, using the embossed thistles and entwined roses as footholds and handholds. From his back pocket he whipped out a big herring to feed to the unicorn.

Its whorled horn was painted gold, chipped at the tip. The unicorn flared its nostrils at the smell of the fish, as the wag swung from the shortened horn using one hand, wailing and singing out,

You are Me and I am You,
I am the Walrus,
I am the Eggman,
Goo Goo Ga Joob—

A group soon came together under the dirty old Mercat Cross and joined right in, and ran to get guitars from wherever guitars could be got, or grabbed hold of a bin, or a bucket, or baton and lid. Or a pair of tongs from a chestnut stand, anything they could clash together and beat the time with.

You are Me. He was glad they were happy. But it wasn't his mood.

a second comer

He didn't remember the best way to the beach. Remembering the best way never came easy, to his benighted, that was the word, to his *benighted* skull. And things were changing faster now.

He was on Constitution Street. Or was it the Boulevard? Peem minded the cold morning in '57, '58 or so the trams had rattled here, their death-rattle as it turned out. Rejected, scrapped, they sat in their serried lines and crackled and burned.

Sometimes he had the feeling, not of having lived long, though that was much, but of having lived through several civilisations. Some more civil than others, just a touch.

The Links were blocked high on either side by the HyperMall and Jumbo Arcade, the UberEye and the RollerCoaster. There was a thinnish strip between, a token alley. It acted like a green arrow, pointing at the Prom, behind which low sands and a restless North Sea moved.

In the green, at the end of Arcadia, a white skeletal shape stuck up. Somebody was before him. And he, like a second comer, needed to get his heart in gear.

Not a whole tree, by any means, though big enough.

No leaves.

No twigs.

No bark.

A single trunk, and two white boughs branching out.

It was rammed in the ground, in concrete.

He reached up, and touched the bough that wasn't empty.

– Have you been here long? he said.

– No, said Lucy. I just arrived.

– Good, he said. I wouldn't want to have kept you waiting.

He looked seaward, but couldn't see the sea.

– Come on up, she said. I've something to tell you. You'll need to be sitting down.

He climbed into the empty bough.

– I've something to tell you, said Lucy.

– Tell me, he said.

– Did you ever meet Alison? said Lucy.

It was quiet at the beach, for the merest moment. The rides weren't working yet.

– Your colleague was it, said Peem, I think. No, I didn't meet her.

– You did, said Lucy, but neither of you spoke. Do you know how old she is, she's forty past.

– Tell me what you have to tell, said Peem. I'm too old for this. I know this tone. Is it, when Alison was first thought of—

– That's just it, said Lucy, she wasn't thought of at all.

I came back from Paris early. I had Alison for six hours. Theo arranged to have her adopted. As for the father, he'd fucked off—

– When he was told to.

– And never appeared again, or wrote, or phoned.

– You said you were on the Pill.

– I said I was *starting*. I hadn't actually taken the first one.

– What an unholy, fucking mess.

– Puts Spectacle in the shade, said Lucy.

– Alison is revving about the place in a stretch Hummer, with bull bars, Lucy continued. God knows where she's stolen it from. I only just got away, through the kindness of trees.

– I've just saved Rookie Marr from choking, he said. Last night.

– Unbelievable, said Lucy. That's unbelievable. The Sixties were quiet compared to this.

– Yeah, I grant you. *Icarus '68*, eh? What was that all about? Like I saw the sun for about ten minutes, and flew sideways as much as up.

– This is a stick I planted earlier, said Lucy. I put it here in honour of Theo. Remember his *Sisyphus,* out in the garden in the snow?

– No, Peem said. I just remember you.

– This stick is into something, said Lucy. Do you know what I found out?

– No, tell me.

– There was another Lucy. And she's under here.

– Too much, he said.

– She'll not be in good shape, said Lucy. It was 360 years ago she arrived. It's not clear in the city record whether she was a Lucy or a Lucky. She worked in an inn, serving ale and oysters. That class of women was nicknamed Lucky. From *Luckenbooth* perhaps. Anyway there was a lot of shit about religion—

– There often is—

– And King Charles wanted one Prayer Book, and the Presbyterians another. Next minute Montrose was riding across the Bridge of Dee to quell somebody, whichever side he was on that day, and a musket got let off, something pre-emptive, or warning, or accidental, and John Forbes stopped the ball.

– You don't have a clue what you do to me, said Peem. And I don't think you ever did.

– Anyway, said Lucy, Lucy had followed him to the Bridge of Dee, and, being pregnant, of course she was demented. John died, with that ball in his head, and she went away and hid, she brought the baby up. She said in public she was fostering, else she'd have been stuck on the stool of repentance for a year, and shelling out a fine.

Five years later, Montrose was in town again, with a troop of Irish dragoons. Montrose was handsome, and a poet, and somebody who would die bravely on a gallows and be distributed on spikes. But he didn't take a line on rape.

Lucy was forced up the narrowness of Adelphi by three or four of them. *Lucky* for her it was that time of the month. They slapped her about and jeered and left her.

Three years further on, and what came visiting? Something smaller than a dragoon, less vainglorious than a leader.

– It seems to be the small things get you, said Peem.

– Plague, said Lucy. Plague ripped the heart out of the people. The rich couldn't get out to their country seats fast enough. They left their servants of course, to prevent looting.

The dear old Council almost stopped meeting. They met only once, in the fresh air of Gallowgate, to agree to issue relevant contracts.

Item: to supply timbers and nails, for the supply of huts for victims of the poorer class.
Item: to supply guards, that none of the poorer class, being with plague taken, may travel back to their homes.
Item: to hire nurses, wherever they may be sought, to be paid a suitable bounty on their survival.
Item: to cut 55,000 turves.
Item: to cart said 55,000 turves to the Links of Aberdeen.
Item: to lay said 55,000 turves on the graves of the dead, who shall be buried at the speediest instance, one with another.

My father's funeral I have to arrange, Peem thought. Together with Ludwig and Amande. Will my tribe of Annie, Hughie, Tammie come back out of the shadows? Not that Lucy ever met them: she read about them, is all.

– Lucy volunteered, said Lucy. Often the nurses would come from a previous haunt of the plague, like Edinburgh. Well if they'd survived, they rode their luck. A paradoxical life. They were shunned and wanted. They performed great mercies. People were glad to see the back of them.

   – Did Lucy survive? he said.

   – Lucy had no immunity. She welcomed in the blackened, swollen, screaming folk, the young, the old, the nursing mothers. She bathed them, held them, given the chance she changed their rags. Tended whom she could tend. She listened to them in the sweat of night, it was all night for them, these huts were built to a budget, they had no windows. I'm sure she tried to console them.

   – What do you think she whispered to them? About heaven?

   – About heaven for some that were furthest gone, maybe. About real things. *Will I really die?* is always on everybody's lips. What can you do but describe a flower by a stream, in the nook of a burn, under a bank, a clump of primrose. Perhaps they remember it. Perhaps they never looked at it. They remember it now. And then one day, she placed her hand inside her petticoat and felt the lumps in her groin.

   – But there is no gravestone for Lucy?

   – None for the 1,400 who died and were ditched here. Written out of history, or never written in, we can only piece one or two together. If I ever did Spectacle again, it would be the story, not of the garish, unjustly famous, but of the unknown.

– Worthy, Peem said. That is worthy.

   – Folk want to know they are connected, said Lucy.

   – Alison does.

   – No, Alison feels betrayed. She brought up Gwen on her own. Alison barely knows Gwen's dad; it was drunken groping at her stepfather's funeral.

There was another silence.

– She had to work right after the baby. So she got a job, and eventually landed up working with her own absentee mother, or Gwen's unavailable granny, take your pick. All unbeknownst. We went out from time to time, a gin from her mother odd Friday nights, that's all a daughter needs. She didn't even know I gave her away till the other day. If Alison wants to kill me, she kills me. If she wants to take us both out, that's what she'll do.

– So we sit up a dead white tree, planted in a charnel house, and wait for our much wronged daughter to come and kill us? said Peem.

– That or the rising sea.

– The fucking sea, he said. Who cares about the fucking sea? Let's go and meet her.

– Wait, she said. Give me time.

– You were there for me, he said, all those years ago. Lucy?

– Your name is Peem, said Lucy. We made love once, a long time ago, and it was very wild, and very beautiful. I was cheeky to you, that was the fashion then. I told you to go away, not quite fuck off, learn to *exist*. I was afraid of commitment, I suppose. It was in my bones.

– It comes full circle, he said. 360 years.

– You slept, you were tired after making love. And you had been running half the night. And you had some problem I didn't take in, about saving the city.

– I was always about to save the city.

– Lots of people are, said Lucy. Anyway, you slept, and I got fresh clothes for you.

He looked across and imagined her nakedness, white on white, against the desperate tree.

– What? she said.

– I was going to say something. But—

– It's not too late, she said. It's never too late. But you don't have to.

– I think that's what I want on my epitaph.

– What?

– *I was going to say something.*

245

She was sinking into herself.

– Have to get up the road, before the tanks— said Peem.

– I'll stay here. My people need me.

– Underneath? he said.

– Underneath everything. Kiss me before you go.

the full story

He headed back up the town, keeping to the wall, ready to dive into any alley.

So he'd held back the full story, at least for now, and perhaps that was best. The years after the fishing, long after he recovered from the bout with the Triplex, the years as a teacher in schools round the country, teaching the distinction between the colon and the semi-colon, attempting to inculcate in the young selected glimpses from the history of doubleness in the Scottish novel. Taking them up hills to recite poems, out to islands to chart the whirlpools in their veins. And away to the theatre, the Citizens, the Traverse, until that fateful night when he allowed himself to get distracted, by an unwise whisky, by jollity behind, and him driving the yellow minibus.

When he came out of his second cracked skull coma, there was no welcome left for him in teaching, not with two kids dead on the Forth Brig slip road. He wasn't breathalysed, he was admonished, he went on supply lists round the country, but whatever teacher shortage might be looming, work for him just shrivelled away. And as it did, so did his sense of purpose and connection. He went wandering then.

He hadn't been home for many's a year, after that second bust-up with his Dad, about *irresponsibility*. Tam was about his only pal, and Iris of course. They gave him a cubby-hole in their house to type in, when he passed through, and Tam looked after his drafts. Iris didn't read them.

The NHS had filed Tam's transcript years ago, and wouldn't release it. Only occasionally did Tam offer comment on the success or otherwise of Peem's reimaginings of the balder facts. Peem's memory came, Peem's memory went, in strange waves. Horizontigo, yes. He feared his past. He wished it away. He sought to recover what was lost.

Writing was mainly therapy, Tam knew that.

As he walked back up the Boulevard, he was composing the core of two speeches. The one he would make at his father's funeral, if he survived, and if Andy's body hadn't got lost in the struggle by then, or abstracted to cover things up by government forces. He wondered if he would meet Annie and them there, and what he could possibly say.

Also what on earth he could say to Alison when he met her, if he met her. It was all so raw, it was war-zone stuff. *Hello – you've never met me – I'm your father – your mother's in deep shock – and your Grandad's just been shot – how are you?*

He wondered what she would look like, Alison, when she was pointed out to him. Decently-built like Lucy, or scrawnier like him? He wondered what she would speak like, too. What would she have inherited of her late Grandad's accents: the emphases with which he had praised, loved, exploded; his subversive laugh?

How are you, love?

no lass in her senses

Was this it, then? thought Lucy.

Would a wee lassie approach behind her, and leave a dead hen and a jug of milk at the base of the tree, then scurry wordless away?

Would a bigger one wander up, dressed in skins, and begin haggering the ground around the tree, with an ineffectual wooden spade?

Would no lass in her senses ever come near her?

kidnapped by time

Alison took her father's arm, it was a brilliant feeling. Peem had asked around and eventually plucked his startled daughter from the massive dance, which had taken over the street. The initial shock, the standing-back, the drinking-in, the blind hug, then, facing each other, running with tears, took longer than you could ever imagine. Then the questions started.

– Sae did ye miss me aa these years? she said.

  – I didna ken you existed. But I missed you, sure I missed you. I've been pretty much on my own for a good while now.

  – Ye didna need tae be.

  – I can cope with aloneness, he said. Sometimes ye get to really like it. Other times no.

  – Bein alane stinks, said Alison, sae dinna ging aff again, okay?

  – I didna go off, said Peem. I was sort o kidnapped. Kidnapped by man and accidents, kidnapped by time. But I'm gettin a grip noo.

  – Gettin a grip soonds good tae me.

  – What is it ye mainly want to do?

  – Get oot o the soss an sotter, Dad, said Alison. I've had it up tae here, ma life's a mess. Far did ye say ma mither wis?

a disgrace tae the deid

Lucy got tired of running history through her brain.

She heard footsteps behind her on the grass.

  There were two sets.

– Come doon oot o that this instant, mither, ye're a disgrace tae the deid!

  Alison's face was red and sweaty, her hair was all over the place.

  – Alison, Alison— she said. I was scared to look round in case it was you. In case it wasn't you, sorry. Oh, god, I'm sorry, Alison, so so sorry. You look so – stressed. Is the revolution over, it all seemed to slip away?

  – Na, said Alison, the revolution's fine. Is yir bum nae numb, sat up that tree? Ye're perchit there like a cross atween a craw an a refugee.

what lenin would have said

– Jist noo there's an amount o dancin that wid fear ye, said Alison, as the three of them made their way up town, hardly touching the big topics, walking side-by-side. There's a Strip the Willow aboot a mile lang, said Alison, atween the Mercat Cross an Holburn Junction. They're roon an roon like a hairy worm, dancin fester an fester tae keep the tanks oot.

Peem and Lucy looked at each other over their daughter's head, and smiled.

– I dinna think tanks dare go near that pavementette, said Alison. There's student blockades at aa weys in, every shity wee lane ye could think o. Hey, fit ye twa sae laughy at?

– A revolution in one street? said Lucy. I don't know what Lenin would have said— ?

– Hae tae start some place, Lenin wid hae said, said Alison. Plus Gwen's got her camera goin. They've cut aff her TV link, but she's streamin the scene on the Internet, tae keep them honest.

– Ye crack me up, said Peem, ye really do. *Every shity wee lane.*

welded

They got up Justice Street and into the Castlegate. Dancers stretched ahead of them, it must be a good few thousand, with all manner of styles and steps and shouts and colours. There didn't seem to be an ounce of misery, no doubt hard to feel miserable when you're so close and patterned with everybody, touching in turn, skirling and birling and moving real fast. Glistening away they were, glowing with something deeply needed, absolved from individualism at last, verging on happy you even might say.

– This maks it aa worthwhile, for me, said Alison. Kinda brings it aa hame.

Her father and mother put their arms round her waist, and the three pulled closer together so they could watch for a moment in content and peace. They could hardly spot a soul they knew, but what did it matter?

– Richt! Ready tae dive in? said Alison.

– I'll gie it a shot, said Peem.

– C'mon, then, said Alison. Quick, afore the music finishes. Ye dance wi Mither, and I'll grab that muckle leerup, tryin tae tuck himsel ahint a pillar like a spare prick at a countra weddin.

She went up to the bloke with the coat collar tugged high.

– Are you gey bored? she said.

He nodded.

– C'mon then, chum.

Dive indeed it had to be, into the long river of folk, which came, as though flowing over old worn stones, swirling towards them, each couple, after miles of dancing, shaking with riffs of surrendered laughter. It was a wonder they weren't pulling bodies out, considering some of the ages. But, as long as music belted from the speakers, they all kept going.

Lucy and Peem, then Alison and Guy, joined at the bottom of the stilled pavementette, just by the Hole, and eddied their way up the lines, as the dance composed and recomposed itself. Pair after pair came birling down, proffering a hand, hooking an arm, pivoting once and surging on, with abiding sense of difference melded, and delicate sense of each other welded.

Peem hardly recognised anyone; he swung on the arms of unknown women from his native city. He did see Charlie pass on the other side, and shouted to him, something daft like *Up the flamingoes!* but it didn't matter, Charlie didn't hear; words were nothing to do with the dance.

Alison swung on the arms of many she knew: councillors, janitors, barmen, Finlay – *Hi hun*! he shouted in passing – and crotchetty old Walty, the Lord Provost's dresser, plus Guy of course. From time to time she gave Guy a stronger haul on the arm, to try to stagger him, but to his credit he pulled hard back. He was either genuinely drawn into the dance, or else he was cunningly fashioning an alibi. Revolutionary situations, she guessed, were often like that, poor souls wondering which side to skulk on. Never mind: this was the best dance that could ever be for her, or that ever was, better than Cossack and Zulu and Breton and Irish, Circassian Circle and Nutcracker Suite.

Lucy saw Zander stuck in a doorway, and waved at him, but he did seem stuck, as though struggling to master such mass activity, a shame really. While she swung with Peem, she couldn't help feeling how light he was, how weak in the bicep. Had he ever done anything real? He was thin as a dream. Thank goodness Alison had inherited a bit of solidity from her, a bit of abiding beef. The music from the loudspeakers stopped; the dancers faltered and looked at each other—

A harsh noise at the end of the street turned swift to a clattering roar.

Then it loomed above them.

An attack helicopter.

Dancers delinked, abandoned partners, stumbled, bumped and fled for the nearest doorway. Under the hammering apparition, Lucy pulled and pushed Alison through a doorway and fell on her, covering her body. What fools they'd been, what happy-clappy fools. They lay without a breath beneath the machine. It shaded across them, its engine thudding, its rotors chopping air.

But no shots came.

– Alison—? breathed Lucy. Alison, love?

– Aye me, Mither. An we thocht it wis bad afore?

– I never knew there were so many forces.

Yet Lucy remembered the baton charges and tear gas in Paris. You went so far. You felt exalted. Then terror stripped all good combination. You felt exposed and loose. If you were still warm, it was only each to each, not each to other.

hug me

Gwen was one of the last to budge as the Lynx made its low passes. She was still speaking to camera as the populace melted through alleys fast. She faced the lens and checked the sky alternately. What was happening on the streets, what was aborting in the very next instant, was too fast to commentate on, although she tried.

– And now, it's an absolute disgrace, the British Government has turned its tanks and helicopters against its own people. Well I say to you, we are not the enemy within, they are. Root these traitors out. Root them out, I say. Bring down this corrupt system, that looks after the useless rich like Rookie Marr and LeopCorp and turns its guns on its own people. This has gone on too long. There can be no greater task.

Then Echo TV's volunteer cameraman said he wanted to go, while he could. She said, Go then, and to Luna, her boom assistant, she said, You too, Luna, go.

– Thank you for getting me out, said Luna.

– Get off the street, said Gwen, before they riddle you.

When she turned away, so as not to watch her brief comrades fleeing, there in the gardens below was a solitary figure.

She bounded down, two stairs at a time. The man was off his head, wielding a hoe and hacking flowers out, where it said *Sonsy Quines*.

Sonsy Quines, in all their white, pink, yellow and chocolate glamour, were being cast aside.

– Who are you? said Gwen.

– Maciek, said Maciek.

– Does it mean *madman*? said Gwen.

– It means *I am staying here*, said Maciek. I can't run. I don't have fast legs, and I can't eat flowers. I will grow my vegetable here, it is less salt in the heart of the city.

– The heart of the city is empty now, said Gwen. Take one look.

– I will grow here, said Maciek, even if it is lettuce.

– I gotta go, said Gwen, I'm a marked woman.

– And beetroot of course, said Maciek. I need my plenty beetroot, after what we are through.

– Put that bloody hoe down, said Gwen.

He leaned it alert on a park bench.

– Hug me.

He did, so that they crushed breasts together, and pressed cheeks. He felt all gnarly.

– Goodbye, said Gwen.

– Goodbye, said Maciek. Look after yourself. You the world needs, if today it does not know it.

a better way

Before you could sort a city out, you had to clean up the source.

They got out of the city just before midnight, when the tide was full, swimming up the slackened river. Peem was the weakest link. Gwen and Pawel did strong versions of head-down freestyle, whereas Peem swam slowly, like a stick insect fond of air, on his back. It was dark enough, with plenty wind on the waters, else they might have been spotted and shot. Then it was a question of moving where it was possible to move, sometimes by brambled dyke or broken woods, or bending their backs along the river path. Bridges they avoided. Humpy stone and swinging slat bridges were choke-points, easily manned.

Gwen thought of her mother's face: it was a real picture once she had tracked her down, sheltering with Lucy, and demanded to know where the stash of spare Semtex was likely to be, from *Calving Glaciers*.

Bear in mind I'm not your wee lassie, she'd said to her mother.

Okay, said Alison.

Because we're well past the days of the wee lassies, she had insisted.

Okay, okay, said Alison, dinna blaw ma heid aff.

Hope I've got better targets, Gwen had replied.

Peem thought of Iris, who had sped them on their way, stuffing the spare space in the poly-lined knapsack with provisions. She kept ramming things in, wrapped in foil or plastic or kitchen roll, or kept for the top, like cake and bananas.

Watch, Iris had warned, and eat your bananas early, or they'll be mush. Do you want a flask?

I'm sure we'll find water, Peem replied.

Iris squeezed his hand.

A flask for after the swim, yes, I think so, said Pawel.

Are you vegetarian? said Iris.

How do you know? said Gwen.

Your skin.

I do take fish, said Gwen.

These are herring I've lightly smoked, said Iris, they'll keep a day or two. Do well all of you, she said to the three.

Thanks, Iris, said Peem, you're a gem.

Never mind that, Iris had said. Bring me something useful when you come back. I need sphagnum moss for keeping the wounds clean. Here. And she'd given them an extra black plastic sack.

Pawel thought of Maciek, trying to tend his absurd garden, and of Lech and the other Poles, forced from their squats and penned in a makeshift camp, pending deportation. He'd show them a better way.

Further upriver they risked a hitchhike, in agricultural vehicles and delivery vans. In Braemar, when they got the length of Braemar, they did something about their lack of bicycles that didn't involve money. They pressed pedals, moved up to Inverey, Linn of Dee, and on to Derry Lodge, seldom separating, taking turns to lead and break the wind. The Linn of Dee was roaring; the snow must be melting on the high slopes of the Cairngorms.

– We don't want to get high too early, said Peem. They stuck instead to the very long valley of the Lairig Ghru, moving off the main path in the lee of Devil's Point and hugging the river, past the white bones of pine revealed in the bog.

– How old are these trees? said Pawel.

– Three thousand years, said Peem.

– And how old are you, grandad? said Gwen. She didn't say it like *Grandad*, not her style, little interest in that.

– Eleven, twenty-two, thirty-five, ninety, said Peem. Two grouse got up and gave their startled call. I don't do age, I leave that for the young to fret about.

– We need to be on the top by dawn, said Gwen. If you guys sleep for a bit, I'll keep watch.

– You need sleep too, said Peem. Nobody knows we're here, none of these sods will guess we're coming. A couple of hours will do us good.

– Yes, said Gwen. We owe ourselves that.

– Che, said Gwen, a little later. I'm thinking of Che.

But in the late afternoon sun, deep in the heather, the other two were already snoring.

love, please, give

When the day was well on, Lucy and Alison risked a brief walk. Despite all the developments out at sea, the oil, the gas, the wind farms, there was still haar, that sudden fog, and the haar came rolling in. All over the Links. Air from the south was flowing over winter-cold water.

They walked past UberSea, then UberEye, rehearsing missed moments and sketching small plans. Lucy had lost her phone and all her numbers. Haar swirled and rose through the pods and girders. They stopped at the white tree of the dead, where the haar hung in skeins.

Alison took her Mum's arm, and they stood in the damp air for a bit.

– It's jewellin the end o yir nose, Ma, said Alison.

Then the fog balled itself up, and billowed off north.

Forty yards from a tent they were – huge, dank, olive.

Strung on the wet grass, higgledy-pig, lay rolls and rolls of razor-wire.

– Oh, god, try them again, said Lucy.

– They'll still be ower high.

– Love, please, give them a try—

i'll take off my clothes

At dawn they'd have to mount a distraction. The bottling-plant for Mountain Heart was sure to be guarded. They had one pistol, which Pawel had captured from the Town House tank.

I'll take off my clothes, thought Gwen, and walk towards them. That's what these fuckers like, anyway, a real good show. Pawel can get them from the back, Peem can disarm them.

They moved up in the May moonlight, well above the oldest tree-line, choosing dark spaces between glittering shields of snow.